Winter
at the
Dog & Duck

JILL STEEPLES lives in a small
market town in Bedfordshire
with her husband and two
children. When she's not writing,
she enjoys reading, walking,
baking cakes, eating them and
drinking wine.

ALSO BY JILL STEEPLES

Summer at the Dog & Duck

Winter

at the

Dog & Duck

JILL STEEPLES

First published as an ebook in 2016 by Aria,
an imprint of Head of Zeus, Ltd

First published in print in the UK in 2017 by Aria

9 7 5 3 1 2 4 6 8

A catalogue record for this book is available from
the British Library.

ISBN (PB): 9781788541046
ISBN (E): 9781786691781

Typeset by Divaddict Publishing Solutions Ltd.

MIX
Paper from
responsible sources
FSC
www.fsc.org
FSC® C020471

Printed and bound by CPI Group (UK) Ltd,
Croydon, CR0 4YY

Head of Zeus Ltd
First Floor East
5–8 Hardwick Street
London EC1R 4RG

WWW.HEADOFZEUS.COM

For Mum
With love always

One

As I walked along Bluebell Lane in Little Leyton that bright and sunny spring morning, I could almost imagine myself to be Snow White – it really was that perfect. Everything was peaceful and tranquil, the only sounds to be heard were the call of birdsong twittering in my ears and the gentle rustle of activity from the wildlife scurrying around in the depths of the woodland countryside. Already this morning, we'd been accompanied on our walk by squirrels and rabbits, come face to face with a startled muntjac deer before it had darted back into the trees, and spotted a heron, standing tall and proud at the river's edge. All around me tiny buds blossomed on the trees offering the promise of new beginnings. I took a deep breath, contentment filling my soul. *Ah, yes. This is the life.* Not even my mobile vibrating in my pocket could spoil the rural idyll...

Okay – so maybe it could. Unable to ignore its insistent demands, I paused, whipping my phone out from the back pocket of my jeans to check my messages before...

'Milo?'

A heavy splash of water and the sound of frantic scrabbling snatched my head up from my phone. I'd only stopped for a moment, not long enough surely for my charge to do one of his disappearing acts.

'Milo!' I tucked my phone in my back pocket again. 'Where are you?'

I looked up and down the lane – the path we'd already traced along the side of Bluebell Woods – but there was no sign of the little cockapoo. Milo rarely ventured very far from my side, and a swirl of anxiety stirred in my chest. I dashed across the path, standing on tiptoes to peer through the trees and then down the steep muddy bank that led to the river. Oh jeez! There he was. My heart stopped. His white curly head was bobbing up and down in the water, his tongue hanging out to the side, a wild look in his normally affable brown eyes.

'Come here, Milo,' I called, more in hope than in expectation, before I clambered over the wire netting and slid down the hill. No problem, I thought, my breathing picking up a pace now. All dogs are natural born swimmers, aren't they?

'Good boy, this way,' I beckoned from the river's edge. I clapped my hands on my thighs and made little clawing motions with my arms so that Milo might get the idea, but he wasn't having any of it. He showed no signs of mastering the doggy paddle anytime soon and instead seemed to be doing his abject best to swallow as much water as possible, making horrible gurgling noises in the process.

'Oh crikey, Milo, come on. You can do this. Please don't drown. Mrs Anderson will never forgive me?'

Looking like he had every intention of ignoring me, I wriggled out of my jacket and threw it on the ground behind me, ignoring the cold nip to the air. There was only one thing for it. If I wanted to take Milo home with me, and I most certainly did – it wouldn't be good publicity for my fledgling dog-sitting business if I inadvertently killed off one of the little darlings before I'd got through the first month – then I was going to have to wade in and rescue the little scamp. Thankful that I was wearing my brand new bright pink wellies, bought especially for my dog-walking adventures, I gingerly took a step into the water. Then another step. Slowly, carefully I navigated my way through a bunch of straggly reeds until suddenly the riverbed dropped several inches beneath my feet, my heart plummeting as I fell with a thud into the murky depths of the river, cold water filling my wellies to the brim.

'Oh no! Eugh' I shuddered. 'That. Is. Disgusting.' Cold seeped into my bones and everywhere else too. 'MILO!' The silly dog had chosen that particular moment to discard his water wings and finally decide to swim... In the opposite direction to me. Terrific.

'Come here.' I lurched forward, narrowly avoiding landing face down in the water, and scooped up the smelly, dripping dog into my arms. I gathered my breath for a moment, before turning around and attempting to wade my way through the surprisingly strong current, muttering all sorts of curses into Milo's ear.

'You all right?' A clipped masculine voice reached my ears. 'Need a hand?'

Tumbling down on to the bank, spilling Milo onto the ground, my hands crawled through the mud as I struggled to attach Milo's lead, not wanting him to repeat his escape routine. Next time he wouldn't even be given the opportunity that was for sure. I heaved my heavy dripping body out of the water, found my legs and stood up, turning around to see whoever it was talking to me. On the opposite side of the riverbank a man dressed in a wax jacket, flanked by two sleek and smooth gun dogs, was observing me keenly.

I gathered my breath and my galloping heartbeat. Tall, dark and inevitably handsome. Oh god – really? Now was definitely not the time nor the place.

'I'm fine. Thank you,' I said, certain that I looked anything but fine. My cheeks flared with heat and my long hair swept all around my face obscuring my view of the man. I shivered, goosebumps running across my skin. Sweeping my hair off my face, I fixed on a smile, trying to give the impression that I wasn't wet through and freezing cold, but I suspected I wasn't fooling anyone. The man's eyes narrowed and his lips, a wide generous mouth I noticed, moved imperceptibly. A puddle accumulated at my feet as the water ran off me and Milo took the moment to shake his body vigorously, seemingly none the worse for his ice bath, showering me all over again. 'The dog got into trouble in the water, but it's all okay now.' I wiped my brow with the sleeve of my jumper and bent down to retrieve my coat from the ground. Not that it would be offering me much warmth now with every other part of my clothing completely sodden.

'You're soaked through. Are you sure you're okay? My place is only across the other side of the field if you want to come back and dry off – get yourself cleaned up?'

It was very nice of him to offer, but quite frankly the last thing I wanted to do was prolong the embarrassment. This particular humiliation was one I had no desire to share with anyone, especially not now I had the opportunity to study the man more closely. Good-looking was probably an insult

4

to his distinctive brand of looks. About six feet two inches, I reckoned, with broad shoulders, messed-up hair and dark all-knowing eyes. Hmmm. Sod's law, isn't it? You scan a dozen dating websites from the comfort of your sofa and don't come across anyone remotely fanciable and then in the freezing cold, soaked through, looking like a bedraggled rat, you happen upon someone half decent. Who was I kidding, he was definitely more than half decent.

'Really, it's fine. I'm not far from home either.' I didn't like the way his dogs were looking at me. With haughty disdain. As though they would never act in such a disobedient fashion as Milo. Judging by the way the hounds stood tall and proud, looking up at their master, watching his every move and listening out for his every word, I imagined they would never dare take a step out of line. Mind you, don't they say dogs are like their owners? The aura of superiority wafting from over the other side of riverbank was palpable.

'Thanks anyway,' I said, giving the man a cheery wave, anxious now to get away as the cold chilled my bones. With as much dignity as I could muster, I turned and marched away, without so much as a backwards glance.

It was only as Milo and I made our way home that I wondered where, in fact, the man might have meant when he'd said he lived on the other side of the field. Admittedly I'd been away from Little Leyton for a few years, but it was only a small village and I liked to think I still knew everyone in the area. Which was ridiculous really. Things had moved on in my absence. I'd been to university, worked three years in the city and qualified as an accountant. I could hardly expect to come home and pick up where I'd left off, as the good-looking stranger had just proved. Little Leyton would always be home to me, but with my parents abroad – Dad had recently secured a nine-month contract in Dubai – and with most of my old friends from school off doing their own thing, I was beginning to wonder whether it had been a good move to come back, after all.

At the top of the lane, I stopped to look back down the hill. I took a deep breath and surveyed the stunning countryside before me; swathes of rolling green fields as far as the eye could see. Despite the sogginess around my nether regions nothing could detract from the beauty of the landscape – a reason, if I'd been searching for one, why I would always be drawn back here. Nestled at the bottom of the valley were the imposing buildings of the Braithwaite Estate. The one time home of the Earl of Braithwaite, the Georgian manor house had fallen into disrepair and had remained derelict for many years, but in recent times it had undergone an extensive redevelopment and now shone like a jewel in the countryside. Beyond the estate, you could just make out the emergence of the new housing estate which had sprung up whilst I was away. That was obviously where the man must have meant. I'd forgotten all about the new development – it had been in the planning stages when I'd left and now it looked to be a busy, vibrant community.

Milo jumped up at my legs, urging me to get a move on.

'Come on then, boy,' I said, 'let's get you home.'

Shivering now from the cold, we picked up the pace and strode past the lovely wooden lychgate that led to St Cuthbert's, the Saxon church where Mum and Dad had married and where I'd been christened, a place that had played such a significant role in my upbringing. I'd attended so many events there over the years: Easter services, summer fayres, harvest festivals and Christingle services too. It was good to know that whatever changes had occurred in Little Leyton, some things would always stay the same.

Definitely, the pleasures of working and living in Little Leyton had to beat doing battle on a jam-packed tube train in London. Okay, so maybe dog-sitting and doing some shifts at The Dog and Duck didn't quite have the same kudos as working for one of the 'Big Five' consulting companies in the city, but for the time being, it suited me just fine. After all, this was never intended as a permanent move.

When I was made redundant, suddenly and unexpectedly, coinciding with the lease on my poky little flat in London coming up for renewal and the landlord deciding it was the perfect time to hike up the rent by an exorbitant amount, I decided, on something of a whim admittedly, that it was an ideal opportunity for me to return home. My sizeable payout from the company had bought me some thinking time and I wanted to make sure my next move was the right one. Three months at home would give me the time to reassess my life and work out what it was I wanted to do next. There was absolutely no need to panic. Not yet. I could walk into another high-paying job in the city tomorrow if I wanted to. And flats to let were aplenty in London. The last thing I wanted was to have a knee-jerk reaction to my change in circumstances.

Rain started to fall on my shoulders and I pulled up the hood of my jacket and tugged on Milo's lead. Absolutely. This was where I wanted to be, living an easy and uncomplicated life with only recalcitrant dogs to worry about. An unscheduled dip in the river was nothing compared to back-to-back meetings and late nights in the office. This new regime would be perfect – it might just take a bit of getting used to, that was all.

Two

Before returning Milo to Mrs Anderson, I made a detour back home. Not something I did as part of my normal range of services but this was a case of desperate measures and all that. I didn't want Mrs Anderson knowing about Milo's unexpected dip in the river and had sworn him to secrecy, but the dank, rank smell emanating from the end of the lead was seriously off-putting and might be a bit of a giveaway. *Ugh.* I screwed up my nose, deciding it might be safer to breathe through my mouth.

In the kitchen, I ran some warm water in the sink, adding some dog shampoo, and gave the stinking hound a thorough washing down. Not an easy job when Milo was doing his best to wriggle out of my grasp and shake the excess water, of which there was plenty, all over the walls. I was only thankful that Mum wasn't around to see the mess we'd made in her kitchen. My parents had already left for Dubai by the time I'd returned to Little Leyton and they were more than happy for me to house-sit for them – saved me from having to pay rent too so it worked out to be the ideal situation all round.

With Milo newly coiffed and me changed out of my soaked clothes and into some clean dry ones, we were just about to leave the house when my phone buzzed into action. It was an unrecognizable number so immediately I went into business mode.

'Good morning, A Dog's Best Friend, Ellie Browne speaking. How can I help?' Every time I said the name of my new dog-sitting business aloud, I couldn't stop the big smile from spreading across my face. My own boss. I could still hardly believe it. Answerable to no one but my clients and their dogs, who all happened to be absolutely lovely. My most demanding client was a boxer called Bertie – that was the dog and not his owner – who pulled on the lead so much he nearly tore my arm out of its socket, but that was as exacting as it got, and besides I was working on training Bertie out of his bad habits. We still had a long way to go but I was a lot more forgiving of Bertie and his funny ways than I was of some of my difficult and awkward clients in London.

The lady on the other end of the phone, Rula, had heard about my services from her friend, another one of my clients, Gemma Jones, and was asking for details on pricing and availability.

'What I'll do is pop some information through your letter box which will give you all the details you need. And if you'd like me to come along and meet Buster then I'd be more than happy to do so.'

I set a reminder on my phone to pop round to Rula's later on my way to my shift at the pub. First though I needed to get Milo home.

'Oh my goodness, Ellie,' said Mrs Anderson when she opened her front door to greet us. 'What on earth have you done to Milo?' My chest filled with dread as she took off her glasses and leaned forward to peer at her dog. 'He looks like a completely different animal.'

My laughter rang out, not entirely naturally.

'Well, he got a bit muddy on our walk so I thought I'd give him a little spruce up.'

Hmmm, maybe I'd overdone the teasing of his white curls – he did look as though he'd just come from the hairdressers with a new shampoo and set.

'That's very good service! You don't get that from me, do you, Milo? Aw, my precious little boy. He always gets filthy on our walks. You were lucky he didn't jump in the river – that's his usual trick.'

'Really?' I said, fixing a grin on my face. And she decided only now to tell me?

'Oh yes, he can be a right little scamp at times. He was probably on his best behaviour for you. He seems to have enjoyed himself though. Shall we say same time next week?'

'Great, I'll pop it in the diary.' With a note not to let Milo off the lead again, although I did hope Mrs Anderson wouldn't now expect the full wash and blow-dry treatment every week.

The bookings in the diary were coming thick and fast. When I'd first come home from London I realised I'd need something to fill my days, something undemanding and enjoyable and that's where the dog walking came in. I made up some promotional leaflets on the computer and popped them through the doors of all the houses in the village. Within days I had my first customers and word of the services I was offering had quickly spread. Growing up, we'd always had dogs at home and I missed not having one of my own. It had been an impossibility in London, and a dog of my own wasn't a viable option now, not knowing how long I'd be staying around, but working with a selection of my four-legged friends meant I really did get the best of both worlds. It was a dream come true.

Along with my shifts at the pub, it meant that my days, and evenings, were as busy as they'd ever been. Not that it felt like proper work at all. Although I was shattered and collapsed into bed each night, falling asleep just as soon as my head hit the pillow, it was a contented, satisfied slumber that greeted me. I didn't come away at the end of the day feeling so overwhelmed with fatigue that I could weep, spending the rest of the night tossing and turning, unable to switch off, before having to get up early and go through the motions the next day. My shoulders didn't groan with tension and my eyes were no longer sore and tired after having stared at a computer screen for eight hours. All the fresh air I was getting meant the pounding headaches which were a permanent feature of my working week in London had all but disappeared. As an added bonus I'd lost half a stone in weight. Hardly surprising really considering all the walking I'd been doing.

Today, I had one more doggy assignment, for my client Mrs Elmore who was recovering from a hip replacement operation. Her little border terrier, Rosie, was an absolute sweetheart, who at almost twelve years old walked even slower than Mrs Elmore, and who stopped at every leaf and every sweet-smelling delight on our route. Still, it made for a very leisurely and relaxing walk around the block – there was no fear of any repeats of Milo's swimming lesson with Rosie – and a pleasant end to the day job. Afterwards I rushed home for a quick sandwich and a cup of tea, before heading to the pub for the evening shift, a stint pulling pints for the locals.

On the High Street nestled between Josh Reynold's Antiques on one side, a quirky shop selling old collectibles and more modern *objet d'arts*, and Polly's Flowers on the other, was the unassuming eighteenth century building that housed The Dog and Duck. Nothing much to look at from the outside, but as soon as you stepped inside you couldn't help but be charmed by the sprawling appealing rooms. Low black beams, an open fire, a bread oven tucked behind the stairs that led to the living quarters, and lots of little nooks and crannies filled with old books and comfy cushions made for an inviting welcome. Walking into the pub always incited a feeling of coming home for me, but then I had spent far too much time in there, propping up the bar, in my formative years.

'I meant to ask you, Ells,' said Josie, taking advantage of the early evening lull and parking her bottom on a stool, 'could you possibly take on any more shifts?' Josie was Eric, the landlord's daughter, and my best friend since... well, it seemed liked forever now.

'When were you thinking?'

'Lunchtimes, evenings. Whatever you can do really. To be honest, I'm ready to stop now. By the end of a shift my legs are killing me and my back...' She winced as she rubbed at her side. 'Besides, I don't think I'm going to be able to fit behind here much longer.' Laughing, she looked down at her bump, which was straining beneath the material of her blouse. She still had six weeks to go until B-day, but now she came to mention it, navigating around her wide berth in the small confines of the bar was becoming tricky. 'Dad's advertising for extra staff at the moment, but I thought, in the meantime, if you wanted some more hours?'

'Sure. I'm happy to fit in as many shifts as I can, around my dog-walking clients, of course.'

Josie lifted her eyebrows, twisting her mouth in an indulgent smile. She was just one of many people who couldn't quite believe how my life had changed in the space of a few months. Gone were the power suits, high heels and polished nails, replaced by jeans and sweatshirts, wellies and the whiff of the great outdoors. I really rather liked the new me.

'Brilliant. You're a lifesaver,' she said.

'It's going to be weird not having you behind the bar though. Who will I have my girly chats with?'

Josie was my oldest friend. Our mums met at The Daisy Chain Mothers and Toddlers group in the village hall, over twenty-four years ago now, and had quickly become best friends, a friendship that had remained strong until Miriam, Josie's mum, died unexpectedly after a short illness when Josie was still a teenager. Like our mums, we'd been besties from day one. Going to school together, sharing birthday celebrations, holidays and everything in between. We'd chosen different paths; Josie seeking out the security of marriage and now motherhood, me opting for a career, but our friendship was as solid as ever. When Josie had found out I was coming home she'd quickly arranged with her dad for me to take up some shifts at the pub which had given us the opportunity to spend most evenings together gossiping behind the bar in the guise of working.

'Mind you, I should take off as much time as you can,'

I told her now. 'You won't get much rest when the baby arrives and, knowing your dad, he'll have you back here before the little one's first tooth has arrived.'

'Well, to be honest, that's what I was banking on, we'll certainly need the money, but I'm not sure it will happen now.'

'Really?' I pulled up a stool and sat down next to her. Our only customers, Bill and Tony, a couple of our lovely regulars, were supping on their pints in the snug, putting the world to rights, so Josie and I wouldn't need to be pulling any pints anytime soon. 'Why not?'

'Dad's tenancy is due to run out and he's not sure it'll be renewed. Apparently the owners are selling up, so we don't know yet what will happen with this place, who might buy it, what they intend to do with it. Dad's thinking it might be time for him to move on.'

'No! Surely not. Your dad is the heart and soul of this place. It just wouldn't be the same without him. Surely the new owners would want to keep him on?'

'Depends on who takes it over. If it's a chain, they'll probably want to implement some changes and bring their own people in. Turn it into a gastro pub, maybe? Or worse still put in a couple of sports TVs and a pool table.'

'Ugh, I hope not.'

We both shuddered trying to imagine what that might be like. The best thing about The Dog and Duck was that it managed to retain its sense of olde-worlde charm. It was a pub in the true sense of the word, a quiet sanctuary away from the pressing demands of the outside world. There were no blaring TVs or loud music, no flashing lights from arcade machines. Eric, Josie's dad, had strived to make the pub a community environment, welcoming to not only the real ale fans, young couples and families who frequented the place, but also to local groups, such as the book club, the conversational Italian class and the group of young men who sat huddled around one of the tables exchanging magic cards. Everyone was welcome as long as they showed respect to their fellow customers and the staff, and if they didn't, Eric was always on hand to discreetly but firmly move them on their way.

'Don't say anything to anyone, will you?' said Josie, looking concerned now. 'I think Dad wants to keep it under wraps until he knows more about what's happening.'

'Of course,' I said, reeling at the news that the pub might change hands after all this time. I couldn't get it out of my head and was still thinking about it later that night long after Josie had gone home. From a purely selfish point of view I couldn't imagine the pub being any other way than the way it was now, in my heart and mind, with everything and everybody that was familiar around me. Working for anyone other than Eric was inconceivable too. Our families had always been so close and we'd shared so many happy and special occasions here – summer parties, charity auctions, Christmas celebrations – it was heart-breaking to think there'd be no more of those events in our future.

'Hello sweetheart.'

I looked up from where I'd been lost in my thoughts, returning clean glasses to the shelf below the bar. There was only one person who called me sweetheart: Johnny

Tay. I smiled, ignoring the flutter of unease in my chest and plastered on my best barmaid's warm welcome.

'Hi Johnny. What can I get you? A pint of the usual?'

'No, I'm not stopping. I just wanted to pop in to say hello.' He stood on tiptoe and leant over the bar taking my face in his hands and depositing a big kiss on my lips. He smelt delicious, of wood chippings, fresh air and grass. 'I'm going down to The Bell to watch the match, but I'll drop in on the way back, walk you home. We could drop off at mine for a nightcap?'

'Oh don't worry about that. I was thinking I'd have an early night anyway.'

'No really, I'd like to. I'll be walking back this way, so it's no problem.' He grinned at me, his bright blue eyes twinkling fondly.

'Okay, I'll see you later then.'

That was the trouble with Johnny. He was just too damn likeable for his own good. Friendly and charming was his default mode. I liked him – no, scrap that, I adored Johnny. We'd become really close friends in sixth form, spending far too much time together in the common room at school, sharing our woes about revision, talking about our plans for the summer when exams were over, lazing in the park, spending hours nursing our beers in the garden of The Dog and Duck, confiding in each other, growing closer with each passing day. It was inevitable that our relationship would grow into something more serious. A teenage romance that had soared that glorious summer and fizzled out just as quickly when I'd gone off to university in the autumn.

Whatever had possessed me to think it was a good idea

to pick up where we'd left off all those years before?

Ugh.

That first weekend when I came home from London I hadn't thought twice about falling into Johnny's arms again – it was all too easy. I revelled in the reminder of his warm voice and the familiarity of his lovely face as we reacquainted ourselves with what had been happening over the last couple of years, catching up on the news about the old crowd from school. Our lives had gone in different directions. Me, studying hard, gaining a qualification that would always guarantee me a decent job, I hoped, and Johnny taking up an apprenticeship with a local joinery company, his innate skills and creativity soon enabling him to set up his own bespoke kitchen company. No surprise there, because as I was rediscovering, if there was one thing you could say about Johnny, it was that he was very good with his hands...

I could see now though that Johnny and I were very different people and we worked much better as friends. The trouble was Johnny hadn't realized it, but he'd taken to calling me sweetheart, turning up at the pub whenever I was working a shift and talking about a future; admittedly only two or three weeks down the line, but it still managed to scare the heebie-jeebies out of me.

Despite what my head was telling me – that I needed to put a stop to what was only ever meant to be a fling – I realized I was getting myself in much deeper than I'd ever intended and the alarm bells were ringing.

Coming home was meant to give me some clarity, to offer me the opportunity to live a simpler, less stressful life, but with each passing day spent in Little Leyton it looked as though life was getting more complicated by the moment.

Note to self: I definitely needed to do something about the problem called Johnny.

Three

'There you go my lovely. These are for you, Ellie.'

It was the start of my shift the next day and Polly Samson from the flower shop next door was standing in front of me holding a bunch of assorted beautiful blooms.

'Wow! They're stunning. Thank you.'

'No problem. I hate to see any flowers go to waste and I know you'll find a good use for them.'

I took them from her, found a vase and placed them in the fireplace, standing back for a moment to admire them.

'Perfect! I was going to take them home with me, but I think they've found their rightful place there, don't you?'

I loved the quiet of the early evenings in the pub when I had the opportunity to potter and chat properly with any customers who popped in. Often, later in the evening, I was too busy to even draw breath so I always made the most of the quiet times when I could.

I plopped some ice into a glass, poured in some orange juice and handed the drink to Polly. Immediately she took a long sip, her eyes brightening as the refreshment hit the desired spot.

'So no regrets then?' she asked. 'About coming back here?

I should imagine life in Little Leyton must seem tame after living in London for so long.'

Polly was a friend who I'd known since my schooldays. We hadn't been close back then; she'd been in the year above me and we'd mixed in different circles, but recently, with her working next door, we'd got to know each other better and had grown much closer as a result.

'It's different, I'll give you that, but this is very definitely my home. Where I belong. I love the sense of community here. You don't really get that in London. Or else I didn't find it. My life seemed to consist of early starts, long days and late nights. It's only now that I'm away from it that I realize how burnt-out I was. I'd gone straight from university into my job, doing my accountancy exams at the same time, and it was really pressurized. Losing my job like that, so suddenly, was devastating, but in some ways I see it as a blessing now. It's given me the chance to step back from it all and decide what I want to do next.'

Polly nodded, taking another sip from her drink. She wriggled her shoulders and exhaled deeply, the tensions of her day seeping from her body. 'Well, I hope you're here to stay now, Ellie? I do love having you around. You've brightened up this place that's for sure.'

Such a lovely thing for Polly to say. She was tiny in stature, but had a huge heart. With her blonde hair cut into a swingy bob and bright blue eyes that shone keenly as she spoke, my mood always lifted just at the sight of her. With her being only next door, I often popped into her shop before or after a shift to have a natter and a cup of coffee. I'd perch my bottom on one of the stools behind her counter and watch transfixed as her fingers tended her flowers, creating pretty bouquets and baskets with expert ease.

'I'm not sure how long I'll be around,' I told her now. 'I love working here and doing the dog-sitting, but I don't see either of them as long-term careers. I'll probably have to go back into accountancy at some stage, it would be a waste of my degree otherwise.'

Which was absolutely true, so why, as I said the words aloud to Polly, did I wonder, not for the first time, if I really wanted to pick up that lifestyle again. Thinking about it, I'd been feeling the strain for months and a stirring of disquiet rumbled in the depths of my stomach as I wondered if the career I had chosen, the one I'd worked so long and hard for, was really meant for me after all.

'So you didn't leave anybody behind in London then?' Polly shifted her bottom on the stool – they weren't the most comfortable seats in the world – and the corners of her mouth twisted in an enquiring smile.

I tilted my head, deliberately misunderstanding the question.

'I wondered if it might have been a man that brought you back here. If you weren't trying to escape a broken heart?'

'Ha! No,' I sighed. 'Four years in London and I don't think I could have had more than a couple of dates.'

'Really?' Polly's mouth gaped open. 'And I thought my love life was in the doldrums.'

'Yeah.' I gave a small chuckle, unable to take offence at her reaction. How could I when it was the sad truth? 'To be honest, for a long time I wasn't really interested in relationships. I was too focussed on my job and then when I was ready to meet someone it never seemed to happen.

Maybe if I had done I wouldn't have come home again.' A pang of sadness swept over me as I was made to consider all those missed opportunities.

'Still, it looks like things are going well with Johnny now. That has to be a good thing, eh? Do you know, I sometimes think these things happen for a reason. That maybe you were meant to come home, to be here at the pub and to be with Johnny.'

'What? No!' I said quickly, hearing the defensive edge to my voice. I jumped up from my stool and cleared away some empty glasses from the top. 'We're not really together, together. Johnny and I are just friends. Nothing more.'

Polly raised her eyebrows at me, her eyes widening in disbelief.

'Really!' I said, feeling a heat rise to my cheeks as I tried to convince us both.

'Hmm, okay. But I'm not sure Johnny sees it that way.'

'Well, he should!' I let out a big sigh. If other people were seeing us a couple then my problem was much bigger than I thought.

'What about you?' I asked, eager now to deflect the attention from me. 'Are you seeing anyone?'

'No.' Polly's shoulders sagged. 'The one thing you can say about Little Leyton is that there is a distinct lack of eligible young men. I'd love to meet someone, but I'm not sure how I'm supposed to do that around here.'

'No.' I sighed in sympathy, looking around us. Bill and Tony, lovely men in their sixties, were supping on their pints in the snug, a group of building contractors had just come in after a long day's work and were discussing last night's football match, and Arthur who had to be pushing eighty was reading his book, sat in the bay window. Hmmm. If The Dog and Duck was anything to go by, then she had a point. 'Don't you meet any nice men through your work?'

'Oh yes, plenty, but they're all either happily married or trying to woo a potential partner. I work in a florist's, remember. It's not the best place to meet single available men.'

'No, I suppose not.'

'One of these days I might try internet dating – I never really liked the idea of it before, but it might be worth a try or else...'

'... a nunnery,' I interrupted her, with a wry smile before turning to greet a customer who'd just walked in through the side door. His head was bent to the floor to avoid the low beams before he rested his hands on the bar and lifted his gaze to greet me.

'Good evening, Sir. What can...' I paused as our eyes met, realization dawning in my mind. 'Oh hello...' *Be still my beating heart.* 'What can I get you?'

Standing in front of me was the man from the lane, minus his two dogs. His large masculine physical presence filled the cosy confines of the snug. Up close, I was able to reassess my first impression of him. Tall – check. Much taller and broader than I remembered, actually. Dark – check. Eyes, the colour of melted chocolate, that flickered with curiosity, and messy dark brown hair that curled on his collar. Handsome – check. Strong features with the finest shadow of stubble across his wide jawline and the faintest hint of a scar above his lip. Oh yes, definitely handsome. From the corner of my eye, I noticed Polly raising an eyebrow at me, her half-smile suggesting that she very much approved of my latest customer. It was almost as if the Goddess of Dating had been eavesdropping on our conversation and had sent down a shining ray of hope, in the form of this man, telling us to keep the faith.

'Oh, hello,' he said, with a warm smile of recognition, 'I'll have a pint of the special, please.'

Why were my fingers shaking all of a sudden? I pulled his pint carefully, grateful to fix my attention on the golden nectar filling the glass, allowing me the opportunity for some much needed pulling-myself-together time.

'So,' he said, after he'd taken a sip from his glass, his tongue searching out the creamy froth left lingering around his lips, 'how's your dog?'

I must have seen that very manoeuvre, the tongue-licking one, performed by dozens of men newly acquainted with their pint of beer, but suddenly it had taken on a whole new level of meaning.

'My dog? Ha ha, oh yes, my dog.' What was wrong with me? Acting as though I'd never met a good looking man before! Well, I suppose it had been a long time. 'She's fine. I mean, he's fine. Milo, you mean?'

The man shrugged and looked at me blankly. *Gawd.* How could he possibly be expected to know the name of my dog? And what must he think of me? The first time we met I was wading about in a river, soaked through, pretending everything was perfectly normal and now I was a giddy wreck, babbling incoherently.

'Yes, Milo's fine,' I said. 'Only he's not actually my dog. I was just looking after him. That's what I do for a living, you see. Well, apart from working in here. I look after dogs. Dog-walking, dog-sitting, that kind of thing. And pouring pints of beer too.'

I was wittering on, divulging far more information than this man probably wanted to hear, but I couldn't help myself. I always spoke rubbish when I was nervous.

'Look, here's my card.' I pulled one out from my back pocket and handed it to him. He took it and turned it over in his fingers, a bemused expression on his face. Poor man. He'd come into the pub for a quiet pint – not to be subjected to my awkward sales pitch, if that's what this was.

'*A Dog's Best Friend, Ellie Browne.*' He said the words aloud, his voice warm like sticky treacle, his effect upon me a bit treacly too, although I wasn't sure if I detected a hint of mockery to his tone. 'A woman of many talents, obviously,' he said, with half a smile hovering on his lips.

'Yes, well, I like to keep busy.'

Scintillating, Ellie. Positively scintillating.

In the background, Polly's head had shrunk into her shoulders, her eyes had narrowed and she wore a painful grimace on her face, as she made a slicing action at her throat. *Shut up, Ellie*, was the message, loud and clear.

'Great,' he said, nodding his head. 'Well, it was obvious you clearly have a way with dogs.'

Sarcastic or what? He was laughing at me, I felt sure, wondering what kind of dog-whisperer almost drowns the animal she's supposed to be looking after and gets sopping wet and muddy in the process. And to think of all the huffing and puffing I'd been doing at the time. I cringed, wishing I could snatch back my card, but he'd already popped it into the safety of his inside pocket. I suspected I wouldn't be adding the man to my client list anytime soon.

Thankfully, Eric wandered in from the back at that very moment, his large and jovial personality cutting through the atmosphere, bringing some much needed warmth to the distinct south-westerly chill wafting in from across the bar.

'Everything all right, love?' Eric greeted me with his customary bear hug. I wrapped my arms round his waist and rested my head on his chest, squeezing him tight. He was like a second dad to me, and in the absence of my own dad, who was living the high-life in Dubai, he made a very good substitute.

'Yes, fine,' I said cheerily, pulling away, aware of the man's gaze upon us. I decided now might be a good time to wash down the pumps just so I could divert my attention away from the man seemingly taking up all the air space in our little pub. Thankfully, any awkwardness seemed to be on my part only. Eric greeted the man fondly, as if they were old friends, and they laughed and joked together, the man seemingly perfectly at ease in his surroundings, even though I'd never seen him in here before. They quickly picked up on a conversation while I was very happy to blend into the background and leave them to it, getting on with my job, my nerves just about back under control.

Polly followed me through into the back bar and handed me her empty glass over the bar, shaking her head.

'Very smooth, Ells, very smooth.'

'What?'

'Maybe this is why you and I don't have any luck on the dating scene. An attractive man walks into the building and you turn into a gibbering wreck.'

'I did not!' I so did.

'I think you may have done.'

'Oh, I was just a bit embarrassed that was all. We met the other day when I was out for a walk with one of the dogs and…' my voice trailed away, not wanting to remember that humiliation, just hoping I hadn't embarrassed myself any further tonight, although judging by Polly's reaction, I think I may have already done so.

Polly giggled.

'I'm going to get off now, but I'll see you soon, right?' Her gaze drifted over into the direction of the man who was now perched on a stool. 'He's bloomin' gorgeous though, don't you reckon?'

'Is he?' I said, determined not to look his way. 'I hadn't really noticed.' Much.

Four

Thankfully I didn't have the time nor the inclination to affirm Polly's view of the man as the pub quickly filled up and I was soon busy serving a stream of eager customers and collecting empty glasses from the tables. The convivial background of chatter, laughter and clinking glasses always gave me a warm glow inside. It didn't really feel like hard work to be amongst people who were intent on enjoying themselves.

It was later as the pub thinned out that Eric came up beside me behind the bar and placed a friendly paternal arm around my shoulder. He turned me towards the man, the one I'd been carefully avoiding all night, the one I could avoid no longer, and asked, 'You know who this is, don't you?'

I smiled weakly, not having the faintest clue, but wondering if I should. Now Eric came to mention it, the man did look very familiar. Perhaps he was a celebrity. He had that kind of air about him. Confident and relaxed, but in a 'hey, check me out' kind of way. Hmmm, he did look a bit like that temperamental chef off the telly. Or maybe he was an actor – from that gritty thriller that was on the other night. Dark mocha eyes, a strong jawline, messy hair and wide generous lips. Mmm, yes, very… familiar. *Oh God, stop it, right now!*

'Ellie?' I felt the benefit of Eric's elbow in my ribs.

'Oops sorry,' I said, turning to look at him. Embarrassingly, I realized I'd been gawping at the man for much longer than would be considered polite. 'No. No, I don't think I do, should I?'

'This is Max Golding, Noel's grandson?'

'Noel?' Who the heck was Noel? And why had Eric decided tonight was the night to audition me for an episode of *Mastermind*? Really, I had no idea what he was going on about.

'Yes. Noel, you know, Noel,' he nodded towards the rocking chair that nestled to one side of the inglenook fireplace.

'Oh my goodness! Noel Golding!' Of course, now I remembered. 'You're Noel's grandson. That's just marvellous.' I beamed, the thought flittering into my mind that this very attractive man – there could be absolutely no denying it – probably had the impression that I wasn't quite the full ticket.

'Yes, that's right. Did you know him them?'

'Oh yes. I knew Noel. He was such a sweetheart, always had a lovely smile on his face and a friendly word. I first started working here when I was doing my A levels, so I remember Noel from those days. He always took a real interest in me and what I was doing. Such a lovely man. One of my favourite customers.'

Noel had been as much a feature of the pub as the stone-flagged floors, the oak beams and the mullioned windows. You could set your clock by him. Every day he would be in at twelve for his pint of ale, savouring it for a whole hour, chatting to whoever was in the pub at the time or reading his newspaper if there was no one around, before making the short journey back to his little cottage, at the back of the High Street, in time for his lunch. In the evening he would be back again, this time for two pints that would last the entire night until chucking-out hour. He was a lovely, charming old man who always had a twinkle in his eye, not dissimilar to the twinkle in the eye of his grandson who was observing me closely now. I felt a heat tingle in my cheeks. Funnily enough I couldn't remember his grandfather ever having a similar effect upon me or knowing even that he had a grandson. Where had Noel been hiding him all that time?

'Thanks. That's good to hear. Everyone always speaks very fondly of him.'

Max held my gaze for a moment looking genuinely touched by my words. It was during one of my reading weeks, home from university, that I learned that Noel had died after a short illness. Everyone who knew him in Little Leyton, and that was most people, was affected in some way by his death. He was that sort of man. The type of person who leaves a lasting impression on you and makes your life brighter just by having known them. For a long time afterwards the pub seemed changed somehow without the old man's presence and his rocking chair by the fire, where Noel would sit when he came in, remained unused for several months in respect of his memory.

'Have you always lived around here then?' I hoped I wasn't overstepping the mark with my question, but I hadn't realized Noel even had any family locally. I certainly couldn't remember him mentioning them.

'No. I came here when Gramps was ill. To look after him. I'm glad I did. He lasted only a few weeks after I arrived, but I was so pleased we had that time together. Then... afterwards, well, I'd grown to like the area so much I decided to stay.'

'Really?' Funny to think that I hadn't run into him before, on any of my previous visits home. 'It is a lovely place to live, isn't it? Such beautiful countryside and so many beautiful walks too, perfect dog-walking country.' But then he probably knew that, having met him in the great outdoors with his two magnificent dogs...

He nodded, with a smile, as though thinking the same.

Quickly I finished up my duties behind the bar. I was just pulling on my jacket when the door opened and Johnny waltzed in.

'All right?' he greeted Max with a broad smile, as if they were old friends too – did everyone in Little Leyton know this man, apart from me? – before coming behind the bar and slipping an arm around my waist. He kissed me enthusiastically, leaving a damp patch on my cheek, and it took all my self-will not to wipe it away with the back of my hand. I gave a sheepish grin to Max, as Johnny proceeded to crush me in a bear hug.

'Nice meeting you... Ellie.' Max smiled and I felt ridiculously pleased that he'd actually remembered my name, the sound on his lips appearing seductive. Max stood up, shook Eric's hand and nodded at Johnny, before walking out of the pub, carefully dodging the beams again. If there was one thing you could say about Max Golding it was that he was definitely all man whereas Johnny who was scrabbling around at my side, all eager-eyed and enthusiastic, was more like a puppy, in desperate need of some training.

*

Later as I snuggled into the crook of Johnny's arms, my hair fanning out on his pillow, I realized I'd probably been a little hasty in my assessment of his manly qualities. Okay, so I hadn't actually planned on coming home with Johnny, but somehow it had just happened. I sighed contentedly, intoxicated by his deliciously seductive scent. He certainly had a magical touch; maybe it was something to do with all those hours spent turning, caressing and carving wood.

'You know, Ells, I'm so glad you're back.' He propped himself up on his elbow and looked down at me fondly. 'In some ways it's as though you've never been away.'

I smiled weakly.

'I'll take that as a compliment, I think.'

'No definitely, you should. Are you glad to be back?' He took hold of my hand and squeezed it tightly, looking at me intently. Maybe it was my imagination but there seemed to be a whole load of meaning in that gesture.

'Yes, it's great. Although strange too in some ways, especially with Mum and Dad being away.'

To be honest, I'd been far too busy lately to really notice Mum and Dad's absence, but this morning in the post I'd received a package from Dubai. Eagerly I'd ripped off the brown paper to find a couple of small gifts, some squidgy dates and a colourful fridge magnet to add to my growing collection, plus lots of photos: Mum and Dad by the harbour, pictures of their plush new villa, the complex swimming pool, the pair of them dressed up to the nines about to go off to some swanky corporate event. Looking at their happy, smiling, tanned faces made me realize just how much I missed them after all.

'Everything here is so comfortable and familiar and yet in some ways it feels as though everything has changed. Things in Little Leyton have moved on – I've changed too, I'm not the same person I was when I was last here.'

'I know, and you've blossomed beautifully, Miss Browne.' Johnny chuckled, taking an exaggerated bite of my neck.

'Stop it,' I said, irritated now, pushing him away. 'That's not what I meant.'

'I know, but it happens. You're older now, Ells. We've all grown up, moved on. It's what happens in life.'

'I suppose. It just feels a bit weird being back, that's all.' For some reason, my emotions seemed to be all over the place ever since my shift at the pub. 'It was great meeting that guy tonight though. Noel's grandson?' I didn't want to say his name aloud to Johnny; I didn't want him thinking he'd made such an impression on me. 'I suppose it got me thinking back to the old days.'

Back to the days when I'd been full of enthusiasm for my future. I'd felt as though I could conquer the world. I didn't have an inkling of doubt that I wouldn't achieve all my goals; getting a good degree, securing a placement with a top company, finding a place to live and meeting someone special, someone equally successful, someone I could share a future with. Was coming back an admission of failure? An acceptance that things hadn't worked out the way I'd imagined?

'Max?' Johnny said now. 'Yeah, he seems all right. You know he lives on the Braithwaite Estate?'

'Ah, I wondered. That place has shot up in less than no time.'

'No, not the new housing estate. The actual estate. He owns it. Lord of the Manor, no less. Apparently, he's spent a fortune renovating the place. Moved in about eighteen months ago. He's a property developer. Seems to have quite a few fingers in different pies. His company was behind the development of the new housing estate.'

When Max had told me he lived on the other side of the field, I'd naturally assumed he meant in one of the new properties on the housing estate. Not in the huge manor house itself.

'Really? Oh... That is interesting.' Fascinating, in fact. He definitely played the part of country squire to perfection. And that would explain what he was doing in the Estate grounds the day I'd met him and why he was so interested in the interloper wading about in his stream. Oh god, he'd probably thought I was a trespasser or something.

Johnny sat up in bed.

'You know what we should do, Ells? We should go away for a holiday. Maybe get one of those last minute deals and head off for the sun. What do you reckon?'

I swung my legs out of bed and retrieved my clothes from the floor, getting dressed quickly. I had an early start in the morning, a date with a Rottweiler called Harry, and it was already past midnight.

'I can't, Johnny. I've just committed to taking on more shifts at the pub and then there's my dog clients. I'm only just getting things established – it wouldn't be the right time to go away.'

I wasn't certain there would be a right time to go away with Johnny. Hanging out with each other in Little Leyton was one thing, but making holiday plans together would mean taking our relationship to a whole other more serious level.

'Well, maybe not now then, but a few months down the line, perhaps?' Johnny climbed out of bed and pulled on his clothes. 'You'll be due a holiday then. I know I could do with one too, I've not had a break in ages.'

I pulled my hoodie over my head and picked up my bag from the floor.

'Sorry, Johnny, I don't really want to be making plans that far ahead. I'm not sure what I'm going to be doing in three months' time. I might well be back in London.'

'Really?' A note of disappointment rang in his voice. I turned towards the door, unable to avoid walking into his embrace, his hands finding my waist. 'I thought you'd had enough of London.'

'Well, I have, at the moment, but that's not to say I won't go back. Coming home – it was only ever meant as a temporary thing.'

He tilted my chin up with his finger, his gaze flickering onto mine. 'Oh Ells, don't say that. Where would it leave us if you decide to go off again? I thought things were going well between us – that we had something special here.'

Gazing into Johnny's eyes, a ripple of dread swirled in my stomach as I realized I couldn't do this any more. As much as I liked Johnny, I knew there was no future for us as a couple. All this talk of holidays had brought it home to me. I needed to put a stop to things before we got in any deeper. I took a deep breath.

'Look Johnny, I really like you. Honestly, I do. We've been friends for years. But I'm not looking for anything serious at the moment. I'm sorry if I've misled you. Given you the impression that I can offer you something more, but I can't, I'm afraid. Maybe we should... you know... stop seeing each other?'

He stepped backwards, confusion and hurt evident on his features as he held up his hands in a gesture of defeat. 'Is that what you really want, Ells?'

'Well, I don't want to give you the wrong idea. I like spending time with you, but that's all it is for me.'

Johnny shrugged and sucked on his lips. 'I see. I didn't realize. I thought we'd been having a good time together. Can't we just carry on the way we are?'

It was true we had been having a good time, but one thing I knew for certain was that it wasn't fair on Johnny to continue like this with him expecting so much more from the relationship than I was able to give. Didn't he deserve my honesty, at least?

'No, Johnny. I'm sorry. This has been a mistake. We should never have got back together again. We work much better as friends, don't you think, and I really don't want to do anything that would jeopardize that friendship.'

Johnny fell silent for a moment.

'Right.' The air between us crackled with tension. 'I hadn't realized we were doing anything to spoil our friendship. That's the last thing I would want too, Ellie, but if you think it's best that we split, then obviously I'd have to respect that decision.' He pulled on his jacket, unable to look at me. 'Come on, I'll walk you home.'

Johnny was doing a good job of hiding his disappointment, but I could feel it emanating from his every pore, making me feel like the biggest bitch in Little Leyton. If I'd needed any more proof that coming back here was a bad decision, then I only needed to look deep into Johnny's eyes.

Five

'I feel really bad about the whole situation. He's so lovely. Good-natured, funny, eager to please – he was everything I wanted and yet things just haven't worked out the way I'd planned at all.'

I knew exactly how Gemma Jones felt. Not that I had a big swanky five-bedroomed house. Or an adoring husband. Or five beautiful children: two boys at school, two little girls at her ankles and a baby in her arms. I certainly couldn't compete with her on the yummy-Mummy front – on account of me not being a Mummy and in my present guise of jogging bottoms, sweat shirt and wellies, failing miserably on the yummy front too. Still, despite our obvious differences, I was feeling her pain; bonding with her, in a way only girls know how, over her distress about the current man in her life.

'I know I've let him down. He's so sweet and loving, but I just don't seem to have the time to devote to him. When he looks at me with those big brown eyes, well, it breaks my heart.'

I nodded in understanding. If I hadn't known better she could have been talking about Johnny. I sighed, reminded of our last conversation. He'd played the puppy-dog eyes trick on me as well, but I was pleased I'd managed to stay firm. Emotional blackmail, that's all it was.

'I know, these boys can be hard to resist at times, but don't worry, Digby will be absolutely fine. Nothing that a long walk over the fields won't put right.' If only all problems of the male variety could be so easily fixed.

'Thanks so much, Ellie.' Gemma handed me the lead and Digby trotted out happily. 'You're a lifesaver, you do know that, don't you?'

Another satisfied customer, I thought with a smile. If I was being honest, Digby was the favourite of all my dog clients. A black labrador, he was the most genuine and affectionate of dogs. Completely obedient too. No running off or jumping into rivers for him and he was perfectly friendly with everyone, including other dogs. With Gemma having so many other demands on her time, naturally Digby wasn't at the top of her priority list, but at least for today, with me, he could indulge in some special one-on-one attention. As soon as we got away from the road, I let him off the lead and he walked to heel all the way around our route, only bounding away from my side when we reached the wide expanse of field.

Watching him run across the grass, his tail wagging, I revelled in the sense of freedom we were both enjoying. Even though I felt guilty remembering my last conversation with Johnny, I realized I'd done absolutely the right thing in making my feelings clear to him. I didn't need the complication of a serious relationship. I was fond of Johnny and liked him as a friend, someone to hang out with, but I knew it would never be more than that. Not for me at least.

Much better that he knew now rather than finding out three months down the line.

Digby stopped in the distance, turning to look at me, his ears pricked, checking on my progress.

I beckoned him, slapping my hands on the top of my legs, and he came running immediately to my side.

'That's right, boy,' I said, leaning down to nuzzle my head into his fur, receiving a wet sloppy kiss for my efforts. 'You're the only man I need in my life right now.'

As I was feeling a deep connection between me and my new beau, and with it being such a beautiful day, I decided to take the long route home and have a meander along the High Street. I felt sure Gemma would appreciate some extra dog-free time and Digby was the perfect companion for such an outing. He would happily meander up and down the paths of the shops beside me, giving a doggy hello – his tail wagged continually – to anyone he might happen to come across.

We walked past Little Leyton primary school and a small gaggle of children came running across the playground to see us through the fence.

'Hey, that's my dog,' said Jake, an adorable boy, who at age nine was the eldest of Gemma's children. He waggled his fingers through the fencing to pat Digby's nose, and was duly rewarded for his efforts with a big friendly kiss on the hand.

'Hey Digby, Digby!' the other children called, all eager to get a similar warm welcome from the dog.

It honestly didn't seem that long ago that it had been me and Josie running around that playground, climbing the fallen oak trunk and playing hide-and-seek. If I closed my eyes and took a deep breath I could still conjure up the smell of the polished wood floors of the corridors in the old schoolhouse. Mrs Abraham, my first teacher, who had been kindly and terrifying in equal measure, was still teaching at the school. Happy times.

Waving goodbye to Jake and his friends, we continued up the High Street which today was bathed in a bright cheerfulness from the last of the spring flowers, their heads still raised defiantly.

Apart from Room No. 4, the new gift shop, which had recently opened in what was the old garage workshop, the shops on the High Street were reassuringly the same as they had always been. There was Edwards, the greengrocers, Medleys, the hardware store, Mr and Mrs Shah at the newsagents and...

'Ellie! Is that you?'

Betty Masters came out from the door to The Bluebell Tea Rooms and beckoned me over.

'Ooh, darling, I haven't seen you in ages. Come on in and have a cuppa with me.' She clasped her hands around me, a big smile lighting up her lovely face. 'You must tell me all your news.'

'I'm afraid I don't have any cash on me, Betty.' I patted the pocket on my jeans. 'And then there's Digby to think about. Maybe it would be better if I popped in some other time.'

'Nonsense, you're here now. Come on inside and bring your lovely dog too. What do you fancy?'

Betty had worked in the tea rooms for as long as I could

remember and she hadn't seemed to have changed at all in that time. With her blonde hair piled high on her head in a bun and her red-rimmed glasses accentuating her twinkling blue eyes, she looked exactly the way I remembered her from when I was a small girl. It always amazed me how slim she stayed, considering she spent her working days surrounded by the most delicious cakes.

Talking of cakes... My gaze ran over the selection of yummy treats behind the glass top counter. I peered in to get a better look. Scones, fruit cakes, brownies, lemon drizzle, muffins, a Victoria sponge, coffee and walnut tray bake, flapjacks – the choice was endlessly tempting.

'A cappucino and...'

'Don't tell me!' Betty held up her hand to stop me. 'A Bakewell tart?'

I nodded eagerly and we both broke into laughter. For a couple of years Mum had worked here and every day after school I would walk to the tea rooms and sit myself on an available table and have a cold drink and a slice of cake – always the Bakewell tart – while waiting for Mum to finish up. Mum and Betty would encourage me to try something new on the cake front, but I'd never wanted to. The soft light sponge with the sweetness of the raspberry jam and the crunch of almonds on top always hit the right spot. Now, I couldn't wait a moment longer to try it again, I took a sneaky bite into the cake and, ahh, it was just as delicious as I remembered. Taking my plate with me I sat down at a table so that I could eat the rest.

Betty sat down opposite me and Digby wedged his body against my leg, his eyes fixed hard upon me, just in case a stray crumb should fall – he was there, ready and waiting.

'Guess who I had a postcard from today?' Betty said. 'Your mum. Seems like they've settled well in Dubai.'

'Oh yeah, I think they're loving it. Their living quarters look amazing and I think Dad is having the time of his life, a bit of a second childhood in fact. He's been paragliding, windsurfing, all sorts. Must admit I miss them though. Still it won't be long before they're back home again – it's gone so quickly.'

'And what about you, lovely? It's super having you back in the village. I do hope you're staying around?'

I smiled and took another bite of cake. It was a question everyone asked me and yet one I had no definitive answer to. Three months was the original plan, a time frame I'd plucked out of the air, enough time to get some perspective on my life, I'd reasoned, but now, well, I wasn't so sure.

'I'll see how it goes. The business is going well,' I said, giving Digby a stroke, 'and I've got as many shifts at the pub as I want, so for the time being I'm happy to stay.' More than happy, in fact. Now that I'd set things straight with Johnny, I'd felt much better about my future in Little Leyton. 'Anyway, what's been happening with you, Betty? How are the family?'

'Yes, they're all fine. Busy with their own lives, of course. Would you believe I've heard from Pip recently? That's a rare occurrence in itself. He tells me he's coming home later in the year.'

'Really, that's amazing!' I only vaguely remembered Pip Masters who was the eldest of the three Masters boys. Tall and with a shock of blond hair, he'd always cut a very striking figure. He'd gone to the boys' grammar school in town. A real high-flyer who was captain of the rugby and cricket teams, he'd excelled in his studies, winning a place at Oxford to study law. He'd gone off with the whole village's expectations on his shoulders, but had only lasted three months, before jacking it all in to travel abroad. From what I'd heard, apart from the occasional flying visit home, he'd hadn't been back properly since. 'You must be excited. Is he planning on staying?'

'Who knows?' said Betty with a resigned sigh. 'To be honest I won't actually believe it until I see the whites of his eyes. With Pip you never know what's he's likely to do next. But it's about time that young man settled down to something at last.'

'Oh, I really hope so too, Betty.' I reached across the table to squeeze her hand. I knew Betty was only managing her expectations, but I hoped for her sake that Pip might decide to stay for a while just so he could get to spend some time with his family.

'Look, before you go, let me find a scone for Digby.' I'd polished off the Bakewell Tart without Digby getting so much as a look in. Now, his ears pricked hopefully at the mention of his name and his gaze didn't leave Betty as she stood up and went behind the counter to remove the cover on a plate of the biggest scones I'd ever seen.

'That's very kind of you, Betty,' I laughed, 'but as he's not my dog, I'm afraid he's not allowed to have cakes.'

'Sorry, Digby,' she said, shaking her head ruefully. 'I did try. Wait a minute, I might have a rotten old dog biscuit out the back you can have.'

With Digby suitably satisfied with the offering from Betty, gobbling it down in a matter of seconds, we said our goodbyes and headed home.

*

With Digby walked and returned to his owner, I turned up early at the pub for my lunchtime shift, grabbed myself a coffee and sat down at the kitchen table with Josie, who'd been idly flicking through the newspaper. She sighed and turned to look at me.

'Are you all right?' I asked.

'Fine, just a bit hormonal, I suppose.'

'Oh, me too. And I haven't even got the excuse of being pregnant.'

It made her laugh, but behind the bright smile I could sense something was troubling her. She clasped her hands around her mug, her gaze drifting out of the window.

'Come on, Josie, tell me, what's the matter?'

'Oh I don't know... I just sometimes wonder if I'm doing the right thing bringing a new life into this world.'

'Oh my god. What's happened? You and Ethan are okay, aren't you? You haven't had a row?' Josie and Ethan were teenage sweethearts and had been virtually inseparable ever since. She was lovely and giving, and had worked as a fitness instructor when she wasn't working at the pub, and Ethan worked at a local garage as a mechanic. He was so friendly and laid-back I couldn't imagine what they might have fallen out over.

'No, it's nothing like that. It's just the news from Calais...' She turned the pages to a double-page spread of photos.

Images that were all too familiar in the media recently. Men, women and children, their faces etched with a mix of fear, defiance and disbelief, adrift and homeless in a foreign land with nothing but the clothes they were standing in.

'It breaks my heart,' said Josie. 'Can you imagine how desperate they must be to put their life and their children's lives at risk to escape from the horrors they've experienced in their own country? It makes me shudder just to think about it.'

'I know.' I reached over for Josie's hand and squeezed it tight. 'Makes you realize how lucky we are to live where we do.'

'But what about the future?' She cradled her bump in her arms, a wistful look on her face. 'What sort of hope is there for my baby in a world where people can do such terrible things to one another? It scares me.' Tears gathered in Josie's eyes, the depth of her emotion resonating with me deep down inside.

'You've got to put it out of your mind, Josie. I know it's upsetting and it's only natural that you're having these feelings now, but don't let it spoil your enjoyment at starting your own family. This should be a really happy and positive time for you. There's so much to look forward to. Really, there is.'

'It puts things into perspective though, doesn't it? There's me worrying about what colour scheme to choose for the nursery and these people are literally fighting for the chance of a life away from fear and violence. It's not a lot to ask for, is it?'

I shook my head, wrapping my arms around my chest. Reluctantly, I could only agree with her.

'It makes me feel grateful and yet guilty at the same time. Grateful that I'm not in the same position as these poor people and guilty that I've got so much stuff for the baby already: clothes, linen, toys. Too much stuff probably – it doesn't seem fair.'

I reached across the table for the paper, my gaze scanning down the text. 'Look if this really means so much to you, why don't we see if we can do something to help?'

Josie's head dropped to the side, her brown eyes growing wide. 'Like what? What can we possibly do?'

'We could have a collection. We could put a call out to all our customers asking for donations, not money, but clothes and bedding, that sort of thing. That's what they're asking for here.' I pointed to the section in the newspaper. 'It wouldn't be too difficult to organize. Didn't your dad do something similar a few years back?'

'Yes, yes he did?' Already I heard a note of bubbling excitement in Josie's words.

'What did Dad do?' asked Eric, wandering in at that precise moment and laying a hand on each of our shoulders, his voice full of warm humour.

'Do you remember that charity appeal?' Josie said, turning to look up at her dad. 'When you drove over to Romania with supplies. It was ages ago now.'

'Yes, we did a couple of runs actually. Filled the van to the brim with black bags full of blankets and off we went. Are you thinking we could do something similar here?' He leaned over, perusing the photos.

'Could we? Would you mind?' I asked him.

'No, of course I don't mind. We should do whatever we can to help.'

'Really, Dad? That would be so brilliant. I know you've got a lot of other stuff on at the moment, but some of these women are like me; expecting a baby. They haven't even got a proper roof over their head. I can't imagine how they must be feeling.'

Eric nodded keenly. 'Well, let's make it happen then.'

'Oh, Eric, that's what makes you the best landlord in town,' I said, standing up to kiss him on the cheek.

'I'll take that as a compliment even though I'm the only landlord in the village.' Eric chuckled.

'Yes, but you would still be my favourite even if there were a dozen more pubs around here. You're the best, Eric,' I told him. 'I'll put some posters up in the window and around the pub, letting people know what we're doing. If that's all right?'

'Of course. And make sure to tell Tim too. He's the editor of the local rag. Comes in every Friday lunch. He'll put a piece in the paper for us. If it's anything like last time, we'll be inundated with donations. We can put anything that comes in straight up in the back bedroom.'

'Brilliant,' I said, fired up now by Josie's strength of feeling, Eric's agreement to the idea and my own growing excitement that we could actually do something to help, however small, and maybe make a tiny difference. 'When I'm out and about with my doggy clients, I'll put the word out too. I'll put together a small flyer and I'll pop them through people's letter boxes as I go past. I can think of a few people already who I know will probably want to help.'

Josie gave a satisfied sigh. 'I know it's not a lot, but it makes me feel better knowing that we're doing something to help.'

'I'm not sure how we'll actually get the donations sent over there, but we can worry about that later.'

'Do what we did before,' said Eric, matter-of-factly. 'Load the van up and drive over. That way we can make sure our aid gets to the right place.'

'But you won't want to be driving to France. You've got a pub to run.' I reminded him.

'Honestly love, I'd be happy to do it. You never know, this might be the last chance I have to get involved in something like this.'

I tilted my head to look at him. I'd put the fact that he might not be running The Dog and Duck much longer to the back of my mind.

'Well, I'm not getting any younger, love, and things are changing around here. I won't be the landlord of this pub forever, and besides, we'll have a baby about the place soon.'

Josie and I exchanged a look and my heart twisted at the realization that Eric was facing an unknown future. The pub simply wouldn't be the same without Eric, but more importantly, how would he fare if he wasn't able to do the job he loved? This place was his home and held so many happy memories. With his wife Miriam, they'd built up a thriving business that had become the heart of the community. They'd made so many good friends in the village and held so many happy and celebratory events at the pub. Special times that our family had been fortunate enough to be a part of too. After Miriam died, over nine years ago now, all the locals had rallied round to help Eric and Josie through the difficult following months. It hadn't been easy, but he'd come through, carving out a new life for himself, needing to adjust again when Josie moved out to start a new life with Ethan. Leaving the pub that formed such a huge part of his memories would be a huge wrench, I knew.

'Of course, you'll have to come with me, Ellie,' Eric said brightening. 'This one here won't be any use in her condition,' he said, nudging Josie in the side.

'Oh cheers, Dad,' said Josie, laughing. 'You're probably right though. I'd struggle to even fit in the van at the moment.'

'We could do it over a weekend,' he continued. 'We can drive down one day, drop the stuff off and then come back the next day. It won't take us long. How does that sound, Ells? A weekend in France with an old geezer. I bet you don't get many offers like that.'

I laughed. Johnny had offered to whisk me away, but I'd turned him down. Thinking about it, this was probably the closest I was going to get to a holiday all year.

'Absolutely,' I said, with a smile. 'I'm definitely up for that!'

Six

Eric was right. Within days of letting people know our plans, we were besieged with offers of help. It was wonderful to see the community rally round, donating old clothes and bed linen, but also bags of brand new items too; baby outfits and hats and blankets, as well as a full range of men's and ladies' clothes, including winter coats and jackets.

'We could start a new shop with this lot,' Josie joked one morning.

'I can't believe it.' I stood back, surveying the heap of clothes. 'Everyone wanted to help. It really does restore your faith in human nature when you get involved in something like this.'

Without exception, all of my doggy clients had given to our appeal and word of what we were doing had spread to the most unlikely quarters. I was out one morning being dragged along at the end of a lead by a highly energetic and eager to please English Pointer called Amber when I ran, almost literally, into Max Golding.

'Oh, hi,' I said, frantically trying to gather Amber closer to my side. At that precise moment she was intent on tying herself up in knots around Max's legs while his impeccably behaved dogs looked on disapprovingly.

'Another day, another dog?'

'Exactly! This is Amber,' I said, not entirely sure why I felt the need to make formal introductions. His long legs stepped over the tangled lead and a smile spread on his lips as he leant down to pat the dog.

'She's beautiful.' He looked at her, admiration shining in his brown eyes and I felt curious, for the briefest moment, what it might be like to be on the receiving end of one of those long, appreciative gazes.

'Yes, she's gorgeous,' I agreed, wondering if it had suddenly become very hot around here. 'Must admit to a bit of a soft spot for her.'

'She shouldn't be on the lead though. A dog like that really needs to be able to run free.'

I smiled. Tightly. *A property developer and dog expert too.* Who knew? I don't know if Max Golding intended it as a slight, but I bristled nonetheless at his words, affronted on Amber's behalf.

'She's only eighteen months old,' I said, a tad defensively. 'If I let her off here, she'd probably disappear into those bushes and I'd never see her again. Her owners haven't had the time to give her the training she needs, so that's what I'm working on with her. Her recall can still be a bit iffy, especially if she gets distracted by other dogs or birds, but hopefully she's improving with every one of our sessions. She's okay in big wide fields where I can keep her in my sight. Pointers have a tendency to roam long distances – she will come back, but it's always in her own time.'

'Fair enough,' he said, shrugging his shoulders. 'Are you going this way?'

I nodded, falling in line with his step as we ambled up

the lane. I was glad that I didn't have to face him full-on, that, instead, I could pretend to be vaguely cool, all the while taking sneaky glances of his profile. In my defence, his profile was very compelling. A strong jawline, wide mouth and the shadow of stubble, together with his sweeping long raincoat, leant him a raffish air that sent my insides a-wobbling. Yes, there was definitely something about Mr Golding that shook my equilibrium. I took a deep breath and focussed on putting one foot in front of the other without falling over. Much less distracting, although no less tricky.

'I hear you're behind The Dog and Duck's latest charity appeal,' he said, turning to look at me.

'Well, it's not just me.' It was a bright cold day and the fresh air stung at my cheeks. 'Josie and I were talking about the situation the other day and we decided we wanted to do something to help. It quickly escalated from there. The response has been amazing.'

'I think it's great, what you're doing. Let me know if there's anything I can do to help on a practical basis. Really, I mean it. If there's anything you need, then just ask.'

'Thanks, Max, that's very kind of you.' Eric had already mentioned that Max had offered to pay our travelling costs and put us up in a hotel overnight, which was incredibly generous of him.

Gorgeous and giving, what a combination. Maybe it was time for me to reassess my first impression of Max as an uptight, arrogant so-and-so.

'Come on,' he said, steering me through a small cutaway in the hedge. 'There's a field here. You'll be able to let Amber have a run.'

'But this is private property,' I said, standing in front of a sign saying exactly that and warning of dire consequences if I was to take one step further.

'Yes, I know,' said Max with a wide grin. 'It's my private property. Come on.'

My mouth dropped open involuntarily and then I laughed, covering up my surprise. I hadn't realized his land extended so far, but then what did I expect? Hanging out with the landed gentry.

As soon as we were in the field, I unclipped Amber's lead and watched her sprint off into the distance, closely followed by Max's magnificent dogs, who I learned were called Bella and Holly.

'She'll be perfectly safe here. There's fencing around the perimeter of the field so she can't come to any harm.'

'Aw, look at her running with your two – she's absolutely loving it.' I wasn't about to admit that she wasn't the only one revelling in the moment. I almost felt like running down the hill myself, arms wide, a la Julie Andrews, but I was still trying for a cool and unwobbly vibe – without much success, admittedly. Walking with Max through the beautiful countryside was more thrilling than I could have anticipated.

'Listen, you can always use this field to exercise your dogs.'

'Really?'

'Absolutely. Obviously keep it to yourself. I don't want the whole village thinking it's a dog's playground, but you're very welcome to make use of it if you'd like to. I know you do some training with your dogs. This would be the ideal spot. You wouldn't be disturbed. Well, maybe only occasionally – by me and these two hounds.'

He gave me a sideways look, his brown eyes shining warmly. He made it sound so inviting, particularly the part where he mentioned I might bump into him again. I had to restrain myself from throwing my arms around his neck and kissing him on the lips. Thankfully the inappropriate bells rang in my head. Instead I thanked him politely and then said the first intelligent thing that came into my head.

'Lovely weather, isn't it? Cold, but warm... No, not warm exactly. You know what I mean. Bright and sunny.'

Not very intelligent as it turned out, but it seemed to make Max smile.

'Isn't this the most stunning scenery?' Max stopped, lifted his head and surveyed the surrounding countryside. 'Every day when I come out here it makes me appreciate just how lucky I am to live in such a beautiful part of the country.'

'Yes, you're right. I grew up here. It was all I ever knew until I went off to university. I don't think I fully appreciated how lovely it was until I went away and then came home again.'

We followed the dogs down the hill, exchanging a smile at their good-natured antics.

'So, are you back for good?' Max asked.

'I'm not sure. It was only ever meant as a temporary thing, but I must admit I'm enjoying the dog-minding and stints behind the bar at The Dog and Duck much more than I could have imagined. It's a simpler way of life, less stressful. But I suppose I'll have to go and do the proper job again at some point.'

'So what was the proper job then, Ellie?'

'I'm an accountant. I worked for one of the big consulting companies in the city.'

'Ah, okay.' Max nodded his head sagely and I wasn't sure if I imagined a look of amusement on his face. As we reached the bottom of the field, the magnificent frontage of Braithwaite Manor came into view just through the hedgerows. The huge country house had formed a backdrop of faded grandeur to my childhood. We'd always called it the big house. Imagined what it might have been like to live there in a bygone age before it had fallen into disrepair. Now the house had been extensively restored. The crumbling brickwork had been repointed and the roof had been replaced, along with the many tall grand windows overlooking the extensive grounds. A sight to take your breath away.

'It's nothing much, but it's home,' I quipped. 'Do you actually live there?' I asked, unable to disguise the incredulous note to my voice.

'Yes.' He glared at me before glancing at his watch and I caught the shift in his mood, wondering for a moment if I'd upset him with my flippancy. 'Look, I'm going to have to go, but it's been great seeing you again, Ellie. And remember, use the field anytime you want to.'

'Thanks Max,' I said, watching him stride off in the direction of the big house, hoping that the look he'd given me hadn't been one of complete and utter disdain.

Seven

'I need a huge favour, Ellie.'

I'd just started my evening shift at the pub when Polly came in for what was becoming her customary after-work orange juice.

'Okay,' I said, trying to decipher from her eager expression just what sort of favour this might be. 'Fire away.'

She took a deep breath. 'Well, the thing is – I've got a date and…'

'Ooh… Really? How exciting! Who is he? Where did you meet him?'

Polly laughed, the faintest hint of colour spreading on her cheeks. 'He's a customer actually. Or else he was. He used to come in and buy flowers for his girlfriend, but I hadn't seen him in months. Then I bumped into him in the supermarket and we got chatting. It turns out he and the girlfriend have split and, well, he asked me out for dinner.'

'Oh my goodness, that's so exciting!' I clapped my hands together delightedly. 'What's his name? What does he do? Where does his live? Come on spill the beans, I'm desperate to hear about this mystery man.' I looked around the snug to check that all my customers were happy and then pulled up a stool and plonked my elbows on the bar, resting my chin on my hands. I was all ears. In the absence of any romance of my own, I was more than happy to live vicariously through Polly's love life.

'That's the thing, I barely know anything about him. I know his name – Rob, but that's about it. I was so surprised when he asked me out, standing there in the middle of the frozen food aisle, I didn't know what to say.'

'But you do like him? He is fanciable?'

'Oh, he is!' She swooned, her face taking on a dreamy expression. 'He's gorgeous. You'll love him, Ells, he's just your type – tall, dark and handsome. Although I'm getting first dibs on this one,' she said with a cheeky smile. 'He seems really friendly too. But I thought it might be a bit awkward, just the two of us, getting to know each other over dinner. I'm so out of practice with the whole dating thing. What happens if we run out of conversation after five minutes or decide we don't really like each other after all? That's why I suggested…'

Her eyes grew wide at me, a tentative smile hovering at the corner of her cute rosebud lips.

'Oh no!' I clapped my hands together, the penny finally dropping. 'Please don't tell me you want me to come along too? Noooo! That would be so awkward. Me sitting there like your mother. I would only get in the way and, if the two of you hit it off, I'd feel like a proper gooseberry. Honestly, Polly, trust me on this, you need to go on your own. It'll be absolutely fine. I'll call you if you like, halfway through the date, to give you a get-out clause if you need it.'

Polly giggled.

'No, I didn't mean just you. Now, that would be awkward! I thought you and Johnny could come along. Like a double

59

date.' She grimaced and scrubbed the words out with her hands. 'No, not really a double date, it's just that I'd feel so much more relaxed with the two of you there.'

Ah. Now I got it. I looked into Polly's bright eager eyes and wondered how I might break it to her.

'The thing is, Johnny and I aren't together any more. I'm really sorry, Polly, but a double date's not going to work.'

'Oh…' She dropped her gaze for a moment, before looking up at me, all doe-eyed. 'Actually I spoke to Johnny and he told me what had happened, that you weren't together any more. And I'm really sorry about that. I know how difficult it must be between you two at the moment, but Johnny said he'd be happy to come along if you were too. He mentioned something about you staying good friends.'

Great. So Johnny had outmanoeuvred me. If I did go, it would mean having to make polite conversation with Johnny and I wasn't sure if it wasn't too soon for that. And if I didn't go, then I would look churlish, as if I didn't want to stay friends after all. It was a lose-lose situation.

'Please, Ellie. I wouldn't normally ask, but it would mean the world to me if you could both come along. Just as friends. Obviously.'

Obviously. I suppressed a sigh. Honestly, it was a wonder Polly had any difficulty in bagging a man. She was all big blue eyes and fluttering eyelashes and even I was finding her hard to resist all the time she was gazing at me imploringly.

'Okay,' I said, reluctantly. 'A double non-date? I don't see why not. It'll be a first for me, at least, and by the sounds of it, it could be fun.'

*

We were less than an hour into the date when I realized I'd probably had more fun on my last visit to the dentist than I was likely to have in the company of Rob. Don't get me wrong, he was everything Polly said he would be. Good-looking in a very clean, scrubbed-up way. Tall, broad and slim, his black hair was closely cut, he had large brown eyes and a magnificent set of white gleaming teeth. Charming too, if in a rather polished practiced way. He had all the boxes ticked but, for some reason, all the parts didn't add up to a very convincing whole. Still, if Polly liked him then that was all that mattered.

'You all right, Ells,' said Johnny, giving me a surreptitious dig in the side.

'Oh yes, yes, I'm fine,' I said, sitting up straight in my chair.

In fairness, I needn't have worried about things being awkward between Johnny and me. If he was nursing a broken heart he was doing a good job at hiding it. His cheeky, lovable personality was on full show tonight and the way he was acting it was as if he didn't have a care in the world. Maybe he hadn't been into me as much as I'd thought.

I immediately focussed my attention back on Polly and Rob and plastered a big smile on my face. I'd drifted off there for a moment, thoughts of Max Golding filtering into my mind. Why, I wasn't entirely sure. I'd been trying to establish what it was that made him quite so attractive, quite so disturbing to my peace of mind. At first I hadn't liked him one bit - okay that was a lie, I'd liked him quite a lot, but I'd found him unsettling, if not compelling. Intimidating, but incredibly sexy at the same time. Something about him messed with my head. Was it the unruly hair or the darkly dangerous eyes that spoke to me? The scar on his top lip or the extent of his wide mouth which lit up in a glorious smile when I was least expecting it? Whatever it was, there was an indefinable quality that spoke directly to my insides, something that ignited in my brain even when he wasn't around.

Anyway, I wasn't here to be mooning over that man. Definitely not. I shook my head to rid my brain of all things Max Golding. I was here to help out my friend Polly and to vet Rob as potential new boyfriend material. Concentrate, Ellie. I peered closer at Rob, dropping my head to one side to get a different view. Nope. That didn't help either. However hard I tried I just couldn't warm to him. Maybe Polly saw something in him that I was clearly missing?

'So Rob, what about when you're not working. What do you like to do then?' I asked, brightly.

For the last fifteen minutes he'd been telling us about his job as manager of the carpet section in a large department store, which would have been fine had he not got sidetracked on the detail along the way. He proceeded to tell us all about the virtues of the extensive range of flooring he sold. You name it, he was an expert in it. Wool, synthetic, tufted, woven – the man was a veritable walking encyclopaedia when it came to carpet, and that was before he got started on wooden and laminate flooring. Who knew there was so much to discover about flooring, well, apart from Rob, obviously. I think we were all desperate to get him onto another subject before we capitulated and put down a deposit on a high pile shag. Anything had to be better than discussing the merits of flooring.

'Fishing. I love it.' Oh dear lord, how wrong could I be? 'There's some lovely spots around here for night-fishing. You need the right bait of course. I like to use…'

'How about we head off to The Dog and Duck for a nightcap,' said Johnny, banging his hands down on the table, making us all jump to attention. Judging by Polly's slightly startled expression, I suspected we were all in need of a change of scene and a livener.

'Well, if you don't mind,' said Rob, addressing me and Johnny directly, 'it's been an absolute pleasure meeting you, but I was wondering, Polly, if you'd like to come back to mine for a coffee. So we can get to know each other a bit better.'

'Oh…' Polly's eyes clouded in alarm, as her gaze darted from me to Johnny. I could have sworn that a little speech bubble appeared at the side of her head. *Help!* Her mouth gaped open, making a false start as the words failed to materialize. Eventually, she managed to form some sort of coherent sentence. 'It's been lovely, but I've got an early start in the morning, so I ought to go back with Ellie and Johnny. You're welcome to join us for a quick drink though, if you'd like to?'

'Fair enough,' said Rob, his mouth curling in disappointment, as though he'd almost closed a deal on a big sale, but had failed at the last moment. He stood up and pulled on his jacket. 'Some other time perhaps. I won't come for a drink – pubs aren't really my scene.'

The collective sharp intake of breath from the rest of us couldn't have been worse if Rob had admitted he killed puppies in his spare time.

'Doesn't like pubs!' said Johnny in mock outrage later as

we walked home through the town, our arms linked with Polly's. 'What's that all about?'

'Must admit it's a bit weird, isn't it?' I said in agreement. 'He's clearly never been to The Dog and Duck.'

Polly gave a heartfelt sigh. 'To be honest, I think that was the least of his problems. Gawd, he was a bit dull, wasn't he? Really I don't know how I pick them. He seemed so lovely and charming when I spoke to him before. Sometimes I wonder if I'm a bit desperate. It's such a novelty to be asked out by a man that I don't stop to think whether it's actually a good idea or not. I was just glad you were both there with me, or else I might still be stuck with him talking about the benefits of loop pile carpets over twist pile or, god forbid, fishing bait.'

'He wasn't that bad,' I said, trying to put a positive spin on the situation.

Both Johnny and Polly stopped, dropped my arms and turned to look at me aghast.

'Oh come on, Ellie,' said Johnny, shaking his head. 'Did you really want to find out more about the stain resistance properties of polypropylene?'

I laughed and walked on. Polly and Johnny ran to catch me up, linking arms again. 'Well, clearly Rob wasn't the right man for you, Polly, but don't let one bad experience put you off. You never know, the next man you go out on a date with might be the special one.'

'Hmmm, I'm not sure I share your confidence,' said Polly with a resigned sigh. 'In fact, I think I'm probably done with dating. It's too much hard work for too little reward.'

Later, sitting on the bench in the snug bar of the pub with a fresh round of drinks in front of us, Polly continued to bemoan her single status. 'The trouble is I think all the half-decent men in my small area of the world are spoken for.'

'Cheers for that, Polly,' said Johnny, shrugging his shoulders and looking forlornly into his beer.

She giggled, and snuggled into his side, and he reciprocated with a friendly arm around her shoulder.

'Oh, you don't count, Johnny. You're my friend. No, I mean fanciable men who are decent and honest, who aren't arseholes or who aren't deadly dull – after tonight, I think that might be even worse than being an idiot.'

'Right, so what you're saying is I don't even qualify. I'm not sure whether to take that as a compliment or feel insulted instead.'

Johnny, who was sat between the two of us, pulled me into his other side and I rested my head on his shoulder. It felt perfectly natural to be together as friends with no other agenda hovering over us.

'Ah well, at least we all have each other,' I said, looking up at him. 'Maybe Rob has a point though. Maybe it's us who has the problem. You have to admit we spend far more time in here than is good for us. You don't think we're all wasting our lives away, drinking ourselves into a future of poverty and drunkenness.'

'Blimey, Ells, you're a little ray of sunshine tonight, aren't you?'

I laughed. 'It's just got me thinking that's all. Where we'll all be in ten years' time? Five years even.' I wasn't sure if it was the wine or Polly's palpable disappointment that had put me in a contemplative mood.

'Oh, that's easy,' said Johnny. 'You'll be Financial Director of a top London firm with a hot-shot city lawyer husband. You'll have three kids, a townhouse, a nanny, and you'll holiday every year in the South of France. You'll be far too busy and important to keep in touch with your old friends from home.' Was that a hint of sadness I detected in Johnny's voice?

'Really?'

'Yeah, I can just imagine that,' said Polly, damning me with her quick agreement, as though it wasn't a huge leap of the imagination. 'What about me?'

'You'll have a whole string of florists throughout the country,' Johnny went on. 'You'll be wildly successful and only have to work a couple of days a week in your shop in Little Leyton just to keep your hand in. You'll have a sweet little cottage in the village, a devoted husband and a baby on the way.'

Polly sighed contentedly. 'That sounds perfect. If you can see all of that in your crystal ball then clearly I have no need to worry. What about you, Johnny? What do you think you'll be doing?'

'Well, I'll still have the business, but I'll have thirty or forty people working for me. I'll be spending most of my time building my own house – I'd love to do that. A barn conversion probably. I'll still be in here most nights though and I'll still be doing the pub quiz once a month.'

'A barn conversion?' said Polly. Her expression took on a dreamy quality. 'That sounds amazing.'

'Don't worry,' said Johnny, ruffling my hair. 'We won't forget about you, sweetheart, even when you're out there conquering the world, we'll be here raising a glass to our high-flying friend.'

I peered into my beer, a stirring of disquiet running

along the length of my body. Inexplicably, I felt a twinge of sadness that they both thought I wouldn't be here in Little Leyton in ten years' time, that I'd be living a different kind of life somewhere else. Daft really, because how could any of us know what lay in our future. The future Johnny spoke about for me was one I'd had planned out ever since I was a teenager at school. I'd wanted to be that high-flyer with the swanky London lifestyle. Only now, I wasn't sure it was what I wanted after all. Especially hearing the words said aloud by Johnny. Could I really turn my back on everything I'd worked so hard for? My qualifications and my career? And how would it make my parents feel to know that the sacrifices they'd made for the sake of my education had all been for nothing?

I closed my eyes, nestling my head further into the crook of Johnny's neck and curled my arm around his waist. I didn't want to think about it. Not now. I was more than content to savour the moment. The familiar sound of clinking glasses, animated chatter and laughter washed over me in a comforting haze.

I could quite easily have fallen asleep there on Johnny's chest without giving a second thought to my future. It was only when I became aware of someone standing over us, interrupting our cosy little threesome that my eyes flickered open. At eye level my gaze settled on a cream cable jumper – snug, warm, huggable – the scent of warm spices reached my nostrils just as my brain registered who, in fact, might be invading my senses in such an insistent way.

My gaze travelled upwards and settled onto the mesmeric dark brown eyes of Max Golding. Mesmeric dark brown eyes that were glistening with amusement as they observed me closely. A stand-off that always seemed to be reached in the company of Mr Golding.

'Hi Max,' I said, shifting myself up in my seat, determined not to be distracted by those eyes. Instead, I attempted to rearrange my limbs into a semi-decent, nonchalant, sophisticated position. Impossible, I quickly realized, in my slightly squiffy laying-sprawled-across-Johnny's-lap state.

'Good evening?' he asked, with a slight incline of his head, still holding on to that permanently amused expression of his that might, if it continued, begin to rile me.

'Great, thank you.'

'We've been on a double date,' said Johnny, laughing, pulling both me and Polly closer in to his side.

'Looks like a lot of fun,' said Max, his dark eyebrows shifting imperceptibly.

His gaze fell on mine and my skin prickled as the air closed in on me. I made my excuses and headed for the bathroom, leaving Max chatting to Johnny and Polly. There was something about that man that got beneath my skin, that made me feel vulnerable and exposed in his company. I needed to clear my head and – *ugh* – judging by the reflection that met me in the loo mirrors, I needed to do something about my hair too. I ran my hand through the wayward curls and wondered what had happened exactly in the period between leaving the house earlier this evening and now to turn my hair into such a disaster. The red glowing cheeks and the thundering heartbeat were all down to Max, but my hair was clearly working to its own agenda. No wonder Max had been sporting such an amused expression when he'd given me the once-over. In the mirror, I turned my head one way and then the other, attempting to flatten my hair down with my hands, but it made not the slightest difference. I sighed. Why was I even worried what Max Golding thought of me, he was just a distraction, a good-looking one admittedly, but one I could certainly do without at the moment. Best to put him completely out of my mind and try to avoid him as much as I possibly could. Absolutely. Out of sight, out of mind. I pulled open the door of the loos and waltzed straight into the path of that damn cream cable jumper. Easier said than done, obviously.

'Oh, hi,' I said, silently reprimanding my body for immediately going into overdrive again. Either it had suddenly become very hot in here or else my body temperature was playing silly beggars again. The corridor at the back of the pub was narrow and tight for space, and the low beamed ceiling only added to the heady atmosphere closing in around me. If I reached out my hand it would be all too easy to feel the thickness of Max's jumper for myself, to rub the fabric between my fingers, to explore and discover the bare skin beneath. Good grief! What on earth was wrong with me?

Judging by Max's worried expression, he was clearly thinking the same. He tilted his head to one side and his eyes narrowed with concern. 'Are you all right. You look a bit...'

I flapped my hands in front of my face. 'I'm fine, it's just a bit hot in here that's all. Don't you think?'

'Well, if you're sure you're okay. It's good seeing you again, Ellie.'

'Yep, great.'

I spread my arms back against the wall and Max squeezed past me, causing me to have a very close encounter with his lovely jumper. I dashed off, eager to get away now from Max Golding. That man was seriously damaging to my health.

69

Back on the wooden bench, I declined Johnny's offer of another glass of wine and instead opted for a thirst-quenching pint glass of lemonade. I needed to sober up and fast – think about getting home. First I leaned across Johnny and whispered to Polly. 'What you were saying earlier about there being no decent men in Little Leyton? What about that Max? You said yourself how gorgeous he is. He'd make an ideal date, don't you think?'

I was half-hoping Polly might want to snag Max for herself then I wouldn't be able to entertain improper thoughts about him.

'Ugh! No.' Polly pulled a face that might have been more fitting if I'd wafted rotten fish under her nose. 'Obviously I can appreciate that he's a very good-looking man, but he's just too... too...'

Johnny and I were hanging on to her every word.

'Too what?' we said in unison.

'He's too much. Too perfect. Too macho, too sophisti-cated, too charming.' Polly rattled off Max's lists of faults, or attributes, whichever way you might consider them, before pausing to give her reasoned argument some further consideration. 'He's just too much of everything. I couldn't be doing with someone like that. Obviously I can appreciate, objectively, that he is a fine example of the male species. Lovely to swoon over and admire from afar, but you wouldn't want to be in a relationship with him. I mean, have you seen the house he lives in?'

I had seen the house he lived in, from a distance at least. It was jaw-droppingly awesome.

'No, men like that are far too demanding,' said Polly, warming to her subject. 'You'd never be able to have an off day. You would have to be thin and lovely and witty and entertaining all the time. You'd be expected to hobnob with politicians and celebrities, rustle up gourmet dinners for his mates and then be a sexual goddess in bed.'

'Nah, I expect he has a man to do that sort of thing for him for him,' quipped Johnny.

'WHAT?!'

'A chef, that's what I meant,' Johnny said, chuckling. 'A chef to rustle up his meals, not anything else.'

'Right, well, whatever he's got going on up at that house, I'm not sure I would want any part of it,' Polly concluded.

I laughed. I knew I'd been guilty of projecting an entire lifestyle onto Max, but I think Polly was taking it to an entirely different level. Johnny shook his head and rolled his eyes.

'There's no pleasing some people,' he said. 'You know, Polly, you should be more open to different people and situations. In your quest for love, perhaps you're being a bit blinkered. Maybe you need to spread your net a little wider.'

'Hmmm.' Polly took a large glug of wine, closed her eyes and reflected on Johnny's words. 'You know, Johnny, you talk a lot of sense. Spread my net further, that's what I'm going to do.'

At that moment, Max returned to the bar and we all turned to look at him, reappraising him in the light of Polly's comments. He had a commanding presence, that was for sure, demanding your full attention as though it was his birthright, and despite my best intentions, I simply couldn't drag my eyes away from him.

'Although, I won't be casting my net in that direction.' Polly went on, just in case we were in any doubt about her intentions. 'Me and the Lord of the Manor over there won't be getting together anytime soon.' She gestured her head towards Max who was now deep in conversation with Eric. 'I'll leave that to some other, braver woman.'

She turned to look at me, a glint in her eyes.

Of course, she was absolutely right about Max. Macho, sophisticated and charming, he was all those things and many more, but I couldn't agree with her on him being too much of a good thing. From where I was sitting he looked pretty much perfect in every way.

Eight

Early the next morning an urgent banging on the front door roused me from my bed. Bleary-eyed, wishing I hadn't drunk quite so much white wine the previous night, I traipsed down the stairs wondering what was quite so pressing at seven-thirty in the morning.

On the doorstep was Gemma Jones managing to look obscenely well-put together in her obviously just-got-out-of-bed look. Pastel-coloured polka-dot pyjamas, blonde hair swept back into a high ponytail and face bare of make-up, she looked as though she'd just stepped out of an advertisement for healthy breakfast cereal. In contrast, in my grey jogging pants and sweat top, feeling like death warmed up, I was certain I'd be cast as the slutty unfit neighbour. I ran my hand through my hair, stood up straight and plastered a smile on my face.

'Gemma!'

'Ellie, I'm so sorry to turn up like this, so early, but I'm desperate.' If this was what desperate did for you, then maybe I needed a small part of it. Looking closer though, beyond the healthy early morning glow, I could see anxiety flecked in her eyes. 'I need a huge favour. I've left the kids with my next-door neighbour, so I can't be long.'

'Of course. If I can. What is it?'

I was clearly the go-to girl for favours in Little Leyton at the moment.

'Nigel's away on business at the moment and he's not back until the weekend. The boys have a sickness bug, Sasha has got her dancing exam today, Eliza's being clingy and the baby's got croup.'

I gulped, hoping to goodness she wasn't about to ask me to look after her kids. I hadn't had a lot of experience in that area and certainly didn't want to be picking up any nasty germs.

'Poor old Digby is not getting a look in,' she went on. 'He's not had a walk in days and keeps looking at me with those sorrowful brown eyes.'

'You want me to walk him?' I asked, relief peppering my words. Dogs I could deal with.

'Please. And I wondered if you wouldn't mind having him stay for a few days too. Just until Nigel's home. Digby's no trouble, as you know. And I'd feel so much happier knowing he was staying with you rather than at the kennels.'

'Yes, sure, that's no problem. He can come with me to the pub. Eric and Josie won't mind. And he'll get plenty of walks with me when I'm out and about with my other doggy clients.'

'Thanks, Ellie.' Gemma surprised me by throwing her arms round me and giving me a tight squeeze. The fresh scent of newly laundered cotton wafted under my nostrils, making me wish I'd jumped in the shower before Gemma's arrival. How did she do it? Five kids, an absent husband, a pristine swanky house to maintain and she still managed to look drop-dead gorgeous and totally on top of things first thing in the morning.

As I watched her drive away to her poorly children, I bent down to give Digby a cuddle, nuzzling my face into his fur. Seemingly she had it all, but I knew, for the moment at least, I wouldn't want to swap places with her for the world.

For that week Digby followed me around everywhere. He was the perfect man; adoring, gorgeous to look at, cuddly and very low maintenance. Just the type of man I needed in my life right now. There was no hidden agenda and no game-playing; you knew exactly where you stood with a loyal dog at your side and that's just how I liked it. In fairness, it seemed that Johnny and I had reached a new level of understanding. He still popped into the pub for a chat and a pint, but he never stayed long and had stopped offering to walk me home ever since our heart-to-heart about our relationship. Bless him, he'd given me the space I'd asked for and for that I was hugely grateful and somewhat relieved too. I'd been worried that our friendship would suffer or things might become awkward between us, but when we had been out together recently Polly had always come along too and there'd been no noticeable tension between us.

'Hello darling, I wasn't expecting you in today. You're not down for a shift, are you?'

I'd turned up early at the pub one morning, with Digby in tow, just as Eric was emerging from the steps of the cellar.

'No, but I was chatting with Josie this morning and we thought it might make sense to make a start on sorting through all the donations. We can put them into piles, similar items together, and then bag them up and label them ready for our trip. That way it will make it much easier at the other end.'

We'd agreed to make the trip to France at the end of the

month, to give enough time for people to get their donations in, but I don't think any of us could have anticipated the response we'd had already.

'That's a good idea. Although I think you might have a job on your hands – you can hardly get in the back bedroom for clothes.'

'Oh, it won't take us long once we get started. Anything that isn't suitable we'll put to one side and then we can decide what we want to do with them – maybe pass them on to another charity.'

'Sounds good to me. Fancy a coffee to get you going?'

'Yes, I'll make them. Josie's at the doctors for a check-up at the moment, but she'll be along in a while.' I wandered into the kitchen, as Digby did a sweep of the floor behind me, picking up any wayward crumbs.

We'd only just sat down when there was a rat-a-tat-tat on the back door.

'Come in,' called Eric.

'Morning Eric, Ellie.' Tim Weston, editor of *The Leyton Post*, wandered in, along with a young woman I didn't recognize. 'This is Victoria,' Tim explained. 'She's just started working on the paper so I thought I'd bring her along to introduce you. I know we put a small piece in the paper a couple of weeks ago about the charity appeal, but we thought we'd run an update in this week's edition, if that's okay? We wanted to get some more details on the campaign and grab a photo of the pair of you.'

'Sure, Ellie will give you all the information you need to know,' Eric offered. 'Come and have a look upstairs, Tim, you'll be amazed by the amount of stuff we've received already.'

Victoria Evans was fresh-faced, twenty-one-ish I reckoned, with long brown wavy hair and barely there make-up, reminding me of a young Kate Middleton. She had a natural, easy charm about her and was clearly eager to do a good job, poised as she was with her pen and notepad.

'So why this particular cause?' she asked, sitting down next to me and sounding like an old pro, as if she'd been doing the job for ever.

'I think we were all touched reading about the plight of the refugees in Calais. These are people, like you and me, fleeing their home country to escape the fear and violence there; it's hard to imagine being driven to such lengths. We wanted to do something to help, to show a solidarity with these people who have found themselves in such terrible circumstances.'

'And what can our readers do to help?'

'We're asking for donations of good quality clothes and bedding. Shoes too. People can drop off any items here at the pub or we can arrange collection if that's easier.'

'That's perfect,' said Victoria, 'we're aiming to get the piece in this week's edition so hopefully it will bring in lots more donations for you.'

'Thanks Victoria.' Immediately I'd warmed to this young woman, especially after Digby had given his seal of approval by resting his snout on her legs and gazing up at her adoringly, which she didn't seem to mind in the slightest. There was an honesty and integrity about her that I hadn't always seen in her boss, Tim. She'd make a useful contact for any future events we wished to publicize. 'Are you local?' I asked her as we stood up to go through to the main bar.

'Kind of. I live in Upper Leyton. At the Old Vicarage?'

'Oh right.' Upper Leyton was the next village along to us, just as picturesque as Little Leyton with its rich honey-colour stone houses surrounding the village green. 'Reverend Trish Evans must be your mum then?'

'Yes, that's right,' she said with a smile that only confirmed the fact that she could be no other woman's daughter.

'Well, look, I hope to see you again, Victoria. If you're interested, the first Friday in every month we have live music here out in the old barn, and every second Tuesday of the month is quiz night, which is always good for a laugh. Aside from that, there's usually something going on here.'

'Great, I'll definitely have to take you up on that.'

After Tim had taken the required photos of me and Eric standing behind the bar with our hands on the beer pumps, he and Victoria stood at the front door about to leave, when Tim turned and asked: 'So come on Eric, tell me, what's this I hear about the pub being sold? I understand this place is being turned into a restaurant, is that right?'

'What?' boomed Eric. I glanced across at him to see a tell-tale twitch of annoyance hover above his lip before he quickly broke into laughter. 'You been listening to the village gossip train again, Tim? You should know better than that. What was it they were saying last year? That I'd bought myself a Russian mail-order bride. Ha ha, well, I'm sorry to have to disappoint again, but there's no changes afoot here. Rest assured though, if there is you'll be the first to know. No, the truth of the matter is the only way I'll be leaving this place is when they carry me out in a six-foot box.'

As Tim and Victoria left and with Eric back down in the cellar seeing to his barrels, I was left wondering what exactly was going on behind the scenes. Clearly Eric hadn't wanted Tim to know anything about the future of the pub, which was understandable, but I was curious to know if there'd been any developments about the new ownership. Perhaps Josie had got it wrong and Eric's tenancy would be renewed after all, but then Eric had intimated to me himself that he might not be around here for much longer. The thought made me shudder. I didn't like to ask him directly as I sensed it was a sensitive topic and I felt sure if there was anything he wanted me to know then he would tell me himself when he was good and ready.

This place was like a second home to me. I knew every nook and cranny, upstairs and down. The old oak wood panelling and dark mulberry walls offered a warm comforting atmosphere and even in the depths of winter with the rain lashing down against the sash windows making them rattle, it still felt like the cosiest place on earth with the fire blazing steadily in the hearth. What I loved most of all was the fact that I could wander in here whenever I chose, help myself to a cuppa, have a chat with Eric or Josie, or anyone of our lovely regulars who happened to be around and generally while away a couple of hours without worrying if I was in the way or making a nuisance of myself. I couldn't imagine being able to do that with new people at the helm. Nor could I imagine wanting to. I sighed longingly. Did things really have to change?

Upstairs I walked into the back bedroom and gulped. What a job I had on my hands. So many clothes! I could barely make out the bed beneath the mountain of items. I took a deep breath, wondering where I should start. Seeing the daisy-sprigged curtains hanging at the window brought a whole rash of memories rushing back at me. When I was small I'd slept in this room on many occasions when staying with Josie for a sleepover. We were always so giggly and excitable, unable to settle to anything, instead running up and down the stairs to collect a bottle of pop, and then some crisps, and then... there was always something else, anything that would give us the excuse to go downstairs to listen in to the grown-up conversations. The sound of laughter, chinking glasses and animated chatter had sounded so exotic and sophisticated to me back then. When we finally made it into our bed, Josie would scare the daylights out of me with her stories of the pub ghost, a young woman in a white flowing dress, who supposedly wafted along the landing in the dead of the night. After that, every creak of the floorboards and every thump on the stairs would have us screeching aloud and burying our heads beneath the duvet.

Now, a cold shiver ran down my spine as I looked over my shoulder towards the doorway. Not the pub ghost, I suspected, but the growing realization that if Eric were to leave the pub, then soon we might only be left with our memories of this place.

I distracted myself by pulling out items from the big heap of clothes all around me. The sooner I started this job, the sooner I'd finish. I inspected each piece, folded them and placed them into piles of mens, ladies and children's wear. Everyone had been so generous. Part of me had been dreading this task, thinking I might have to rifle through old and smelly worn pieces that had seen much better days, but without exception everything was of high quality.

I'd just filled to the brim another bag, fastening the top with a tie, when I stopped, rooted to the spot, alerted by a stomach-churning crash from downstairs followed by an anguished cry.

'Eric?' I called.

When there was no response, only a muffled groan, I sprinted down the stairs.

'Eric? Are you all right? What's happened?'

'Aargh, Ellie, I'm down here.'

I peered down into the darkest depths of the cellar. Usually I avoided going down there if I possibly could, but now was no time for sissiness.

'I'm coming,' I said, sounding much braver than I felt.

Carefully, hanging onto the handrail, I navigated the steep stairs, the sounds of Eric's distress getting louder with each step that I took. When I reached the bottom I saw him, sprawled on the ground, surrounded by the contents of a crate of Belgian beer bottles, now shattered across the floor, the smell of hops meeting my nostrils.

'Oh goodness, Eric. What have you done?'

'It's my leg. I think it might be broken. You'll have to call for help, love. I can't move. Be careful of that glass. It's everywhere.'

I'm not a medical expert, but I could tell by the way Eric's ankle was sticking out at an awkward angle, that he'd done some serious damage. His skin had taken on a pale cast and suddenly he looked every one of his sixty years.

'Don't worry, Eric. I'm going to call for an ambulance,' I said, trying to quell the panic rising in my chest when I realized there was no phone reception down in the cellar. 'Don't go anywhere,' I said, wincing at my choice of words. 'I'll be straight back.'

I hated to leave Eric alone, but I knew I had no other

choice. Seeing him completely helpless, unable to move and groaning in pain, made my heart twist in sympathy. Nothing else mattered now but him. My mind flittered back to the last words he spoke to Tim as he left the pub, "the only way I'll be leaving this place is when they carry me out in a six-foot box." *Oh no!* I really hoped it wasn't some kind of unlucky omen.

I rushed up the stairs, grabbed the phone and put the call into the emergency services. I was just on my way back down to the cellar, armed with a blanket, when Josie wandered, unsuspecting, through the front door.

'Oh Josie!' A surge of emotion filled my chest at the sight of her. I hadn't wanted her to witness this, not in her condition. It took all my self-control not to break down in front of her, but I bit hard on my lip to keep the tears at bay. 'Your dad's had an accident,' I told her, my voice wobbling. 'But don't worry. The paramedics are on their way.'

'What's happened?' I saw the concern in her face. One hand flew to her mouth, the other instinctively cradling her bump. 'Is he all right?'

'He's had a fall. It looks like he's damaged his leg.' She began to follow me down the stairs and I turned to stop her. 'Don't come down. Please. There's glass all over the floor and we don't want you falling over too. Try not to worry, he'll be fine once they get him to hospital, I'm sure.'

'Tell him I'm here, won't you?' she said, squeezing my hand.

Dan, the barman, alerted by the frantic text I'd sent him, bowled through the front door just at that moment.

'Is he all right?' he asked, looking from me to Josie, placing a hand on my shoulder.

'He's in the cellar. Broken his leg, I think. The ambulance is on its way. I'd better get back down there now to see him.'

Dan followed me, immediately going to Eric's side, and I felt so grateful for his reassuring presence. Meeting Dan for the first time, you might look at him twice to check out the full visual feast in front of your eyes: black spiky hair, multiple tattoos and piercings all over the place, but beneath the whole gothy vibe, he was the sweetest, most gentle guy you could wish to meet. He'd worked at the pub for the last few years, and was such a steady hand, always ready to stand in and do extra shifts when needed. And he took on most of the heavy work down here in the cellar too. Apart from today, of course.

'I would have got these beers shifted,' he gently scolded Eric.

'I know.' Eric grimaced as he spoke. 'I wish you had now,' he said, just about managing to raise a smile.

Thankfully the ambulance arrived within a matter of minutes and the paramedics worked quickly to make Eric comfortable, offering him oxygen to ease his breathing, before manoeuvring him out of the cellar on a stretcher. As they carried him out through the pub, Josie was waiting, her face etched with concern as she strained to see her dad.

'Oh, Dad, I'm here, are you all right?'

Eric gave her a weak smile and a thumbs up from beneath his blankets.

'Don't worry about anything here. Dan and I will take care of everything,' I said, patting him on his shoulder.

'And I'll follow you down to hospital in the... car,' said Josie. 'Oh... my... god! What's happening?' Josie looked down in horror at the flood of water pooling at her feet.

'Looks like your waters have broken, love' said the paramedic matter-of-factly.

'But they can't! The baby's not due for another couple of weeks.'

The paramedic laughed ruefully. 'Well, it looks as though your baby has other ideas about that. Come on, you'd better get in the ambulance with us. We can check you over on the way.'

Nine

They kept Eric in for a couple of nights before he returned home with the addition of a metal plate and five screws in his ankle, a plaster cast, a bag full of painkillers and, despite the pain he was suffering, a huge grin on his face from the news that he had become a grandfather for the first time to a beautiful baby girl. Stella Darcy Martin was born at 3.35 a.m. weighing a bonny six pounds and five ounces despite being two weeks early, and Mum, Josie, Dad, Ethan and new granddad Eric were all doing fine.

News had quickly spread amongst the locals about Eric's fall and the arrival of the new baby and a crowd of well-wishers gathered in the snug bar at the end of the following week wanting to check on Eric's progress and, more importantly, to wet the baby's head.

Eric sat in Noel's favourite place, in the rocking chair next to the fireplace, his leg supported on a padded stool, and was at the end of some good-natured ribaldry.

'You know Eric, you really should take a bit more water with the booze these days.'

'And what were you doing getting sozzled on the Belgian beers at ten o'clock in the morning, anyway?'

Eric took it all in good part.

'I don't know about sozzled. I was certainly drenched – all I could think about lying flat out on the floor was what a waste of good beer! I still don't know how I managed it. I do that journey up and down to the cellar every day, and have done for years, without any mishap and yet that day I tripped over the bottom step, landed flat on my back and couldn't have caused more damage if I'd tried.'

'You don't do things by half, that's for sure,' said Johnny laughing. 'I reckon you're going to be out of action for some time though, even when that cast comes off.'

'I know, it's a blimming nuisance,' said Eric, his voice heavy with frustration. 'There's so much I should be doing instead of sitting around here getting in the way.'

'Hey Eric, you're not in the way,' I said, bending down on my haunches beside him. 'You're in prime position to direct operations from the hub of the pub.' I gave the rocking chair a gentle nudge. 'Me, Dan and the other bar staff have got it all covered. Really, there's nothing for you to worry about. And at least you're here to tell us where we're going wrong.'

'I suppose, but you know me. I don't like sitting around with nothing to do.'

'I know it must be difficult but honestly these next few months will pass in next to no time. You'll look back on this period and laugh. Really you will.'

Eric raised his eyebrows, looking doubtful.

He'd been putting on a brave face, but I knew Josie was worried about his state of mind. When I'd popped round to see her to meet her lovely little baby she'd asked me to keep a close eye on him.

'This is a setback he could have done without, Ellie. What with the uncertainty about the pub and if he'll still have a job and a place to live in a couple of months' time, I know he's been feeling really out of sorts. I just hope this doesn't drag him down further. He doesn't confide in me as much as he used to, I don't think he wants to worry me now I have the baby to look after.'

'He'll be fine. He's got a lot of people looking out for him, people who love and care for him. And besides, he has this little lady in his life now.'

I took Stella from her mum's arms and cradled her in my own, lifting her up to kiss her tiny cute nose. Her milky sweet scent was delicious and gave me a lovely warm fuzzy feeling inside.

'You are the most beautiful baby I've ever seen,' I whispered into her ear.

Josie laughed. 'I think so too, but then I'm probably biased.'

Happiness and weariness radiated from every pore of Josie's body, and I was so delighted to be able to share in my friend's joy.

'You really are very clever to have produced this amazing little thing. Well, you and Ethan too, but obviously you did the most important bit. Let me know when you need me to babysit and I'll be straight round.'

I stroked Stella's wispy hair around her perfect head, wondering if that strange sensation stirring in my stomach could be mistaken for something like broodiness. Babies had never featured in my plans and yet now, transfixed by the newborn in my arms, something stirred deep down inside me. How very odd. I quickly banished the thought and handed the baby back to her mum.

'Dad's coming round for Sunday lunch and when we get

back to some kind of normality...' Josie snorted as if she couldn't quite believe that would ever happen again, '... then I'll be popping in to see him regularly, but can you just keep an eye on him for me in the meantime when you're down at the pub.'

'Of course I will,' I said, kissing Josie and then her baby on the cheek. 'Don't worry about a thing. You've got your hands full with this little one here. I'll keep a close eye on your dad and if I'm worried at all, I'll let you know.'

'Thanks Ellie, you're a star, do you know that? It's been lovely having you back in Little Leyton. You've been such a great support, not only to Dad and me, but to everyone. Not sure what we'd all do without you. And no, you can't leave now, even if you want to. Now we've got you back in the village, we're never going to let you go again.'

I'd laughed, and gave my two favourite girls a big hug. 'Well, I'm not planning on going anywhere just yet.'

Now, in the hubbub of the pub, remembering Josie's kind words brought a warm smile of contentment to my face. Not that I'd done anything special. This was my home, the place I knew best. I was amongst friends, people I'd known for years. It was only natural that I'd want to help them. I looked at Eric who was sporting his best disgruntled expression.

'The thing that upsets me most is that I won't be able to make our trip. I know how much it means to you girls to deliver these donations to the people who need them most and now I won't be able to come. I've let you down.'

'Of course you haven't let us down. It was an accident.' I pulled out a stool next to Eric and parked my bum. 'You didn't do it on purpose, or at least I hope you didn't. I mean, if you really wanted to get out of a trip to the continent with me then you only needed to say so.'

Eric gave a rueful smile.

I'd been trying to lighten the tone, but judging by his expression I wasn't sure I'd succeeded. To be honest, with the drama of the last week I hadn't given a second thought to our forthcoming trip, but Eric had reminded me it was less than a week away now with everything booked and paid for. I really didn't want to be driving all the way to France on my own, but if I had to then I would.

'Don't worry, we'll sort something out,' I said breezily, sounding more confident than I felt.

'Shall I see if I can arrange something? Dave Roberts has his own transport company – I'm sure he'd be happy to send one of his men over there if I ask him to.'

'No way. There's no reason why I can't still go. I know Josie would want to go if she could so I'll go instead as a one-woman representative of The Dog and Duck.' I waved my non-existent flag in the air.

'You can't go on your own, love. I wouldn't be happy about that.'

I sometimes felt that in my parents' absence Eric had taken on the role of being my surrogate father a little too seriously.

'Honestly, Eric, I've backpacked alone in the Far East, a little jaunt to France really isn't going to trouble me.'

He shook his head gravely. 'No, if anything should happen to you, I'd never forgive myself. Perhaps I could come with you after all, we've still got a week to go – the pain might have settled a bit by then.'

'Absolutely not. Sorry, Eric, but I don't want you coming

89

with me like this. You'd be a...' I stopped, but it was too late, my foot was firmly engaged in my mouth.

'... a liability? I know.'

We'd reached an impasse and I still wasn't sure how to get out of it. The crowd around us had been engaged in their own conversations, oblivious to ours. I looked across at Johnny who was giggling with Polly.

'Hey, Johnny,' I called, hit by a sudden brainwave. My words cut through the noisy babble and everyone fell silent to listen to what I was about to say. 'What are you doing next weekend?'

Johnny gave a tilt of his head, his oh-so familiar cheeky twinkle shining in his eyes.

'Fancy coming with me across to France to drop off the donations? I need a co-driver.'

A million emotions spread across Johnny's face in that instant, I recognized a few of them: horror, surprise, shock and confusion. Quickly, he covered up his feelings with a shrug and a warm smile.

'Sorry Ells, I've got a big job on next weekend. A new client. I won't be able to get out of it.'

'Ah, never mind, it was only an idea.'

A stupid idea admittedly. What had ever possessed me to ask Johnny? Mind you, a few weeks ago he was proposing the idea himself, albeit in a somewhat different guise to a charity trip. If I was being honest, I'd been surprised at how readily he'd backed away from our relationship. Part of me had expected him to put up more of a fight, to try and persuade me to give him another chance, but he hadn't. Which was just as well probably. It would be all too easy to fall into our old patterns if we were thrown together over a long weekend. No, definitely not one of my better ideas.

'I wish I could come and help,' said Polly, 'but I can't leave the shop at such short notice.' She shrugged. Sitting with Johnny, they both managed to look sheepishly apologetic.

'No, don't worry about it,' I said, waving my hands carefreely, trying to ignore the small knot of concern building in my stomach.

Dan sidled up beside me, and placed a hand around my waist. 'You know I'd help you out if I could, but I'm probably better off staying here, supervising this place.'

'Thanks for the thought, Dan, but as you can't drive I'm not sure you'd make the best co-driver,' I said, laughing. 'Don't worry about it. I'm sure something will come up.'

'Ellie?' Through the hubbub I heard someone call my name, the deep smooth tones instantly recognizable, speaking to my insides in a way that I suspected wasn't totally appropriate. I looked up to see Max appraising me from across the snug. I met his gaze with a smile, my eyelashes doing their own thing and fluttering involuntarily. *What the hell?* Cool, calm and collected – most definitely not.

'Next weekend?' he asked. 'I can run you over there if you like.'

What? No! Who asked him anyway?

'Oh no, don't worry... there's no need... I can...'

'Would you, Max? That'd be great,' said Eric, his mood immediately brightening.

'What a good idea,' said Johnny.

'That's so lovely of you to offer,' said Polly, beaming.

I turned to Dan who lifted his palms to the air and

shrugged as though it was a complete no-brainer.

I glared at them all. These people were supposed to be my friends.

'Well, only if Ellie's okay with the idea, obviously,' Max said, filling the awkward silence.

I gulped, feeling my cheeks redden, suddenly aware of everyone's attention on me.

'Of course, it's just I don't want to put you to any trouble. I'm sure you have much better things to be doing with your weekend.'

'Absolutely not. And it's no trouble at all.' His gaze landed on mine, hovering for a lingering moment. 'I'd love to help.'

What possible reason did I have to say no? I could hardly admit I had a growing infatuation for him that sent my whole insides spinning and had me acting like a teenage girl in his company. I needed to put my personal feelings to one side.

'Perfect then,' I said brightly, 'that sounds like the ideal solution.'

Ten

Early the following Friday morning I met Max at the pub, and with the help of a couple of the locals who'd volunteered their services, we loaded up the van. Eric gave me a hug, banged the back of the van with his crutch and waved us off as we drove away on our mission.

Since Max had offered his services as my driver I'd given myself a stern talking-to. There was no need for me to feel awkward or apprehensive about being holed up in a van for two days with an admittedly drop-dead gorgeous man. It would be absolutely fine. As far as Max was concerned I was just a local girl who worked at the pub and who loved dogs – at least we had that one thing in common. If the conversation ever ran dry we would always have our canine friends to chat about, and besides, Max wasn't to know I'd been harbouring all sorts of deliciously inappropriate thoughts about him. Thoughts that had intensified ever since I'd found out he would be accompanying me to France. In my other life, as an auditor, I'd been expected to present a professional demeanour on all occasions and for the sake of this trip I just needed to consider it as another business assignment and not a romantic getaway.

I quickly realized it was going to be easier said than done

though when we hadn't even ventured out of the village and the subtle scent of Max's aftershave, rich with chocolatey musky undertones, was playing at my nostrils. Business head on, I focussed my gaze steadily on the passing view outside.

'It's really lovely of you to take time out of your busy schedule to do this, Max. There was a moment there, after Eric had his accident, that I thought I might be going it alone.'

'Absolutely not a problem.' I watched his hands as they tapped lightly on the steering wheel. Large strong capable hands that were clearly used to manual work – I liked that. Oh God, I really shouldn't be fantasizing about his hands already!

'I know how disappointed Eric was at having to miss the trip. He's such a good guy and does so much for the community. I know if the shoe was on the other foot he would be the first person to volunteer his services.'

Of course. I knew I shouldn't have read anything more into Max's enthusiasm for accompanying me abroad. He was only helping out a good friend.

'That's true. He's had some rotten luck lately. I really hope he doesn't have to leave the pub. The place just wouldn't be the same without him.'

'Leave the pub?' Max turned his head sharply to look at me. 'Why would he need to do that?'

As soon as the words left my mouth I realized what I'd said. What had I been thinking? I grimaced, shrugging my shoulders.

'Oh nothing's sorted. It's just that the tenancy on the pub is coming up for renewal and Eric thinks it might be sold to new buyers. If that happens, he's not certain he'll

94

still have a job, or a home, come to that. The thing is, I'm not sure it's common knowledge yet. I shouldn't really have said anything. You'll keep it to yourself for the time being, won't you?'

'My lips are sealed,' he said, zipping them shut. He grew pensive for a moment. 'Like you though, I'd be sad to see Eric leave the pub.'

One of the joys of living in Little Leyton was that if you let slip a tiny nugget of information you could guarantee it would be round the whole village in the space of a morning. I just hoped I could trust Max not to say anything. I certainly didn't want Tim Weston getting hold of this nugget of information.

'Must admit I've not done anything like this before,' I said, eager now to change the subject. 'The whole idea of us doing something to help the refugees just seemed to snowball once Josie and I started discussing it.'

'Sometimes it's good to step outside of your normal daily routine and do something different once in a while.' He turned his profile to look at me, an easy smile lighting up his face. 'But then you'd know all about that.'

'Yep,' I nodded. My life and working routine had been turned on its head these last few months. 'Despite your best plans, life has a habit of throwing you a few curveballs every now and then, just to keep you on your toes. I could never have imagined coming back to Little Leyton to work, but I have and so far I don't regret a thing.'

'That's the best way. Life's too short to harbour regrets.'

I couldn't imagine Max being the type of person to have regrets or second thoughts about anything. He was confident, self-assured and go-getting. Just the sort of personality I was attracted to and just the sort of person you needed as a chauffeur. I smiled, my gaze flittering over the strong lines of his profile as he concentrated on the road ahead. Definitely, I was in very safe hands. I closed my eyes and let my head fall back on the headrest.

*

When we arrived in France later that day it was only a short drive to the area where the makeshift camps that we'd seen in the press had sprung up. Although no amount of photos could have prepared us for the rambling desolation of these sprawling new villages. There was a high security presence and the razor-wire fencing surrounding the camp only added to the feeling of gloom and despair. Rows and rows of small tents dotting the muddy ground merged into a messy blur in the distance. We were directed to an area where we were told we could unload all our black bags.

Climbing out of the van, my feet landed deep in a boggy patch, splattering my jeans with mud, and I glanced around to see the whole site was in the same state, one huge waterlogged swamp. Above me, dark clouds loomed ominously, matching the grey desolation of our surroundings. I shivered, and wrapped my arms around my chest.

'These are always very welcome.' Zak, one of the guys handling the distribution of the aid donations, was going through our bags and pulled out a pile of woolly blankets. 'Although the days are getting warmer, the temperature drops significantly here at night so these will come in very useful, thanks.'

'Are there many women and children here?' I asked, my

gaze flittering over his shoulder to a milling crowd of men.

'The majority of the people here are young men, but there is still a significant proportion of women. Those tents over there' – he pointed at a collection of threadbare tents flapping bravely in the wind – 'are for families.'

My heart broke at the thought of families with young children having to live in these conditions.

After we'd unloaded all the bags, and with Max deep in conversation with Zak, I took the opportunity to wander off towards the tents Zak had pointed out. Josie and I had put together some small personal kits filled with soap, a flannel, a toothbrush, toothpaste, sanitary items for the women, and shaving gear for the men. I wanted to be able to return to Little Leyton and tell Josie that the items so generously donated by the community had reached the people we'd intended them for. A plume of smoke from a small campfire and the sound of music coming from a tinny radio greeted my arrival.

'Hello.'

A young woman dressed in navy tracksuit bottoms and matching hoodie, rocking from foot to foot, a baby at her hip, looked at me warily.

'Hi,' I said, more brightly this time. 'My name's Ellie. I've just come over from the UK today with my friend.' I swept my head in the direction of Max. 'We brought some supplies. Blankets, clothes, that sort of thing. I just wanted to come and say hello.'

She gave a small nod of her head in understanding.

'What's your name?' I asked.

'Ima,' she said softly.

'And what about your baby?'

I couldn't help but think of Josie and Stella. What if it was them standing here instead?

'Samir.' A hint of a smile played at the woman's lips as she said her child's name.

'He's gorgeous. How old is he?'

'Six months.'

She bounced him on her hip as his little fingers played with her long dark hair. He had the same big brown eyes as his mum which were appraising me in a similar distrustful fashion.

'Have you been here long?' I asked.

'About one month.'

'Look...' I rifled through the big holdall I carried over my shoulder. 'Can you use this?' I pulled out one of the packs of toiletries we'd prepared. 'It's only a few things but they might come in helpful.'

I was conscious of not offending or patronizing Ima. Nothing in my life before had prepared me for something like this and I was struggling to find the right words. All I knew was that I wanted to reach out to her, one woman to another.

Ima took the pack gratefully. 'Thank you. You people are kind. We have plenty clothes, blankets. But here, living like this, it's not right.' She gestured towards the desolation behind her. 'We are like animals, caged together.' Her words delivered flatly tore at my heart. What if it was me standing in her place? My family living in these terrible conditions? I could only nod in agreement, as my gaze skittered around the camp. The pictures in the newspaper had been grim, but nothing could have prepared me for facing the reality of the situation. The harrowing sights alone were disturbing enough but with the sound of the place, everyday noises pitched against an oppressive stilled silence and the stomach-churning smell of the place, it was something no picture could ever capture. It was a human wasteland; cramped, filthy and cold, with litter scattering the ground and a rancid stench filling the air. I suppressed a sigh of frustration and a creeping feeling of shame. Had I honestly believed that I could turn up here in the van with some old clothes and think I could make some kind of difference? It was laughable. Whatever I'd been expecting it hadn't been this.

'I'm sorry,' I said.

Ima's dark eyes seemed to penetrate my soul. I needed to explain.

'I'm sorry that this has happened to you, that you're living like this. I wish I could do something more to help but...' My words trailed away at the realization of my own impotency. 'I really wish there was. I hope I haven't offended you coming here, talking to you.'

Ima gave a resigned shrug of her shoulders, her lips curling ruefully. 'It is good that you come, that you see me. The person. Not animal. In my own country I was teacher. My husband, he's engineer. We have good life, a home. We do not want to leave our country, but it is impossible to stay. Bombs, shooting.' She shook her head. 'It is too unsafe. For us, and our child. We must find new home in a new country where we can be safe.'

I had to bite on my tongue to stop myself from saying, 'Come with me back to Little Leyton. Bring your husband and your son. You can live with me in our house. We'll sort something out.' But I knew it wasn't the answer even if it were allowed, and besides, Ima and her family were only one of many such families. And this was just one of many such camps.

'Well, I really hope you get to move on very soon,' I said, feeling wretched with helplessness. My words sounded hollow. I reached out for her hand and she took mine with a small smile. 'I wish you every luck for the future and for Samir's future too,' I said, squeezing her fingers tight, before letting go and turning to walk away, tears filling my eyes.

With guilt threatening to overcome me, I quickly handed out the remaining kits from my holdall to the small crowd of onlookers that had gathered around us before going off in search of Max. I found him still chatting with Zak and another aid worker.

'Are you all done? I asked, neutrally, when there was a natural lull in their conversation. I felt desperate now to get away, but didn't want to show it.

'Yep sure. You've got my card,' he told Zak. 'If there's anything else you can think of then just let me know.' He shook hands with the two men and turned to me, the warmth of his expression providing a much-needed contrast to the stark realities of our surroundings.

'You okay?' He gave me a sideways glance as we climbed into the van.

'Yep fine.' I turned away, curling my body away from him, staring out through the window, yet seeing nothing.

In truth, I was anything but fine. I hadn't given a second thought to how our visit here might make me feel and I hadn't expected to be so overwhelmed by the reality of the living conditions in the camp. Meeting Ima, I couldn't help but compare her situation with that of Josie and her new baby. Josie was full of joy and hope for the future – what hope did Ima have and what chance in life her baby, Samir?

Thoughts of Ima and Samir swam round in my head. I turned and looked across at Max, grateful for his presence.

'What were you talking to Zak about?'

'He was telling me that they intended building some permanent structures in the camp. I volunteered a couple of my guys to come over with the van and their tools for two weeks to lend a hand. The offer's there if they need it.'

'Really? That's so lovely of you. Being able to do something constructive. Something that will make a difference. I felt so helpless back there. Talking to that woman with the baby, I felt ashamed that she was in that situation, as if it were my fault, and there was nothing I could do to help.'

'It was certainly an eye-opener, that's for sure. But you shouldn't feel ashamed, Ellie. You came here because you recognized these people's struggles and you wanted to help. That's a good thing. I'm just glad I came along with you too, Ellie.'

'Oh me too,' I said, gratitude peppering my words. 'I'm not sure I could have faced this on my own.'

Who was I kidding thinking I could have come out here alone? Max had no idea just how safe, secure and protected his presence made me feel. There were a few moments, when we arrived at the camp and when I was chatting to Ima, that tears pricked at my eyes and it had taken all my self-restraint not to have a major chin-juddering wobble. Knowing Max was there, and seeing the way Ima held and conducted herself, made me realize I had no right to give in to my feelings of pity and distress over the situation. My reason for being there was to be helpful, to provide some kind of support, however minimal. Not to turn into an emotional wreck. Besides, what right did I have to cry when I could go home to a lovely warm house. The refugees had no such luxury and were having to live like this every day, yet still managed to survive somehow.

A little way down the road Max pulled into a lay-by, stopped the van and turned off the ignition. He undid his seatbelt and turned to look at me.

'Come here,' he said, opening up his arms. 'You look as though you could do with a hug.'

I hesitated a moment before I unclipped my seatbelt and shifted towards him, my whole body relaxing into the strength of his embrace. Feeling his protective arms around me, his warm sweet scent filling my nostrils, that was when I knew I could let go, that I couldn't hold on a moment longer. Tears ran down my cheeks and the emotion buried tight inside me escaped in raw, heartfelt sobs. Max stroked my head, pulling me closer into his chest and it didn't matter to me in the slightest, nor it seemed to Max, that I was leaving the dampest, snottiest wet patch on his lovely white shirt. I could have stayed like that forever, shielded from the horrors of what we'd witnessed earlier, but Max pulled away to look at me.

'Look, I know that was tough for you. Me too, but you did brilliantly back there. There's something about seeing the reality of the situation for yourself that is deeply humbling, but you can't take on the responsibility for that woman, for all those people. We did what we came here to do and that has to be enough. For the moment, at least.'

Max leaned across to mop up my tears with his thumb,

before pulling out a tissue from his pocket and finishing the job properly.

'I suppose you're right. Thanks Max,' I said, my breathing under control now. 'For being here. At my side. I couldn't have done it without you.'

'Come on,' he said, with a warm smile. 'Let's get you to the hotel.'

Eleven

Fifty minutes and a leisurely drive later we turned up at a small seaside resort and it was as if we were in another country entirely. Which we weren't, of course, but this old-fashioned French town with its elegant architecture and olde-worlde charm was a million miles away from the harsh realities of the place we'd just visited.

'I thought we'd stay away from the camps. I didn't know what the hotel situation was like around there, and besides I know this area quite well.'

'It's fine by me,' I said, mesmerized by the beauty of the landscape. Wide sweeping sands, the rolling sea and colourful elegant villas lining the promenade.

'I should have mentioned it, but we're in a twin room.' Max pulled into a small gravel car park behind a quaint hotel. 'I hope that's okay? When I booked for you and Eric the hotel was fully booked apart from this one room, which I knew wouldn't be a problem for you both. I should have said something earlier, but it completely slipped my mind until now. We could always have a look round to see if we can get into somewhere else?'

'No, no, don't worry about that, it'll be fine. I'm okay with it if you are too.'

Spending the night in the same room as the man I was currently nursing a major crush on – what could possibly go wrong? I mean, it wasn't as if there was anything remotely romantic about this trip, despite the closeness I'd felt towards Max when he'd comforted me in the van earlier. Besides, I was definitely not at my best right now. My skin was red and blotchy on account of all the crying I'd been doing and I was nursing an almighty headache for my efforts. To be honest, I would be happy to lay my head down anywhere tonight.

After checking-in at reception, which gave Max the opportunity to show off a masterful command of the language and demonstrate his most delicious French accent, we were shown to our bedroom at the top of some wide steep stairs.

'Oh my goodness,' I said, dropping my rucksack to the floor as the door opened onto an oasis of calm.

The room was high-ceilinged with a central chandelier, cool cream walls and pretty glazed doors that opened out on to a small balcony. The twin beds, pushed closely together to make a double, were covered in white linen with a rich gold eiderdown folded over the bottom of the bed and big white opulent cushions resting against the bedstead. It took all my self-control not to launch myself at it and land face-down, spreadeagled on the sumptuous loveliness.

'You like?' asked Max, clearly amused by my open-mouthed reaction.

'Oh, it's lovely. So sophisticated, yet cosy and…' I paused. Yep, romantic was definitely the word stuck at the back of my throat, but I quickly pushed those thoughts straight out of my mind.

'We can push the beds apart, if you like,' Max offered, sensing some hesitation on my part.

'Oh no,' I said, rather too quickly, waving my hand at him to put a stop to any such ridiculous idea. We could be grown up about this, surely. 'Please don't go to any extra trouble. It's just lovely as it is.'

'Well, I aim to please,' he said with a sidewards glance, his dark brown eyes sweeping over me. My gaze caught his and I gulped at his words.

He dumped his bag on the floor and walked towards the French doors, opening them up. I followed him out on to the balcony and stood beside him in the cool breeze, looking out on the tree-lined avenue below. In the distance was the sea and we watched transfixed by the white waves rolling back and forth over the wide stretch of golden sand. The sight took my breath away. Max broke the silence by turning to look at me.

'Would you like a shower?'

My heart stopped for the briefest moment, a trickle of anticipation running down my backbone.

'Excuse me?'

The faintest hint of a smile played at his lips. 'I wondered if you wanted to take a shower.' There was a pause. A discernible pause. 'I'm going to have one, but if you'd like to go first?'

'Oh yes, of course,' I said, hoping the heat in my cheeks wasn't visible to Max. I wandered back into the boudoir, I mean, bedroom. A shower was probably a good idea. It was beginning to get decidedly hot in here.

*

After we'd freshened up we ventured outside. I felt refreshed and with a new energy after my lovely invigorating shower. It was early evening but still warm enough for us to wander along the seafront in just our long-sleeved jumpers. The beach was a hive of activity with Segways whizzing along the sand, dogs lolloping into the sea, and other people, like us, just enjoying the last of the good weather for the day with a leisurely walk. Despite the beauty of our surroundings I still couldn't erase from my mind the injustice of what we'd witnessed earlier.

'It hardly seems fair that people are here enjoying their freedom in this beautiful landscape, able to do what they want, when they want without a care in the world, and yet down the road those poor people are herded into camps like animals, not knowing what their future holds.'

Max nodded, his mouth turning up ruefully. 'Yes, it certainly makes you stop and think.' He took hold of my hand and squeezed it lightly, his touch awakening all sorts of sensations within me.

'Poor Ima and her baby, and all those other people too are stuck inside that camp tonight without the freedom to come and go as they please. It makes me feel bad to think that they don't have the same rights and privileges that we have. It's all wrong.'

'I know, Ellie, and I understand perfectly where you're coming from, but don't let it eat you up. You did what you came here to do and that's a hell of a lot more than most people will ever do in their lifetime. Now, well, we're here, we might as well make the most of it.'

Max spoke a lot of sense. Me moping around wasn't going to change a thing and as he'd been kind enough to volunteer to bring me here in the first place the least I could do was try to be reasonably good company. After all, it wasn't really a hardship being alone with Max, in a beautiful coastal location, with the sea breeze whispering against my skin. Actually, it was only then I realized that Max still had hold of my hand. I thought it had been the cool wind heightening my senses, causing goosebumps to ripple along my body, but looking up into Max's eyes I sensed it was something else entirely.

'You know we should go and get a drink,' he said, holding my hand up, looking at it intently and giving it a little shake, as if he'd only just realized too that we were still holding hands. With a smile, he squeezed my fingers and let go, leaving me with an intense feeling of longing.

We found a small bar tucked away down one of the cobbled backstreets, where we sat on high stools and drank cool long beers. Animated chatter rang around us, which was all the more enchanting for the fact that it was in French. My ears strained to catch the odd word or two that was recognizable to me from my days of GCSE French, but Max clearly had no such problems as he chatted away happily to the bar staff and locals.

Back in Little Leyton I was more used to serving Max with a beer, exchanging idle small talk about the weather, his day, my day, the dogs, before moving on to the next customer, never standing still long enough to have a full conversation with him. Here, there were no such restrictions. My gaze travelled around his face, as he uttered something wholly incomprehensible to the barman. His features were achingly familiar and yet I realized I barely knew him at all.

'Where did you learn to speak French so well?'

'At school. And then I spent a couple of months grape-picking in the South of France, and a few months as a bar-back in Paris. It's amazing how quickly you pick up the language when you're living and working in a country. *Et toi? Parlez-vouz des langues?*'

There was something about his French accent that spoke directly to the pit of my stomach, warming my insides.

'Er... um... un petit peu... je parle... le francais,' I said, showing off my entire vocabulary in one fell swoop.

He smiled a lazy smile, his eyebrows lifting in a way that suggested he wasn't remotely impressed with my language skills.

Later Max told me that he'd actually been asking the barman where the best place to eat was and after finishing our beers we made the short walk to the cosy bistro that he'd recommended, Chez L'Ami Pierre, which was tucked away in a back alleyway, somewhere we wouldn't have stumbled upon by ourselves. It turned out to be the perfect choice as the small eatery was full of rustic atmosphere with Gallic charm oozing from every corner, and it had the most amazing smells wafting in the air.

As I tucked into my cassoulet – well, when in France and all that – attempting to stop the succulent juices from running down my chin, it occurred to me that this was the closest I'd come to a proper date in months. I couldn't really remember the last time I'd been out with a man sharing a romantic meal together. My alcohol-fuelled nights with Johnny couldn't be classed as dates or in the least bit romantic. Being here with Max though, across a candlelit table, sharing good food and wine, it crept upon me, slowly, surprisingly, what I'd been missing out on all this time.

'So, how are you enjoying being back in Little Leyton? You always seem so busy what with all your dogs and the pub shifts.'

'Oh, I am, but I just love it that way. It's great. Much better than I could ever have imagined actually. I suppose for me it's such a change of lifestyle – less demanding and stressful, and it's a joy not being stuck in an office all day, having to deal with demanding clients. Nowadays, my clients are always so pleased to see me – I'm always greeted with wagging tails and the occasional lick too.'

'I bet,' said Max, with a chuckle. 'Can you see yourself going back to your old career?'

'Hmm, not sure. That was the plan, but now, I don't know. It's lovely having all my friends and neighbours nearby. Maybe when my mum and dad come home I'll rethink it. I love them both dearly, but I'm not sure it would be a good idea for us all to live together again, it's been too long. What about you?'

I knew nothing of Max's living arrangements; if he had a wife or a partner, or a brood of little Maxes running about the place. I could just imagine them now; dark haired, wide-eyed, and with mischievous smiles lighting up their faces. There it was again, that funny feeling I'd experienced when holding Stella in my arms. Most strange. My gaze flittered over Max's handsome features and I hoped, with a selfish pang, that he wasn't living out his own personal happy ever after up in that big country manor.

'Me?'

'Yeah, are you in Little Leyton to stay or are you just passing through?'

'No, I'm staying put. I first came to Little Leyton to look

after my grandfather, but I quickly grew to love the place and realized it was somewhere I could put down some roots. It's ideal for me as I work from home, but it's near enough to all the major transport links so I can get into London easily if I need to, or anywhere else I might need to go. It might sound daft but it makes me feel closer to Gramps. Growing up, we moved around a lot with my dad's job so there was never anywhere that really felt like home. Little Leyton is the closest I've come to experiencing that sense of... I don't know, family... community. Can you understand that?'

I nodded, understanding perfectly. 'What about your parents? Do they live in the area?'

'My dad's no longer with us. He died when I was sixteen and my mum, well, she quickly re-married. She moved to Spain with her new husband, and took my younger sister, Katy, with them. They love it out there. So I hear. I don't really see much of them these days.'

'Oh right.' I detected the hint of sadness in his voice. 'I'm sorry about your dad.'

Max shrugged and gave a rueful smile. 'One of those things.' He took the opportunity to refill my glass of wine from the carafe on the table and I sensed that particular line of conversation was dead. 'So, how about you and Johnny?' he asked, his voice lifting. 'How's that going?'

'Me and Johnny? Oh, we're just friends, that's all, we have been for years. Nothing more.'

'Really?' Max raised a querying eyebrow, looking entirely doubtful.

'Well, we had a bit of a thing a while back and then when I came home again, we picked up where we left off, but it's all over now. We're much better as friends.'

'Ah right.' Max gave a knowing nod of his head. 'I did wonder. I thought you two were together, but then when I saw Johnny out and about...' His eyes flickered over my face, his lips twisting. 'Well, that would explain it then.'

Okay, I admit it, I allowed myself a small, self-satisfied smile. Max Golding had clearly given my relationship status some thought. And there could only be one reason for that. I wasn't just a mad dog lady and barmaid to him. Looking back, I wondered if it was any coincidence that my feelings for Johnny had waned at about the same time that Max had wandered into my life. Sensing my opportunity to find out more about Max's personal life, I asked him, nonchalantly, 'So what about you then? Is there anyone special in your life?'

'What, apart from my gorgeous girls, you mean? Bella and Holly?'

I smiled, remembering his dogs, but I was under no misapprehension that they might be the only beautiful women in his life. Nor was I going to let him off that lightly. I lifted my eyebrows and tilted my head, when he showed no sign of elucidating further. 'Well?' I teased him.

He shook his head slowly, and I noticed a flicker of amusement in his eyes. 'Not really. Well, nothing serious at least.'

Which told me everything and nothing. Clearly, Max didn't want me probing into his private life, which was fair enough. As much as this might feel like a date, it wasn't one. I was having trouble remembering that. His private life had absolutely nothing to do with me.

'I once had a bit of a thing with a French girl,' he said, unexpectedly. Now his expression had taken on a wistful quality, his chin uplifted to the beamed ceiling of the restaurant, a smile spreading across his lips.

'Really?' I said, eager to find out more.

'Yep.' He turned his attention back on my face. I still hadn't got used to the effect his direct gaze had upon me. Every single time. It was unnerving. There it went again, my heart, giving a little fillip. 'Long time ago now. Not sure why I was reminded of it. I guess it's being here in France, the sounds, the smells, it brings it all back.'

'What was her name?'

'Nadine. I met her when I was working in a vineyard. Her family took me in and we became very close, we were inseparable for the summer.'

So that's where he'd learned to speak French. All that pillow talk had clearly done wonders for his mastery of the language.

'What happened?' I asked, mopping up the remainder of the delicious juices on my plate with some fresh bread. Despite being desperate to know all the gory details, I didn't want to appear over keen. Striking the balance between interested friend and slightly obsessed fan-girl, wanting to know every single thing about his French girlfriend, down to her dress size, her hair colour and what she liked to eat for breakfast, was proving difficult.

'It was just a summer romance. When I went back to England we kept in contact for a while, exchanged letters for a couple of months, but then, well, it just fizzled out. As these things do.'

'Aw, shame,' I said, not entirely sincerely. 'Have you ever thought about looking her up again?' *No. Really?* As soon as the words left my lips, I wondered what had possessed me to ask such a thing.

'What? No.' Thankfully his rebuttal was wholly convincing. 'It was just a teenage thing. And I'm not sure it's ever a good idea to go back. You can't dwell on the past or what-might-have-beens. Some things have their special moment in time and that was very much of its moment. It's the here and now that's important and I'm a great believer in living in the moment.'

There it was again, that gaze, assessing me, sweeping over me in a warm caress. I had to agree with him, the here and now was definitely the place to be.

Twelve

Later, we walked along the cobbled half-lit pavements of the
town, peering into the shop windows, Max's amusement
evident as I gushed over the expensive handbags and designer
clothes, swooned over the boulangeries and marvelled over
the patisseries on our way back to our hotel. Honestly, it
was as if I'd never been out of Little Leyton. Occasionally
Max placed a firm guiding hand into the small of my back
steering me one way and then the other, his assured touch
feeling entirely natural and comfortable, if not a whole lot
enticing too.

It was only when we were back in our hotel room that
the self-consciousness I'd experienced earlier put in an
unwelcome return. Hardly surprising when I was so out of
touch at being alone with a frankly drop-dead gorgeous man
in what was a very warm and welcoming room, a bedroom
no less, the said bed looking even more inviting now in the
soft golden hue of the bedside lamps. Two beds maybe, but
in my eyes it looked like one big open invitation. I mean,
how were you supposed to act in these circumstances? I
gulped, my earlier exhaustion having done a bunk and
now every inch of my being was alive with anticipation and
intoxication. How on earth could I be expected to get any

sleep tonight? I had to keep reminding myself that I was being daft to even entertain any romantic notions when there was absolutely no suggestion that Max was remotely interested in me in that way.

'Do you want to use the bathroom first?' Max asked, whipping off his jumper over his head and pulling up his shirt in the process, giving a tantalizing glimpse of bare bronzed skin.

'Good idea,' I said, reluctantly dragging my eyes away from his body, scooping up my bag and dashing into the sanctuary of the bathroom.

I greeted my reflection in the mirror with a grimace, immediately quashing any ideas that there might be any chance of romance. I wasn't looking my best. Still in jeans and sweatshirt, and wishing I'd brought along a dress or at least a pretty top to have changed into, my long brown hair which had started the day in a neat ponytail was now sticking out at all angles, a frizzy halo framing my face. The quick dash of mascara I'd applied earlier had all but disappeared apart from an unbecoming black splodge beneath my right eye and the bloom of bronzer had been replaced by a mask of weariness. What did it matter? Max probably hadn't given a second thought to how I was looking.

Quickly, I pulled off my clothes, splashed my face with water, cleaned my teeth, brushed my hair and then climbed into my pyjamas, grateful that I'd remembered to bring some. All scrubbed up and freshly prepared like a turkey at Christmas, I wandered back into the bedroom busying myself with the contents of my bag so I wouldn't have to face Max head on.

'Oh... ha ha... yeah, I like it.' His gaze travelled from the top of my head down to my bare feet. He was trying and failing not to laugh, which wasn't quite the reception I'd been expecting.

I looked down at my cotton pyjamas and shrugged. 'What's so funny?'

'I love the jim-jams, my three-year old god-daughter has a pair just like them.'

Perfect. I smiled sweetly, trying to pull off a sophisticated, sexy and elegant vibe in my Hello Kitty Primani two-piece, but in reality it was never going to happen. Maybe if I'd known I'd be sharing a room with a gorgeous man I might have come better prepared, but I hadn't given it a second thought. An image of Gemma Jones flittered into my mind; she'd managed to rock the bedtime look in her pastel spotted nightwear. I wished I had an ounce of her style and pizzazz. Or the foresight to ask to borrow her pyjamas at least.

I stuck my chin in the air and brazened it out. My whole purpose for this trip was to come and see the conditions people were living in in the refugee camps and to hand over our donations, even if, having witnessed at first hand their hardships, I'd realized what a token effort it had been. Being here with Max was just a distraction; admittedly he was a very good-looking, eminently distracting distraction, but this time tomorrow I'd be back at home and all this awkwardness would be just a vague memory. We could get back to bumping into each other occasionally down the back lanes while walking our dogs or exchanging pleasantries in the pub.

First of all, I just needed to get through one night in the same bed as this man – I mean, how hard could it really be?

*

'Oh, for god's sake, what's the matter?'

Max's irritated voice broke through the oppressive silence in the darkened room. The bedside table lamp flickered into life and my eyes screwed up against the sudden light.

'What? What is it?'

'You,' said Max, shifting himself up the bed and looking at me accusingly. 'What's the matter? You haven't stopped fidgeting all night. Tossing and turning, sighing, fighting with your pillow – what's the problem?'

'Ooh sorry,' I said, sheepishly. 'I didn't mean to wake you, it's just… well, I'm not sure why but I can't get to sleep.' I knew exactly why I couldn't get to sleep, but I could hardly admit that to Max.

'I would never have known.' He sighed and swung his legs out of bed, raked his hands through his hair and placed his elbows on his knees, cupping his chin in his hands as he observed me. Even with bedhead hair and dark weary eyes he still managed to look gorgeous. 'Do you want a drink?' he asked.

'Oh no, really, I didn't mean to disturb you. Sorry. Just get back into bed and I promise not to make another sound.' I cringed, realizing I was in danger of sounding like his mother. 'Really, don't worry about me, I'm sure I'll fall asleep eventually.'

'Hmm, somehow I doubt that very much.'

'When I was a kid and couldn't get to sleep, my mum would always say, "Lie on the edge and you'll soon drop off!" I always smile when I think of that.'

'Really?' Only Max wasn't smiling. He was scowling at me through narrowed eyes.

Guilt fluttered through my veins knowing that I'd woken

him, especially after the busy day we'd had. Really, I should have fallen asleep as soon as my head hit the pillow – we'd been up since five o'clock but, alone with only my thoughts in the dark, my mind had been a maelstrom of emotions. The events of the day played over and over in my head; my first impressions on finally reaching the camp, experiencing for myself the damp and cold and squalor, meeting Ima and her baby, wondering if I would have the same strength of character and determination in her position. Then, spending an intimate evening with Max. I was too wired up to be able to switch off. It hadn't helped when Max stripped down to his black boxers and T-shirt and padded around the bedroom as though he owned the place, before slipping into the bed next to mine. Way too close. Close enough to touch if I moved my hand and yet, oh so far away too.

Definitely, it was all Max's fault. His presence was all-encompassing, filling the room with his overt masculinity. His subtle natural scent, citrusy and elusive, taunted my nose buds as I lay there chasing sleep, all the time listening out for his breathing, steady, effortless and strangely enchanting. Max was equally compelling asleep as he was when he was wide awake. Clearly, my presence in the bed beside him hadn't troubled Max in the slightest as he'd had no problem dropping off straight away.

'Right, well, I think I might have a drink,' he said, rubbing his eyes. 'Wine?' He held up a bottle of red he retrieved from a tall oak cabinet.

Really I fancied a warming hot chocolate, but looking around it appeared wine was my only option and having dragged Max from his sleep it seemed rude not to join him in a nightcap.

'Lovely,' I said, with a smile, wiggling myself up the bed.

'So, do you always have trouble sleeping?' he asked, handing me a glass. 'Or is this a special occasion?'

'Normally I sleep like a log, but you must admit it's been an eventful day. My head is just full of everything. Too much stimulation, obviously,' I said, with a wry smile. I failed to mention that he had seeped into my innermost thoughts too, and showed no signs of moving out soon. Especially now he was sat up beside me in bed looking deliciously rumpled from sleep.

'Don't worry about it,' he said, with a rueful smile. 'I wasn't really tired anyway.' We both knew that was a blatant lie, but at least it went a tiny way to making me feel better. He poured the wine into flutes, chinking his glass with mine and climbed back onto his bed.

'I hope you're not regretting coming with me now,' I said lightly, taking a sip of my wine which gave me a little shudder. Eugh. Red wine hadn't improved any since the last time I tried it. Maybe, with a bit of practice, I'd get used to it.

'Not at all. I'm pleased to have been of some help.'

'You know, it's made me realize how lucky we are to live somewhere like Little Leyton. It's such a beautiful spot – we don't have to worry about not having a proper roof over our heads, there's very little crime in the area and there's such a lovely sense of community.'

'Not to mention a great pub!'

'Absolutely. We have so much to be thankful for. Things we take for granted. Like being able to wander down the pub and have a beer. Honestly, if there's one thing today has taught me it's that it's really not worth worrying about the small stuff.'

'I try not to,' said Max drolly.

I gave him a sideways glance. Thinking about it, Max was definitely not the type to be sweating the detail. From the little I knew of him, he was a go-getter, someone who made things happen, a successful businessman, someone who wouldn't think twice about offering to drive a virtual stranger to another country all in aid of a good cause – I liked that about him.

I turned my head to look at him properly and with it came a sharp reminder of just how good-looking he was, especially so reclined next to me on the bed, dressed only in a T-shirt and his boxers. Oh dear lord! How could I have forgotten about those boxers? Snug and leaving very little to the imagination, although I couldn't help myself from imagining it all anyway. His legs were bronzed, firm and muscular, a rugby player's legs, I wouldn't mind betting. My stomach lurched and I averted my gaze back to his face. In profile, his prominent cheekbones and the sharp cut of his jawline covered in a light stubble made him look like a model who'd just turned up for his photo-shoot – designer underwear, obviously.

'Yeah, you're right,' I sighed, deciding it was probably safer to focus on the watercolour painting on the opposite wall, a summer garden depicted in pretty muted colours, rather than the brooding sex-god next to me. 'Something you said earlier about living in the moment resonated with me. I know I've been guilty in the past of not stopping to smell the flowers – instead, focussing on passing exams, getting to uni, finding a good job, saving money – always looking to the future and a time when everything would be perfect. Now, I realize that it's so easy to wish your life away doing that. Being back in Little Leyton has taught me that it's the little things in life that bring the most pleasures: taking a walk in the lovely countryside with the dogs, sharing a coffee or a drink with a friend, feeling you belong in a place. What wouldn't all those people living in the refugee camps give to have those luxuries?'

'Yup, definitely. I told you, it's the here and now that's important.' He chuckled to himself. 'Come here,' he said, placing his arm around my shoulder and pulling me gently into his side, my head falling naturally onto his shoulder. 'You're very talkative in the middle of the night, aren't you? Why don't you close your eyes and try to sleep?' I took the hint and shut up. Besides, now I had other more important things to focus on.

Through the thin cloth of his T-shirt I could hear the rhythmic beating of his heart resonating in my ear. Oh god, my eyes closed involuntarily, and his proximity, the delicious scent of his skin, sent my body into free-fall.

I snuggled into his warm firm body, not knowing for a moment what to do with my free arm until I let it rest across his waist, finding its rightful position. There was absolutely no chance of me sleeping, not now. I tilted my head to look up into his heavy dark eyes and felt myself lost there wondering how we'd got ourselves into this position. His dark gaze perused me intently and my insides melted into a molten pool of desire. His lips, full and wide, drew me to him like a magnetic and I couldn't have resisted even if I'd wanted to, which I didn't. I really didn't. My mouth on his sent waves of desire rippling through my body, making my toes curl and my fingers ache with desire. His kisses were tentative and sweet, and yet tantalized with the promise of so much more. His tongue teased open my mouth, as he held my face in his hands, his taste deliciously robust and enticing, all at the same time. The here and the now. Wasn't that what he'd been telling me all night long? I turned my body, reaching up an arm to pull his head down closer to mine, to feel the strength of his kisses, deeper and harder. His eyes flicked opened to look at me, unease clouded behind the flame.

'Ellie...' he took a breath. 'Ellie, Ellie, Ellie, while this is a delightful development, I really don't think we should be taking this any further.' He dropped his arms and actually shifted his body away from me, looking at me as though the last few delicious moments had been an aberration.

'Why not, what's wrong?'

'Nothing's wrong,' he said, with an unconvincing smile. 'I just don't think this is a good idea. Not here, not now. We've got an early start in the morning and neither of us want to do something we might end up regretting.'

'Oh right, okay,' I said, affronted, but doing my abject best not to sound it. Pretending to be absolutely cool with the whole situation when I wasn't. I couldn't imagine what there might be to regret. I was only doing what he'd been recommending, living in the moment, savouring the moment, hoping the moment would grow into a bigger, better, more memorable moment. Had I totally misjudged the situation?

'Is it the pyjamas?' I asked, trying to defuse the underlying tension sizzling between us.

He laughed and put his arm back around my shoulder,

but now it just felt awkward. 'It has nothing to do with the pyjamas, the pyjamas are extremely fetching. But trust me on this, Ellie, you know that wouldn't be a good idea. We're friends, I'd really like to keep it that way.'

Friends? God, how totally embarrassing and humiliating. Max couldn't have made it any clearer if he'd sent me an official memo. He didn't fancy me. Not in the slightest and I'd misread his charm and friendliness for something more. The shame! How would I ever live this down? Would I have to spend the rest of my life avoiding Max Golding? Or perhaps leave Little Leyton altogether so I wouldn't run the risk of bumping into him again.

'Yeah, you're right, of course,' I said, dead nonchalantly. So much for all that rubbish Max had been spouting about the here and now. I pulled the duvet up to my chin and slid under the covers, turning away from Max. 'I'm actually feeling really tired now. I might even be able to get some sleep.' I conjured up an extravagant yawn, purely for his benefit. 'Night, Max.'

'Night, Ellie.' Whether I heard humour, warmth or relief in Max's words, I couldn't tell. I was way past second-guessing his feelings and emotions. I closed my eyes to blank out the humiliation and surprisingly fell fast asleep.

Thirteen

Max, being the perfect gentleman, never alluded to our middle of the night kiss, our almost something more moment. That's not to say there wasn't any awkwardness on our trip home but I took the opportunity to catch up on the sleep I'd missed out on the previous night and had my eyes closed for most of the journey. Well, it spared me from having to make conversation with Max and I suspected he was as relieved about that as I was. When he dropped me off back at my house I thanked him once again for his help and was rewarded with a chaste kiss on the cheek. It was as if that night in a romantic French hotel room had never happened.

Thinking about it, it was probably for the best. If we had succumbed to our desire, or rather more accurately, my desire, then where would that have left us? Embarrassed, having to avoid each other, which in our little village would have proved very difficult, or worse still, having to pretend to make a go at some kind of relationship when it was blatantly obvious that neither of us wanted that. No, it didn't matter that my pride was a bit bruised, I'd soon get over that and in the meantime perhaps it would be best if I kept out of Max's way as much as possible.

Since our return I'd done plenty of shifts at the pub and

hadn't seen Max once, so I suspected he was of the same mind as me and was keeping well away.

'Ellie, can I have a word?' I was just wiping down the pipes after a busy lunchtime session when Eric hobbled in from the back. He was moving around a bit easier now on his crutches, but judging by his pained expression it was still a struggle for him, especially in the small confines of the pub.

'Sure,' I said, joining him at one of the tables in the bar. I sat down opposite him, looked into his eyes and knew whatever it was he had to say wasn't going to be easy for him.

'Well, Ellie, you know Tim Weston was in here a few weeks back digging for dirt, well, I certainly didn't want to say anything to him at the time, but he was right, it does look as though I could be moving on soon.'

'Really?' My shock was genuine. Although Josie had given me the heads up that there might be changes afoot, that was some weeks ago now and in the absence of hearing anything further, I'd been hoping, against hope, that we'd be in the clear now and wouldn't be facing the possibility of change after all. Hearing the words from Eric's mouth made it so much more real. I really couldn't ignore it any longer.

'Yep, I don't know if Josie's mentioned anything to you, but my tenancy on the place is coming up for renewal and it looks as though the current owners will be selling up.'

I shook my head, feigning ignorance. In fairness when I'd popped in to see Josie the other day we'd been far too busy discussing my trip to France and baby Stella's progress to talk about what was happening at the pub.

'Really, what will that mean for you, and for the pub then?'

'Well, the pub's been bought by a chain, Hunters Inns, so they'll want to bring their own managers in. I should imagine they'll do a complete refurbishment too.'

'Oh no, that's awful. Hunters are a huge chain. I can't see how this place would ever work as a carvery.'

At the moment we didn't serve food at the pub. The kitchen simply wasn't big enough. Besides, The Dog and Duck was an English country pub at its heart, not a restaurant. Over the years Eric had occasionally considered serving meals but he'd always discounted the idea when he realized that it would change the core of his business. That was something neither he nor his loyal customers would want. For special events we would bring food in, but it was always something very basic, and never on a regular basis.

'I expect they'd extend out the back and make this whole area a dining room,' said Eric, his mood contemplative.

'But why haven't they taken the trouble to speak to the local community? To see what they want. The villagers don't want a restaurant, this place works perfectly well as it is.'

'I know that, you know that...'

'Well, we can't let it happen! To think that Little Leyton would lose its only independent pub, it's heartbreaking. This pub has so much history and character, it's depressing to think that it's going to be changed into some soulless franchise.'

Eric shrugged and picked up a bar mat from the table, tapping its edge on the table. 'I know, but what can you do. It's big business. There's no room for sentimentality. It's all about making a profit these days.'

'Where will it leave you?' I asked Eric.

'Not sure yet. I'll have to find somewhere to live, obviously.

Work-wise, who knows? All I've known for the last twenty years is this place. I don't know how much call there is out there for old publicans.' He chuckled ruefully. 'And I can't see myself picking up a new career, not at my age.'

'Don't be daft. Something will come up, I bet.'

'Well, if not, I've got little Stella to keep an eye on and I can always get myself an allotment or take up bowls. Isn't that what men of my age are supposed to do?'

'Somehow I can't see you doing that.' I reached across the table for his hand, intertwining my fingers with his.

'Anyway, I wanted you to know, Ellie, because obviously it will have an impact on your job here. You know if it was up to me then I'd keep you on forever, but with new owners, I don't know what's going to happen or what it will mean for you and the other members of staff. Hunters might decide to keep you all on, but then again...'

'To be honest, I'm not sure I'd want to stay if you're not here at the helm. It would be a completely different working environment and I'd be expected to wear that silly uniform.' I rolled my eyes and we shared a smile. 'I can't see that happening somehow, can you?' I sighed, thinking what an awful shame it would be for the whole village, but most importantly for Eric of course.

'Well, obviously as soon as I hear any firm news then I'll let you know, but I thought you'd want to be pre-warned. You know, so that you can make other plans.'

'Thanks, Eric.'

Plans? I'd spent my life up until now making plans. I really didn't want to make any more. Why did things have to change? An image of Max's face flittered into my mind. It was becoming a bit of a regular habit, him popping into my head when I least expected it. Even though I'd been doing my best to avoid him since we got back, without the pub it was unlikely I would run into him as much and for some reason that thought made me inexplicably sad.

'Don't look so downbeat, love. It'll be a few months at least before they'll be able to throw me out on the streets and we've got lots coming up in the meantime. It's the pub quiz next week and we're bound to be busy over the summer period with the extra visitors the good weather brings in, and then there's the beer festival to look forward to. With thirty-five guest beers and a visiting oompah band, it's going to be our best one yet.'

That was the thing about Eric, he never rested on his laurels as far as the pub was concerned. He was so much more than a landlord. As well as the numerous social nights and charity events he organized, The Dog and Duck provided a meeting place for various clubs. On the numerous shelves around the pub, there was a huge selection of books; romance, crime, biographies, gardening and cookery books, which customers were welcome to borrow and return once they'd finished with them. All done on trust, of course. If board games were more your thing, then there were plenty of those to choose from too. More importantly for the regulars, Eric was known to keep a good, clear pint, for those who were aficionados on the matter, and there were plenty of those who flocked to our pub, but he also brought in guest beers to ring the changes for the locals if they wanted to try something new. The Dog and Duck was not just a pub; it was the warm and homely heart to our village.

'Do you want me to get some posters organized?'

'Too true. Until they push me out of that front door then

business will carry on here as normal. Let's make the next festival one to remember, just in case it is our last one. If you could put together something on the computer, love, that would be terrific. The usual sort of thing.' He picked up a beer mat, pulled out a pen from his shirt and scribbled down some details, before handing it to me. 'Thought we might put on some food too, bratwurst, German cakes, that sort of thing.'

'Hmm, sounds great.' It was hard to believe that Eric's special evenings, the laughs and the friendship might soon be a thing of the past.

Eric was making light of the situation, I knew, but his commitment to the pub would mean he would continue to play the part of mine host to perfection until he was forced to close the pub door behind him for the very last time. One thing was for sure though, when it did happen it would be the end of an era for the community of Little Leyton and the end of an era personally for me too.

Fourteen

'Amber! Come!'

I stood at the top of the field and hollered. In the far distance, the sweet English Pointer stopped in her tracks, hearing her name. She turned to look at me, her ears pricked keenly, before setting off with gleeful abandon, charging towards me, her long legs making short work of the distance between us.

'Good girl,' I said, rewarding her with a treat when she stopped in front of me, looking up at me with those adorable brown eyes.

Training of the young English Pointer had come on in leaps and bounds ever since I'd begun using Max's private field for some intense sessions. It was ideal because I was able to let her off the lead, safe in the knowledge that she couldn't escape. She was proving to be a quick learner, responding eagerly to my commands. She still got distracted, of course, by the taunting of birds swooping around her, or a scent on the ground that was too tempting to resist, but generally her recall had improved immensely.

I leant down to ruffle her ears and sent her off again, watching as she bounded across the field. I glanced at my watch. Ten more minutes and then we would have to head back home. While she mooched around the open countryside, her nose fixed to the ground, I took a leisurely wander around the edge of the field. No great hardship. What other job would give me the opportunity to work in such a beautiful setting without a care in the world, relishing the sensation of the warm air brushing against my skin and breathing in the fragrant fresh summer scent. Being on Max's private property I couldn't help wondering where he was and what he might be doing. I half hoped I might bump into him here, while he was out walking his dogs, but no such luck. I'd been on tenterhooks for ages thinking that he might be the next person to walk through the door of the pub, imagining how cool, calm and collected I'd be with him, how relaxed, but I didn't even get the opportunity and each time it wasn't him standing there in the doorway my stomach slumped in disappointment.

I looked up at the sky and shook my head, trying to rid myself of all thoughts of Max. He'd clearly managed to put all thoughts of me straight out of his head as soon as we'd arrived home from our trip and here was I mooning over him, projecting hidden meaning into the intimate conversations we'd shared while away, and generally behaving like a love-struck teenager. Honestly, it was ridiculous. Sometimes I wished I'd never even met Max if it might have saved me from feeling so wretched about him now.

Mind you, if I'd never met Max then I would never have been given the opportunity to use this field for training my dogs, so I had to be grateful to Max for that at least. Especially on a day like today. The countryside of Little

Leyton was shown off to its absolute best advantage. The sun was shining high in the sky, casting a warm glow on the bare skin of my arms. In the adjacent field, sheep grazed on lush green grass and buttercups and cow parsley heralded the arrival of summer at last. It was all so peaceful and serene, with not even a dog barking. In fact, I noticed now, there wasn't even a dog in sight!

'Amber!'

I'd only taken my eyes off her for a moment and, in that moment, wouldn't you know it, she'd disappeared out of view. Panic rising in my chest, my gaze scanned the field trying to pick out her distinctive orange colouring, her white-tipped tail held straight behind her, but I couldn't see her anywhere.

'Amber, come!' I called again, expecting her nose to pop out from behind the clump of bushes at the bottom of the field. When she didn't appear I pulled out the whistle from my pocket and gave it a short sharp blast. 'Amber!' I cried, hearing my panic resonating across the field.

I started to jog down the hill and across the grass to where I'd last spotted her, calling out her name all the time. As I reached the bottom of the field my panic abated as I spotted a flash of colour within the bushes until a pair of dark worried eyes peered out at me.

'What's the matter, Amber?'

She gave a small whimper, but she wasn't budging so I bent down onto my haunches and pulled apart the shrubbery. Somehow she'd become caught in a tangle of branches and her legs and body were draped with brambles. Her forlorn expression, fear in her eyes, melted my heart.

With my hands I tore at the undergrowth, the brambles tearing at my skin as I pulled the thicket from her body. When she was finally freed, she wandered out gingerly and it was only then I noticed the deep gash to her side. She sat at my feet, reluctant to move and I was able to take a closer look at the cut. Gently I held her collar while examining her injury. She'd managed to put a great big open hole in her side and she had blood seeping from the wound.

'Oh, Amber, what have you done?'

Looking at her huddled body with her tail tucked tight beneath her legs, I knew she wouldn't be able to walk the distance back to her house. It took at least twenty minutes going at a decent rate and in her current condition I knew she wouldn't be able to make it. I pulled out my phone from my pocket, cursing when I realized I had no reception. I looked around hoping to see someone, anyone who might be able to help us; a tractor driver, a fellow dog walker, Max Golding – where was he when you needed him? – but there wasn't a soul in sight.

'All right, girl,' I said, stroking her face. 'It will be okay, I promise it will.'

There was only one thing for it. Over the other side of the barbed wire fence was Max's home, Braithwaite Manor. It was the last place I wanted to go but the only place by a long chalk where there would be any chance of getting some help. I attached the lead to Amber's collar and scooped her up in my arms, carefully avoiding the injury to her side. I walked to the far corner of the field where the fencing was a little lower and lifted her up and over the fence, depositing her gently on the other side.

'Wait, sweetie,' I told her, but I knew she wouldn't be

running off anywhere. Her reluctance to move at all told me she must be in a lot of pain. Grabbing hold of the end fence post, I scrambled over the barbed wire fencing, narrowly avoiding doing myself some serious injury in the process.

'It's all right, sweetie,' I said, giving her another hug. 'We'll get you sorted just as soon as we can, I promise you.'

All the time scary thoughts were running through my head. What if Amber had done herself a serious internal injury, damaging her organs? What if she lost consciousness now, here in my arms? What would I do then and how on earth would I explain to her owners what had happened?

I picked her up again and started the walk down the hill towards the big house, trying to ignore the growing sense of unease in my chest. Every now and then I would need to stop and put her down on the ground to take a breather. She wasn't a huge dog, but all those defined sleek muscles made her an athletic powerhouse.

As the front facade of the house came into view for the first time, I gasped in wonder. Until now, I'd only seen snatches of the house from a distance, but up close you couldn't help but be overawed by the sheer magnificence of the classical Georgian property. Approached by a tree-lined drive, the sight was breathtaking, a classic English country house that wouldn't have looked out of place in a period drama like *Downton Abbey*.

Come on, Ellie! I chided myself. Now wasn't the time to be hanging around admiring the architecture.

I just hoped to God Max was at home or else I didn't know what we would do next.

Breathless and flustered, I reached the imposing front door and rapped hard on the brass knocker, putting any embarrassment aside at seeing Max again for the moment. When there was no answer I knocked again, more urgently this time. Finally, after what seemed like an interminable wait, I heard footsteps approaching the door.

'Oh, thank...'

'Hello. Can I help you?'

It certainly wasn't Max who answered the door and it didn't look like the hired help either. The woman who was standing in the threshold, framed by the imposing Georgian entrance, must have been about twenty-eight years old. She was taller than me, slimmer too, and her hair, in a luscious chestnut hue, fell in loose, but perfectly formed waves onto her shoulders. Cheekbones to die for, brown intelligent eyes and clear flawless skin completed the look of perfection.

'Oh er hi,' I said, my mind doing mental gymnastics trying to work out who this woman might be. 'Is Max around?'

'No, I'm afraid he's not. He's away at the moment on business. Is it something I can help with?' she asked, her gaze travelling over me. 'Or can I leave a message for Max?'

There was something about the way she said his name in a warm caressing tone that made me suspect she knew Max very well. An uneasy sensation stirred in my tummy. She looked relaxed and totally at ease in her expensively cut designer jeans and tight fitting white T-shirt that showed off a firm, high embonpoint. Very firm, very high, very distracting. I dragged my eyes away, not wishing to appear rude. I could just imagine what a glamorous couple they made though; Max with this gorgeous lady on his arm. I thought back to that night in France when I'd asked him about his love life, recalling how coy he'd been on the subject. Remembering how I'd been all too willing to take things further made me shudder with embarrassment now. No wonder Max had shown no interest in me when he had this beautiful woman waiting for him at home. How desperate I must have seemed.

'It's just... my dog,' I said, remembering what I was doing here. This wasn't about Max. I couldn't care less about him now, but I did care about Amber. 'She was having a run in Max's field, he said it would be okay to use it, but she's had an accident. She's got a big gash to her side. I need to call for the vet but I'm not getting any reception on my mobile. Could I use your phone please?'

'Oh no, poor little thing,' she said to Amber, running a beautiful manicured fingernail under the dog's chin, and then looking for herself at the cut in the dog's side. 'Come on,' she said, dashing back behind the door and returning a moment later with a jacket thrown over her shoulders. 'I'll drive you to the vets, it'll be much quicker.'

'If you're absolutely sure,' I said, as the woman took Amber from my arms and walked the short distance over to the jeep, opening up the back doors and laying Amber down gently on a pile of blankets.

'No problem at all,' she said, with a wide generous smile that lit up her face.

She started the car and set off, turning the car around in the gravel turning circle surrounding an ornate water fountain. 'I'm guessing you're Ellie,' she said with a sideways grin, looking perfectly at home in the driver's seat of Max's jeep.

'Yes, that's right,' I said, feeling a mix of relief that we'd be able to get Amber to the vets very soon and curiosity about the woman sat beside me. What had Max told her about me? That I'd made a pass at him. Had they laughed together over a glass of wine at my ridiculous behaviour? So many questions, but knew I couldn't ask any of them. 'Sorry, I don't know your name.'

'I'm Sasha,' she said in a way that suggested it would make things much clearer, but it didn't. Perhaps sexy Sasha was Max's sister or his cousin or his business partner or his neighbour from down the road or...

'Max's girlfriend?' she added helpfully, as though she'd heard my unasked question.

'Oh right, yes of course,' I said, as though I'd had a momentary lapse and Max had told me all about her and I'd forgotten about it, when, of course, he hadn't said a word. If he had, then my stomach might not have plummeted now to the bottom of my wellies and my heart wouldn't be sulking around about my knees somewhere. Not that he'd had any reason to tell me, it was his private life and if he wanted to keep it private then that was fair enough. I couldn't help wondering though, as we rumbled along the narrow country lanes in the jeep, why Max had been so secretive about his lovely girlfriend. There had been plenty of opportunity for him to tell me about Sasha; he could have dropped it in naturally when I'd told him about me and Johnny or he could easily have said something when he'd been waxing lyrical about his teenage French girlfriend, but for some reason he'd chosen not to. Hell, I'd even asked him outright if he had anyone special in his life and he'd fobbed me off by saying 'nothing serious'. I took a sneaky sideways look at the lovely Sasha and wondered how she might feel being described that way. To my eyes, she looked absolutely serious, absolutely gorgeous and very much of the here and now.

Cramping pains twisted in my stomach. Anxiety probably over Amber... and the realization that Max had a very real and gorgeous girlfriend. Could I really have expected anything less?

At the vets, we were rushed inside into a consulting room while Sasha sat in the waiting room. I thanked her for her help and told her there was no reason for her to wait, but she insisted on staying, and to be honest, I was grateful for her support.

When I emerged from the consulting room half an hour later with a tentative Amber at my side, Sasha jumped up to greet us, concern etched upon her lovely features. If I'd been hoping that my first impression of Sasha had been mistaken and that she wasn't as totally gorgeous as I'd first thought, then sadly I was wrong.

'How is she?'

'She's fine, thankfully, although I think she's probably feeling a bit sorry for herself right now.' Me too, I could have added. 'She's had her fur shaved off and eight staples put into her side, poor little thing. They've given her a course of antibiotics and some painkillers. She'll be on restricted exercise for about a week until the stitches come out, but other than that they think she should make a full recovery.'

'Oh thank goodness for that, Amber.' Sasha dropped down on her haunches and put her arms around the dog's neck. 'You had us worried there for a moment.'

'Thanks, Sasha, for everything. I'm really not sure what

I would have done if you hadn't been at home.'

'Honestly, it was no problem. I was only too happy to help out. Come on, I'll give you a lift back,' she offered.

Ever since I'd met Sasha, admittedly only an hour or so ago, I'd been trying to find something to dislike about her. I mean, no one could be that perfect, could they? She was impeccably groomed with a catwalk figure, had beautiful skin and eyes, an open friendly nature and was kind to small animals and anxious frazzled strangers who turned up unexpectedly at her door. I gave her a surreptitious glance and sighed inwardly. Really, knowing that she was Max's girlfriend, I wanted to hate her, but try as I might, I just couldn't.

'Max told me the trip went well,' she said, turning to look at me as she clipped her seatbelt on.

'Oh yes,' I said, wondering what else Max might have told her. 'It was really kind of him to step in like that to drive me over there.' I forced a smile. 'It seems that both you and Max have come to my rescue in recent times. I really can't thank you enough.'

'Don't worry about it. I know Max was very impressed by the way you organized the pub's charity appeal. And Max always likes to help out for a worthy cause.'

I smiled ruefully, wondering if that was how Max viewed me – a worthy cause. I cringed inwardly thinking of our moment of intimacy. We'd kissed for heaven's sake, lips and tongues and everything, although that had been at my instigation admittedly, and now I was sitting here next to his unsuspecting girlfriend. Guilt washed over me, especially as Sasha had been nothing but kind to me. Although in fairness, I would never have even attempted to kiss Max if I'd known he had a girlfriend in tow, but he had failed to mention that little snippet of information. I'd thought, stupidly, that Max had been similarly attracted to me as I'd been to him – surely I hadn't imagined the way he looked at me with longing in his eyes – but obviously it had just been a moment of madness.

Our emotions had been running high. The intensity of the day we'd spent together; visiting the camp, sharing a cosy meal, and being alone in a beautiful hotel bedroom together had created a false intimacy. It would have been all too easy to give into the moment and we nearly had, only Max had finally come to his senses, presumably when he'd remembered his beautiful girlfriend. Or perhaps he'd never forgotten about her in the first place. Perhaps Max had felt sorry for me and hadn't wanted to reject me, knowing what a bad day I'd had and had given me a kiss by way of consolation. Ugh. Not expecting me to want to take things further. Double ugh. Taking a sideways glance at Sasha it seemed unlikely that he could have forgotten her even for a moment. She was a natural beauty. Kind and compassionate too. I felt slightly sick.

'Thanks again,' I said, when she pulled the car up outside the house of Amber's owners. I'd already rung to tell them about the accident so hopefully they wouldn't be too shocked at seeing their lovely pet with a fresh wound in her side.

'No problem,' Sasha said, leaning across the passenger seat and smiling at me through the window. 'I'll make sure to tell Max what's happened and I hope it hasn't put you off using the field in future.'

I laughed, returning the bright smile. 'No, not at all.' Although Amber's accident wasn't the reason I wouldn't be using the fields or going anywhere near Max's property from now on.

Fifteen

Thankfully, Cathy Harvey, Amber's owner was really lovely and understanding when I sat down with her over a cup of tea and explained to her exactly what had happened.

'Honestly Ellie, don't beat yourself up over it. It could have happened at any time and it might just as easily have been me walking her. You know what she's like. She's a little daredevil. If there's a scent or an interesting bush to explore, then she'll be in there. She's a fearless little thing. I was only grateful that you acted so quickly and got her to the vets in time.'

'Well, it was lucky that Sasha was at home.'

'Sasha?'

'Oh, she lives at Braithwaite Manor with Max Golding. I hadn't met her until today, but when I couldn't get any phone reception I went straight there, it was the nearest place we could get to. Thankfully she was in and drove me straight to the vets.'

'That was good of her. I've never really had much time for that Max Golding, but maybe I'll have to reassess my opinion. Eh, Amber?' she said, joining the dog on the carpet in front of the hearth for a cuddle.

'She doesn't look too distressed by her unplanned visit to

the vets,' I said, feeling relieved that Amber was thumping her tail on the floor, enjoying Cathy's attentions.

'No, she'll be fine in a day or two. I have a feeling it might take you a little longer to get over it.'

I laughed, nodding in agreement.

'So?' Despite my best efforts at letting Cathy's comment pass, my curiosity had got the better of me. 'What is it you don't like about Max Golding then?'

'Well, have you seen him swanning about the countryside in that ridiculous coat and hat of his as if he owns the place? He's an arrogant upstart.'

I suppressed a smile, thinking back to the first occasion when I'd met Max in the lanes. With his clipped tones, and the way he held his head high, his chin jutting forward, I could see exactly where Cathy was coming from. He'd been wearing the same hat then too. I called it his country gentleman gear, but was that the real Max Golding? In France I thought I'd seen a different side to his character, but now I wasn't so sure.

'Have you seen what he's done in the valley?' Cathy went on. 'Building all those houses. Little Leyton doesn't need that sort of development.'

'No, but I suppose it's happening everywhere, not just in Little Leyton. Besides, I didn't think they were too bad. I've not been inside any of the houses, but from the outside they look lovely and in keeping with other properties in the area. I suppose it provides housing for the local community. As far as estates go, it's rather a nice one.'

It sounded as though I was defending Max, but I could tell Cathy wasn't convinced.

'Hmm, but where will he stop? I've heard he's already put

in a planning application for a further development. I spoke to him once. He's very charming and can talk the talk, I'll give you that, but I'm not sure I trust him. He's an outsider wanting to make some money out of our beautiful piece of countryside.' I nodded, tight-lipped, wondering if she had a point. 'Still,' she went on, 'I'm very grateful to his girlfriend for helping you out today. I should thank them both.'

'Well, I'll make sure to pass on your thanks when I see them.'

I wondered if Cathy was being unfair about Max Golding, but then how much did I really know about him myself? I'd certainly experienced his charm at first hand, but was it possible I'd been so seduced by his good looks and easy manner that I hadn't seen beyond that. Oh God, I hoped not! I like to think of myself as a good judge of character, but finding out that Max had a girlfriend who he hadn't deigned to tell me about had left a bad taste in my mouth and the sneaky impression that I might have made a fool of myself in front of him.

For some reason I couldn't get it out of my head and I was still thinking about him later that night when I made way to the pub. I wasn't working a shift, thank goodness, the events of the day had put me in a reflective frame of mind and I was more in the mood for drinking beer than serving it. So I was meeting up with Johnny and Polly and I suspected we might be dragged along on another of Polly's dates.

'What do you recommend then?' asked Johnny, as he and Polly pored over the menu of craft beers.

'Well, we have the new range of summer beers in. There are some really special ales on here and they all have their merits,' I said, with a sideways grin. Although I wasn't working, I couldn't help giving the sales patter. 'This one's lively.' My finger travelled down the menu, landing on a description of one of the beers. 'Crisp and tangy with the hint of lemon peel and a touch of spice. Thirst-quenching and perfect for a summer's evening like tonight. Or, you could go for this lovely fruity beer. Strawberries and cream ale. It has a wonderful golden colour, a delicious aroma and is very smooth on the palate, very quaffable. Or else...' I worked down the list of ales.

'Oh, how on earth are we expected to choose?' said Polly. 'You make them ALL sound totally delicious. I think we should start with the lemony one and then move onto strawberries and cream. What do you reckon, Johnny?'

'Summer fruits galore, I can't think of anything better,' said Johnny, whereupon they both dissolved into giggles. My gaze travelled from Johnny to Polly, who were both completely oblivious to my bemusement, and I got the distinct impression I was missing out on some hilarious in-joke. Either that or they were a few glasses ahead of me on the alcohol front.

'Look why don't you two go outside and grab us a bench. Make the most of this sunny weather while we can. I'll be out in a moment.'

I went up to the bar and ordered the drinks from Dan, who was single-handedly manning the bar.

'Let me know if it gets any busier and if you need any help, Dan. I'm only out the back.'

'Will do, but it should be fine, thanks. Eric's around here somewhere.'

As Dan pulled our beers, I wondered if he was aware that the pub might soon be sold. Eric would have mentioned something, I felt sure, but I didn't like to say anything just in case he hadn't. I felt a pang of sadness standing there in the heart of the pub I loved so much knowing that our tight-knit family might soon be disbanded. Dan lived on a narrow boat on the canal with his girlfriend Silke and I knew his shifts at the pub helped to fund their bohemian lifestyle. What would he do if he found out there was no longer a job for him at The Dog and Duck any more? I suppressed a sigh. It was all too much to think about now. I'd come out this evening to get away from my worries, not to add to them.

With my tray of drinks, I wandered through the pub and out the back doors. The pub garden was at its finest in the summer with its array of hanging baskets and tubs, full of billowing pink petunias, fuchsias and geraniums, supplied and lovingly cared for by Polly. Tonight the air was fragrant with their heavy scent and surprisingly warm too.

'So,' I said, placing the drinks down on the bench, 'how have you both been? Seems like ages since I saw you.'

'Good,' said Polly.

'Great,' said Johnny.

They turned to look at one another and beamed in unison, as if they were the holders of a treasured secret. My smile dropped and a feeling of unease crept up on me. I really hoped to goodness that they hadn't signed me up for some awful double date scenario again and were working their way up to telling me about it.

'Did you ever hear from Rob again?'

'Rob?' They both looked totally baffled. Honestly, what was the matter with them tonight?

'How can you have forgotten about Rob? The carpet man?'

'Oh God no!' Polly gave an exaggerated shudder. 'Well, he did call a couple of times, but I explained to him, nicely, that I didn't think we were compatible. He was fine about it though. I'm sure he'd make a lovely boyfriend to someone, just not to me.'

'And no other dates since then?' I asked.

'No, not really,' said Polly sheepishly.

'Well, that's not strictly true,' added Johnny.

'Really? Come on then,' I said, taking a sip from the gorgeous smooth beer in front of me. 'Spill the beans.'

'Well, um, it's a bit awkward.' Polly's cheeks turned as pink as one of her posies of peonies. 'I've been meaning to tell you, but...' her voice trailed away into the summer night's air.

'What Polly is trying to say is that we...' Johnny picked up Polly's hand and for one godawful moment I thought they were going to announce their engagement. My mouth fell open involuntarily and I quickly closed it shut again.

'Well,' Johnny went on, 'we're together now, seeing each other, dating, courting, whatever you'd like to call it.'

Not quite an engagement then, but almost. I gulped inwardly and felt sure my eyes widened to the size of dinner plates.

'Really?' The summer fruits flavoured ale suddenly seeming to have an almighty kick to it.

'Yes. Oh Ellie, I hope you don't mind,' said Polly, leaning over the table and grabbing my hands. 'I felt a bit embarrassed about it, knowing you and Johnny had a thing going on for a while, but Johnny told me not to worry and that you'd be absolutely fine with it. It's not as though it was ever very serious, what you two had going on, was it?'

'No.' I shook my head vehemently.

Wasn't it?

Not on my part at least, but I'd thought Johnny had been serious about me. He'd certainly been persistent, enthusiastic and had looked at me longingly and lovingly, in much the same way as he was looking at Polly now. Clearly he hadn't wasted any time in pining over the demise of our relationship. I'd been the one to let Johnny go and yet I couldn't help feeling hurt by the speed at which he'd moved on. Obviously I hadn't been that difficult to replace.

'Of course I don't mind,' I said, lying through my teeth, 'it's just a bit of a surprise that's all.'

'Well, I wanted you to know because it's pretty much common knowledge around the village now, but I wasn't sure if you knew or not, and I wanted you to hear it from us rather than from someone else.'

'No, I didn't know,' I said, my gaze drifting around the garden. How long had everyone else known? I was reminded of Max and the way he'd gently probed me about my relationship with Johnny that night in the restaurant. Clearly he'd known. Possibly I was the last person in the world, or the last person in Little Leyton, at least, to know. 'Well,' I said, plastering a big smile on my face, channelling my best Oscar-nominated leading actress impression. 'That's just brilliant news. I'm really happy for you both.'

Peering into my beer, there was no reason not to be happy for them. They were two of my favourite people in the world and thinking about it, they were probably very well suited to each other. Much better suited than I'd ever been to Johnny. It might take some getting used to the idea, that was all.

'I'm so pleased,' said Polly, who proceeded to clamber

over the rickety bench to give me a hug. 'I didn't want any bad feeling between us.'

'Don't be daft. That would never happen.'

'Right, well, in that case, I think we should have another drink,' said Johnny, who'd been studying his beer mat intently for the last few minutes and was now looking mightily relieved to have the awkward conversation out of the way.

'Go on then,' I said, finishing off the beer in front of me quickly. 'Tell you what, I'll have one of those strawberry and cream beers next, I think.'

Definitely, in times of emotional shock or celebratory news, whichever way you looked at it, strawberries and cream beer was definitely the way to go. I pulled my cardigan over my shoulders to ward off the sudden cold nip to the air. Change was inevitable, but at the moment the changes in Little Leyton were happening far too quickly for my liking.

Sixteen

For the first time since I'd moved back to Little Leyton I had a completely free Saturday with no dog walks on the schedule or pub shifts to work. Which, on this particular Saturday, was a complete and utter blessing, considering the humungous hangover I was nursing.

The summery beers had been delicious but surprisingly potent and although I'd only had three – or maybe it was four, it was all a bit hazy now – I really couldn't remember the walk home, only that Johnny and Polly had bundled me through the front door and pushed me up the stairs and into my bedroom. That's what friends are for, I guess.

So much for Polly complaining about the lack of men in Little Leyton. She'd snapped one up, after all. Probably the last remaining single eligible man in the village. And I wasn't sure why but my heart groaned at that thought. Not that I'd wanted Johnny for myself. No, I was clear about that in my head, but knowing that he was now unavailable brought a finality to our situation that I hadn't anticipated.

On reflection, I was entirely okay with the knowledge that two of my best friends were now acting out love's young dream. Together. I suppose there was still a tiny part of me that was smarting at the dent to my pride, but if I put that to one side, then yes, I think I was happy for them.

Coming back home hadn't been about rekindling old relationships or even starting a new one. It had been about getting away from the pressures of my full-on life in London and taking some time out to decide what it was I really wanted to do next. To find some balance too. And while I was already reaping the benefits of my new work regime, enjoying the freedom of the outdoor life and the conviviality of working in a bustling pub, I'd come to realize there was still something missing. For years I hadn't wanted to be tied down in a relationship, to have the pressure of rushing home from work, conscious of someone waiting for me there or having to consider another person's needs and feelings. I'd been too focussed on my career goals to worry about those sort of things. But it was in these last few weeks that I'd become aware of a subtle shift, deep down inside me. A stirring in my stomach that had me recognizing an emptiness I hadn't been aware of until now. It was a revelation.

In my fuggy-headed state I rolled out of bed and wandered off to the kitchen in search of painkillers. Never again, I swore, popping a couple of pills and washing them down with a glass of water. Mind you, I always had a good time with Johnny and Polly and last night had been no exception. Witnessing them together, so caught up in each other, laughing and joking, finishing each other's sentences – yes, already! – and clearly full of excitement and hope for their future, had brought it home to me that I might want something similar.

Perhaps now was the time for me to meet someone; invest some energy into my personal life and find that someone special to share the good things in life with.

I slumped down on to the stool in the kitchen and rested my head in my hands. Ugh. Dreadful didn't even come close. When the painkillers kicked in, I'd feel better. Everything would seem clearer. Now, well, everything just seemed a little fuzzy.

I eased myself up from the stool and pulled a frying pan out of the cupboard, found some bacon in the fridge and turned the hob on, pouring a splash of oil in the pan. Flicking the kettle on, I popped a teaspoon of coffee into a mug. Within minutes the aroma of gently sizzling bacon wafted up my nostrils, making me feel marginally better. Quickly, I buttered two slices of thick white bread, poured my coffee, put the cooked bacon on one piece of bread, a dollop of tomato ketchup on the other, and sandwiched the bread together. Sitting back down on my stool, I bit into the sandwich, not caring one jot about the trail of grease oozing down my chin and onto my vest. Grease, carbs and ketchup – it was too good and hit the spot perfectly.

Feeling somewhat more human after tucking into my bacon sarnie, I wondered what had got into me this morning? Mooning over my single status. Just a blip, obviously caused by an excess of beer the previous night. There was no need to panic – there was still plenty of time for me to meet someone – okay it might not happen in Little Leyton, but then I hadn't intended on hanging around here for long. It was only ever meant as a stop gap, so why I'd begun to entertain thoughts of staying here permanently I didn't understand. It was a ridiculous idea. Besides, Mum and Dad would be home in a couple of months. That would focus my mind on moving on. Not that I didn't love this house, I did. It was my childhood home, full of happy memories, but

I was twenty-six years old now – still living in my parent's house at this age hadn't figured in my plans.

Still there was absolutely no need to panic at all. For the moment, there was no more convenient or picturesque place to live than at No. 2 Ivy Lane Cottages. The double-fronted stone cottage was situated right in the centre of Little Leyton in a row of similar-looking properties, overlooking the village pond, and only a five minute walk away from the pub. Approached through a wrought iron gateway, a stone paved pathway, flanked by lawns, lead up to the white wooden front door. At this time of year, Mum's hollyhocks, foxgloves and delphiniums, were a blaze of colour, all vying for attention while rambling pink roses framed the wooden porch way.

From the outside the cottage appeared tiny, old-fashioned and quaint, but as soon as you stepped over the threshold, you were in for a lovely surprise. The cottage was flooded with light, and was airy and spacious, giving a modern contemporary feel, thanks to Mum's eye for design. Over the years my parents had done extensive renovations to the house, knocking through the small cramped rooms to make one large open-plan living area, laying oak wooden flooring throughout, and installing a huge farmhouse style kitchen which was at the heart of the home. Despite all the modernization, the original qualities and charm of the old cottage had been enhanced and retained.

Hearing the letter box rattle, I wandered over to the front door to collect the post. Mainly bills and bumpf, but there was a postcard from Dad, the sight of his distinctive sprawling handwriting making my heart flutter. I turned over the bright card showing towering skyscrapers lit up against a night sky.

Life in Dubai is good! The sun's always shining and Mum's suntan is coming along a treat. Missing you, and having a pint down at the local, although missing you much more, of course! Will call soon. Love Dad xx PS Remember to water the garden x

Smiling, I placed the card on the fridge, securing it with a magnet. Knowing they were happy and enjoying their new adventure abroad made me happy. Water the garden – hmmm, I'd been a bit hit or miss on that front over the last couple of weeks so I'd put that on my list and do it today. First though I ought to do something about the state of the house. My gaze drifted round the kitchen and through into the open-plan dining and living room. It's wasn't exactly messy, but the place hadn't had a proper top to bottom clean since I'd moved in. Wasn't cleaning good for the soul? And hopefully it would help take my mind of the hangover – that was my Saturday sorted then.

Six hours later, after having done a quick swoosh upstairs and down, loaded the washing machine and dishwasher, sprayed some polish around, run the hoover over the rug and flung open the windows to let some fresh air in, I was done. In fairness the swooshing part had only taken an hour and the rest of the time had been spent recovering, reclined on the sofa drinking tea and eating chocolate truffles – hair of the dog and all that – while watching back-to-back episodes of *Dinner Date*.

I was just considering getting up and having a shower when the doorbell rang. Looking down at my grease-stained attire, I thought about ignoring whoever it was, but when it quickly rang again I levered myself up off the sofa, chocolate wrappers falling to the floor in my wake. I staggered towards the hallway, my legs heavy and achy from so much prolonged inactivity, and pulled open the door, thinking it might be a dog client.

'Hi Ellie.'

No such luck. Not a dog client, but wouldn't you know it, Max Golding standing on my threshold looking as though he'd just walked in from a menswear catalogue. Gorgeous. Far too gorgeous for his own good. Trouble was, he seemed to have an unerring knack of finding me at my worst. Every single time. Why couldn't we bump into each other when I was dressed up to the nines in a little cocktail dress and high heels? Not that I got to wear my glad-rags much these days.

In contrast, in brown thick-ribbed cords, a red check shirt and a warm engaging smile, Max looked every inch the country gentleman. Our eyes met fleetingly. In a way that did funny things to my insides. In a way that disturbed me because really I should have been so over him by now after not having seen him for so long, and finding out too about his secret girlfriend Sasha.

It was too late to close the door in his face and pretend I wasn't at home, even though the thought crossed my mind.

'Hi Max. I haven't seen you in a while,' I said, nonchalantly as though I hadn't been obsessively counting the days.

I found a smile and my manners from somewhere, inwardly cursing that I hadn't jumped into the shower half an hour earlier. I looked a wreck. I hadn't even brushed my hair today or changed out of my pyjamas, the ones that had bacon fat splattered down the front. I was a bit sweaty too from all the housework I'd done. Crossing my arms in front of my chest trying to obscure the stain, I looked him up and down. What exactly was he doing here looking drop-dead gorgeous?

'I just wanted to check how Amber was doing. Sasha told me what happened.'

He'd said her name. Sasha. I'd been holding onto the remote hope that the gorgeous girlfriend had been a figment of my imagination, but Max had just gone and dashed that hope.

'Oh right. Yeah. Thanks for asking. She's fine now. Doesn't seem any the worse for her accident. By the way, Cathy Harvey, Amber's owner, asked me to pass on her thanks to you both for helping out that day.' I didn't mention that she had plenty of other, less flattering, things to say about him too.

'That's good. And you?'

'Me?'

'Yes. You. How are you?' The corner of his lips curled in a smile. 'Have I called at a bad time? I could come back some other time if you're busy.' His gaze gave an imperceptible sweep of my body.

'No, it's fine.' I didn't want him coming back again. I didn't want him here now, really. We'd spent two whole days together and hadn't been stuck for conversation for a moment. Now, as he loitered on my doorstep, it couldn't be more awkward. Maybe he'd take the hint and leave.

His gaze perused me, his dark eyebrows raised questioningly. He made a show of looking behind him and then peering over my shoulder into the hallway beyond me as if I might have someone waiting there. A wry expression settled on his face as he clapped his hands and twisted his lips in amusement.

'Right. Well then...'

When he showed no sign of taking any hints and moving on, I asked, only out of politeness, 'Did you want to come in?'

A wide smile spread across his lips. 'Thank you, Ellie, if I'm not disturbing you at all.'

'No, it's fine. Come through.' If nothing else I'd be curious to know what it was he wanted.

He walked past me and gravitated toward the kitchen. Parking himself on a stool, he looked totally at home in my surroundings. He took up my offer of a coffee and I was pleased to have something to busy myself with. Anything to stop myself from having to look at him. I pulled two mugs out from the cupboard and flicked on the kettle.

With Max seemingly in no hurry to tell me what exactly he was doing here, content enough to just observe me pottering about the kitchen, I felt the need to break the silence.

'Sasha was a complete lifesaver the other day. I'm not sure what we would have done if she hadn't been at home.'

'Don't worry about it. I know she was only too pleased to have been of some help.' There was no self-consciousness on Max's part as he spoke about him and Sasha as a couple, as if it was common knowledge between us. 'We were relieved that it wasn't any worse. I feel kind of responsible that it happened on my property.'

'Oh, don't be. It was just one of those things. It could have happened anywhere.'

I passed Max his coffee and sat on the stool opposite him, carefully avoiding looking directly in his eyes. It was thoughtful of him to come and ask about Amber, but now

I wished he'd hurry up and finish his coffee and leave. Making polite conversation with him in the familiar and cosy surrounds of the pub was one thing, but being here in my home felt altogether more intimate, more awkward too.

'Sasha seems lovely?' I said.

There, I'd said it. Asked a direct question in relation to his girlfriend. The one he failed to mention to me. The one I was deeply curious about.

'Yep,' he said immediately without a flicker. 'She's a great girl.' He had the good grace to look away, pausing for a few seconds before swiftly moving the conversation on. 'How's life these days at The Dog and Duck? I've been away on business for the last couple of weeks. I've not had a chance to pop in.' If I'd wanted to find out more about his relationship with Sasha it was clear Max wasn't going to be the one to tell me.

'Oh, you know, same as always. Busy. Eric was saying they've found a buyer for the pub.'

'Really?'

'Yep. A restaurant chain apparently. I can't imagine it myself. The place isn't big enough to swing a cat.'

Max shook his head, seemingly lost in thought for a moment. 'No. I can't see it happening either.' His brow furrowed as he lifted his mug to his lips. 'The last thing I heard they were still in negotiations. I suppose we just have to keep our fingers crossed that it doesn't come to anything.'

I shrugged, a sigh escaping my lips. 'The trouble is if these people don't buy the pub then I'm sure it's only a matter of time before another buyer's found.'

'What are Eric's plans, do you know?'

'When he leaves the pub? I don't think he knows yet. I'm

not sure he's thinking that far ahead. What I do know is that it'll be a major upheaval for him. He's trying to appear as if it doesn't bother him, but I can tell he's really concerned about the future. The pub has been his whole life for so long. He'll find it a huge wrench to leave.'

'Hmmm, I bet. And he's not the only one either. Think of all the locals who use the pub as a meeting place. That won't happen if the place is turned into a restaurant.'

'Exactly. It will have a real impact on the local community.'

'And you personally, I guess? If you were to lose your job.'

'Yeah. I'd be sad to leave the pub, but that doesn't really matter. I can always find another job. It's more the loss of the pub to the community that concerns me. And what it will mean for Eric, of course.'

'Maybe he'll take the opportunity to retire?'

'Maybe.' Although I couldn't really see Eric as the type to sit at home in his slippers watching *Tipping Point*. It was the pub that gave him a purpose, a reason to get up in the mornings. My gaze drifted out of the kitchen window as we fell silent for a few moments, both lost in our own thoughts.

'Look, do you fancy a drink? I'm going to call in to the pub on my way back – do you want to come with me?' Max's deep brown eyes appraised me warmly. A look I'd seen before. A look I'd previously misinterpreted as desire. Now, in the unflattering lights of the kitchen, in my grease-stained PJs, I saw the look in his eyes for what it really was: friendliness, politeness. That was all. There was no hidden meaning behind the seductive gaze. No desire to rip off my clothes and take me on the carpet. What had I been thinking?

'Thanks, but I've got plans,' I said with as much dignity as I could muster.

'Shame.' He nodded, his gaze sweeping over me. 'Maybe some other time?'

I smiled and showed Max to the front door.

Some other time? I highly doubted it. Max had a girl-friend. And as much as I liked him, I didn't really want him as my friend. I had plenty of those already and spending too much time alone with Max was likely to do serious damage to my peace of mind.

Seventeen

'Why don't you go off for an hour or two, love, and enjoy the celebrations outside?'

It was the August bank holiday weekend and Little Leyton's summer fayre was well underway. The sun was shining high in a cloudless sky and already we'd seen a steady trickle of customers through the doors of The Dog and Duck. We had jugs of cold Pimms filled to the brim with strawberries and mint and oranges, ready for serving, and the garden was bathed in a warm glow, festooned with colourful bunting and an array of billowing hanging baskets and pot plants.

'Would you mind?' I asked, already undoing the ties to my apron. 'I don't suppose I'll be long.'

'Take as long as you like, darling,' said Eric fondly, who I suspected wouldn't be going far, but instead would be happy mooching around his pub all day, chatting with his customers.

Outside, the warm sun caressed my bare arms. I popped my sunglasses on and wandered down the High Street and around the village green, stopping at all the stalls to inspect the goodies being sold. Already, I'd bought a jar of green tomato chutney, some plum jam and a lemon drizzle loaf.

I was just walking past the stall for St Cuthbert's when I heard someone calling out my name.

'Over here, Ellie!'

Standing with her head and hands through the wooden stocks was the Reverend Trish Evans who was smiling at me broadly and waving as best she could with her hands locked down.

'Oh, hello,' I said, dropping my head to the side to talk to her.

'Would you like to have a go at throwing some wet sponges at me? Three for 50p. You know it's for a good cause.'

I didn't like that idea at all. It didn't seem right somehow to be throwing wet sponges at the vicar, but if she insisted... And as Trish had mentioned, the proceeds from today's fayre would be split between two worthwhile charities, a local children's hospice and a fund towards building a permanent structure for the refugees in France.

When Max and I had returned from our trip, me, Josie and Eric had all agreed that we wanted to continue our fund raising activities for the refugees in Calais. Max had volunteered the services of a couple of his men to go and help with the construction of the new building, but they still needed donations towards building materials. We saw it as an on-going campaign and had decided to continue collecting clothing donations in the pub too, with a view to making further trips over to France in the future. Although one thing was for sure, if I was going over to the continent again, I certainly wouldn't be taking Max as my co-driver. No way. That route led only to disappointment and heartache as I'd already found out to my cost.

Now, I popped my 50p in the bucket and picked up the first sponge. I threw it half-heartedly in the direction of Trish, but it fell far short of reaching her.

'Come on, Ellie, you can do better than that,' urged Trish.

Thankfully my second and third attempts were just as bad, one went flying over her head and the other hit the wooden board to the side of Trish's face. Mind you, I did wonder if it had been anyone else locked in those stocks, someone like Max Golding, whether my aim would have been much better. The way I felt about him now I'd probably pay fifty quid to throw wet sponges into his face. I sighed, wondering how one man – one gorgeous and unavailable man admittedly – had managed to lodge himself into my head quite so firmly, and was now refusing categorically to move out.

Waving goodbye to Trish, I wandered on, past the tombola and the coconut shy.

At the Daisy Chain Mother and Toddlers stall, I spent a lovely time browsing through their selection of paperbacks, before picking out a romance, a crime thriller and an historical saga. I loved a bit of bedtime reading and once I'd finished with them they'd be able to go on the bookshelves at the pub.

'Oh, hi Ellie, how are you?'

It was Victoria Evans, the young woman from the local newspaper. With sunglasses worn high on her head and with her notepad and pen in her hand, she looked every inch the roving reporter.

'Great thanks. And you?'

'Yes. I'm doing a write-up of the event for the paper so

I'm just getting round trying to see as much as I can.'

'Well, my highlight has been throwing wet sponges at your mum,' I admitted, with a smile.

'Ha ha, yes, you've reminded me. I need to go and have a try at that too. I don't get too many of those kind of opportunities,' she said, laughing.

'If you have a chance, Victoria, could you mention in your article that there is still a collection point in the pub for any donations that people might want to make towards the refugee fund.'

'Of course, I will,' she said, hurriedly scribbling it down in her notebook.

'Oh, and if you've got any other free spots in the paper in the coming weeks, perhaps you could do a little mention of the German beer festival that we'll be holding soon. There'll be music and dancing and regional German foods and some great beers too. It's always a brilliant event, it would be good to spread the word.'

'We've got an "upcoming events" feature in the paper now, so I'll make sure it goes in there, if you like?'

'Thanks Victoria, you're a star.'

I felt much more at ease asking Victoria for help, rather than her boss Tim Weston, who I'd always found a bit slippery and sleazy. I knew if I'd asked him for help in promoting our events he would only have probed me on what was happening behind the scenes at the pub and I really didn't want to be drawn into those kind of conversations. Not that I would have anything to tell him. There were low-level mutterings sweeping around the village that the pub might be changing hands soon, but it was still just rumour and intrigue at the moment.

Half an hour later, I eased myself up from the grass where I'd taken the opportunity to lie in the sun, dipping into the romance I'd bought and relishing the sensation of the sunrays caressing my skin. Hot and sultry days like these were few and far between so you had to make the most of them when you could. Wandering back to the pub, I passed Paul and Caroline, my parents' next-door neighbours, who were standing in the queue to the refreshments tent.

'Why don't you come and have a cup of tea with us, Ellie?' Caroline beckoned me over.

That's what I loved so much about Little Leyton. That I could wander through the village and meet so many friends, people who looked out for me and cared about me. In London, I could go for days without talking to anyone but the people I worked alongside. Here, if I hadn't drawn my curtains by eight-thirty in the morning, then I knew someone would be knocking on my door asking if everything was okay.

Relative newcomers to the village, Paul and Caroline had only moved in a couple of years earlier, but they'd quickly become good friends with our family, and Mum and Caroline were always popping into each other's houses for a cuppa and a chat.

'Oh, I do miss your mum,' she said now, as we sat down at a table in the sun.

'I know, me too, but they are loving it in Dubai. I'll be speaking to her later, she'll be sorry to have missed the summer fayre, she always enjoys it so much.'

'Well, send her my love, won't you? And you know if there's anything you need or if you ever want to pop round to ours for a meal, then you know you'll always be very welcome.'

'Aw, thanks Caroline.'

Definitely, there were so many lovely friends and interesting characters to be found in Little Leyton. Talking of which... Over on the other side of the green I saw Max Golding and my heart lifted. Very interesting... Showing off his tanned legs in khaki shorts and with a fitted black T-shirt, sculpting the contours of his chest, he looked more than interesting. There should be a whole different category for the likes of Max Golding. Sexy, dashing and... I shook my head. *Forget about him, Ellie. Move on,* I chided myself. But where was the lovely Sasha today, I wondered with a pang. Really, I should go over and chat to him, show him that I was perfectly cool with the whole situation. Definitely, after my tea, I'd go and seek him out.

As I took another bite into the delicious comforts of my cream scone, a flash of lightning forked through the sky and a dark rumbling of thunder indicated its intent.

'Crikey, that sounds ominous,' said Paul, looking up to the heavens. Just then the clouds opened and heavy rain poured down upon us. I held my arms up into its path. Cool, refreshing and potent. People stood up, surprised by this unexpected change in the weather, running for cover under the marquee and into the surrounding shops and houses.

Paul chuckled, getting up from his seat. 'I think that might be the guvnor's way of telling us that summer is well and truly over.'

Well, either that, or an omen to me that I should keep well away from Max Golding at all costs.

Eighteen

In the following weeks I took heed of that warning from the heavens and duly kept my distance from Max Golding. Fortunately, I didn't run into him at the pub even though I knew from Dan that he had been in on a couple of occasions. And I didn't bump into him on any of my walks either. I took that as a sign from a higher authority that this was the way it should be. Max Golding should come with a government health warning, I'd decided, and the sooner I got him out of my system the better. Luckily I'd been very busy and I hadn't had chance to think about him... much. Although now on the last night of the beer festival with all our friends and locals in, suddenly I was feeling his absence much more keenly.

The pub was alive with excited chatter, laughter and, yes, some raucous behaviour too. The place was filled to the gills with happy punters intent on sampling the array of beers served in traditional steins and soaking up the atmosphere provided by the oompah band, the Bavarian Buskers, who played an array of lively pop songs in folksy Bavarian style.

Eric, Dan and the other guys had thrown themselves into the spirit of the evening and were sporting lederhosen, which gave rise to a great deal of good-natured ribaldry.

Josie and I wore jaunty Tyrolean hats and had plaited our hair into bunches. With our white tie-front blouses and blue gingham aprons over black dirndl skirts we certainly looked the part of Bavarian serving ladies. All of the bar staff had been called in to assist on what we knew would be one of our busiest evenings of the year and Eric presided over proceedings with his usual flair and good humour.

It was lovely having Josie back behind the bar, she'd only just started taking on a couple of shifts in the week leaving Ethan at home on babysitting duties. Not that we'd have much chance to chat this evening, but she had shown me the latest photos of Stella on her phone, totally adorable, and I'd made a promise to pop round to hers later in the week for a catch-up and a cuddle with little Stella.

After serving behind the pumps for a couple of hours, I swept around the bars, collecting glasses from the tables, a job that took much longer than usual as everyone was in high spirits and wanted me to stop and chat with them. I even got roped into some energetic dancing with a couple of the buskers. A group of men who had come in from a neighbouring town by minibus had taken over the small back bar and were getting louder and merrier by the moment. Eric was keeping a close eye on them. He certainly didn't want to spoil anyone's fun, but he wouldn't tolerate behaviour that would spoil the enjoyment for the rest of the customers.

As I manoeuvred around the group of guys, collecting their empties, one of the guys grabbed me around the waist and pulled me towards him.

'Hello, Heidi,' he whispered in my ear, 'You are looking very... lubb... very ludd... very luv... luverly...' He sighed contentedly, pleased with himself at getting his words out, albeit not an actual word, but I knew exactly what he meant. 'Can I just touch your plaits?' He waved his hands around in front of his face trying to get a grip on my hair, but fortunately his aim was well off.

I laughed and extracted myself from his hold. 'I wouldn't if I were you. My boyfriend is the strong, possessive type. Doesn't like anyone messing about with his girl.'

'Aw, well, I won't tell him if you don't,' said the man, who was clearly the worse for wear, having downed several pints of strong German beer over the course of the evening. His friends, who had been watching our interaction intently, threw back their heads, laughing at his antics.

A little while later, I was back in the kitchen loading dirty glasses into the dishwasher.

'Not causing you too much grief, are they?' asked Eric, who was free of his plaster cast now and moving around much more freely.

'What, that group of lads? Nah, it's nothing I can't handle.'

You couldn't be a shrinking violet or easily offended if you'd worked as a barmaid for as long as I had. I was used to the backchat, the cheeky comments and the innuendo that came with pouring pints of beer for a living. I gave as good as I got and could usually deflect a tricky situation with a sharp retort or a witty quip. If things ever got more out of hand then Eric was always around to step in and take control of the situation, but it rarely came to that.

We were taking advantage of the much-welcome lull in the evening's proceedings. Josie had left after the main rush wanting to get home to her little one, and Dan and Andy were out the front manning the bars. Eric poured us both a long cool lemonade topped up with ice and lemon, and we took a moment, away from the hubbub to take a reviving sip and remark on what a great evening it had been.

'I haven't seen it so busy since… well, since the last beer festival.'

'Ah yes.' My mind cast back to the previous year when there had been a 'Beers of the World' festival. Then, I'd come home from London for a long weekend especially to attend, as a customer mind, not as a member of the bar staff. Johnny, me and a crowd of locals had sat in the front bar, sampling a variety of beers, and slowly and surely getting ourselves very, very merry. I couldn't remember much of the detail, naturally. It was all a bit of a haze then and more so now. Although I do remember the laughs. And the feeling of warmth and love I'd felt curled up in the crook of Johnny's arm. I sighed. Tonight it was Polly snuggled up in Johnny's arms. A pang of longing for that lost evening whirled its way around the pit of my stomach. Where had that suddenly come from?

'So, Ellie?' Eric's voice nudged me out of my reminiscing. 'Do you want to hear the good news or the bad news?'

'Ooh go on then.' I ran my hands under the tap and pulled a clean, fresh tea-towel out from the dresser, tucking it into the apron on my skirt. 'I could do with some good news, what is it?'

'Hunters Inns? The company that were buying the pub? They've pulled out.'

'Really?' I couldn't help a big smile from spreading across my lips. 'That is good news. But why?'

'Apparently their surveyors looked at the pub and gave

it the thumbs-down. I think they had plans to extend the place, but with the restrictions on it because of its listing, they realized it wasn't going to be a viable option.'

'Well, we could have told them that,' I said, laughing.

'Exactly.' Eric nodded. 'I can't tell you how pleased I am though that it's not going to be turned into a carvery.'

'Oh, me too.' I threw my arms around his big chest, giving him a squeeze. 'Such good news, but what's the bad news?'

'Ah yes, well, there was another buyer waiting in the wings. A new deal's been done.'

'Already?' My moment of joy was short-lived.

'Yep. A private buyer apparently, so I don't have any details. And that's the thing. At least with Hunters we knew what they had in mind for the pub. It's anyone's guess what this mystery buyer might intend to do with the old place.'

'Hmm, I see what you mean. Well, it can't be any worse than turning it into a carvery, can it?'

Eric grimaced and gave a slow nod of his head.

Thinking about it, there were a dozen other terrifying options for the pub, but perhaps it was better not to even contemplate those. 'We're just going to have to stay positive and hope to goodness that whoever buys the pub loves it as much as we do and wants to keep it just as it is.'

Eric sucked on his lips, before a wry smile appeared. 'That's what I love about you, Ellie. Your sunny nature and your ability to look on the bright side of every situation.'

'I try!' Just then the distinctive sound of glass shattering across the old stone floor followed by an almighty cheer resonated from the snug bar. 'Uh-oh, the natives are getting restless, I'd better go and see what's happened.'

Grabbing the dustpan and brush from the under stairs cupboard, I went back into the bar and proceeded to sweep up the remains of a broken beer jug, to a chorus of encouragement from the revellers. The guy who had been so fascinated by my plaits just a little while earlier joined me on the floor, on all-fours.

'Please be careful,' I told him. 'There's glass everywhere. Why don't you go back to your friends? I'll have this all cleared up in a moment.'

'But I'd like to help, Heidi. Here...' He shuffled forwards on his hands and knees, reaching for a shard of glass. 'Oh fuck! Ouch. Shit. Ooh look, it's bleeding.'

Typical! I thought I'd managed to sweep up all the glass, but there'd been one remaining piece and my new friend had only gone and found it and embedded it into his hand.

'Oh dear. Come on,' I said, offering him a hand up so he could get up off the floor. 'Let's get you cleaned up.'

He grabbed hold of my arm with his good hand, and held his other hand up in the air, all the time dripping blood down his arm and across the floor.

'Are you going to take me home with you?' he asked, as I led him through the bar, carefully avoiding the other customers so as not to splatter them with blood.

'No,' I laughed, 'I'm taking you to the kitchen so we can get that finger cleaned up and get a plaster on it.'

'Oh, that's a shame.'

'Everything all right?' Eric asked, meeting us halfway, a look of concern on his face.

'Yep, fine. Just a little accident. Nothing that can't be

sorted. I'm just taking...' I stopped and turned to look at my drunken charge, who was actually being very compliant. 'What's your name?'

'Kirk.'

'I'm just taking Kirk to get his finger sorted.'

Eric nodded and went on his way, checking on the other customers, a relieved smile on his face.

In the kitchen I ran Kirk's finger under the tap and wrapped some kitchen roll around it to stem the bleeding. Then I found a plaster from the first-aid tin and placed it gently over the cut.

'Thank you, Heidi,' he said, gratitude shining in his glazed eyes as he looked down at his finger and then back at me. Honestly, the way he was looking at me, adoringly, you would have thought I'd just performed major life-saving surgery. Not just stuck a plaster round his finger. 'You're lovely you are, do you know that?'

'All part of the service,' I said with a smile, placing my hand in the small of his back and guiding him through the pub back towards his friends. Nurse, friend, confidante – I was all things to all people in my role as barmaid.

My gaze swept around the bar. Some customers were making moves to leave but there was still a huge swell of people enjoying the festivities. It was going to be a late night, I knew. Once we shut the door on the last customer, then I could look forward to sitting down at long last, taking the weight off my feet and rewarding myself with a long cool glass of beer. Still, that was a long way off yet, I realized, glancing at my watch.

With Kirk patched up and reunited with his friends, I

picked up where I left off, collecting glasses and giving the tables a wipe down.

It was only then that I spotted Max Golding standing at the bar. As I looked up, cloth in hand, he acknowledged me with a slight incline of his head and that distinctive half smile of his that made his dark brown eyes flicker with mischief. He must have only just turned up or else I would have noticed him before. Max wasn't the blending into the background type. His presence very much demanded attention. Or maybe that was just the effect he had on me. Or rather the effect he used to have on me. I'd been trying my best to put Max out of my mind, but it wasn't easy, he had a habit of seeping into my thoughts unbidden. Still I was determined to treat him just like any other customer – one that was probably worth avoiding at the moment.

Thankfully tonight we were very busy so I could almost forget he was there. Almost. Trouble was, every time I looked up, he was looking over at me. Or perhaps it was me looking across at him. Oh God. That was it. There was me thinking, hoping, that he was taking surreptitious glances at me when actually it was wishful thinking on my part. What was wrong with me? Taking sneaky peeks thinking he wouldn't notice, when all the time he was observing me, that wry amused expression on his face. Get a grip, Ellie. *Before you make a complete and utter fool of yourself.*

I disappeared behind the bar, out of sight of Max, hopeful that he would leave just as quickly as he'd arrived. I shuddered, annoyed at myself for letting Max get under my skin in such a way, darkening my previous light-hearted mood. Grrr. That man was seriously beginning to annoy me. Why couldn't he just get out of my head and leave me alone.

'Heidi!' Kirk's plaintive call echoed to the rafters of the pub. 'Heidi! I'm going home now.'

Smiling, I lifted the bar and wandered out to the front to see Kirk and his group of mates getting ready to leave. Kirk's face lit up when he saw me.

'Thank you lovely Heidi lady, for such a brilliant night and for looking after me, like.' He held up his finger proudly, before enveloping me in a bear hug.

'That's all right,' I said, laughing, extracting myself from his hold. 'I'm glad you had such a good evening.'

'Aw, it was great.' He leaned into my side, almost losing his balance as he did so, grabbing on to my arm to steady himself. He giggled. 'Are you sure you wouldn't like to go out with me sometime for a drink, like?'

'Thanks, Kirk, but I'm taken for. Remember.' I placed my hands on my shoulders to firm his balance. 'You have a safe journey home.'

'I will, lovely Heidi. What's your proper name?'

'You know what? I like Heidi. You can call me Heidi,' I said laughing.

'Yeah, that's what I thought it was,' he said, as though it was the funniest thing in the world. From his pocket he pulled out a note of paper. 'Look if you ever change your mind about that drink, then phone me. I promise you we'll have the best bloody time ever.' He popped the scrap of paper with a scrawled telephone number on it into the pocket of my apron and gave me a gentle squeeze on my arm and a cheeky kiss too.

'Right mate, that's enough now. Time for you to go on your way, I think.'

I span round, startled by the familiar voice, even more startled to see Max standing far too close to Kirk, his body almost touching the other man's, his eyebrows drawn tight together and his face as dark as thunder.

Nineteen

'Max!'

'Uh-oh.' Kirk's head rolled on his neck, he narrowed his eyes and looked up at Max, and then at me, his face a picture of confusion. 'Is this your boyfriend then, Heidi?'

'What? No.' I turned to Max, hoping he was about to explain exactly what he thought he was doing, because I had no idea whatsoever. Why was he wading into something that had absolutely nothing to do with him? 'What's the problem, Max?' I said sharply.

'This guy. He's the problem. He's been hounding you all night.' He towered over Kirk and I had the impression if he even so much as blew on Kirk then my drunken friend would probably topple over in front of me. Instead, Max said, 'Just leave the girl alone. Can't you tell she's not interested?'

Kirk's brow furrowed and his bottom lip jutted out. 'Sorry, Heidi, have I been a pain. I'm sorry.' He scratched his head. 'I… well, I'm sorry if I've been out of order.'

'No, it's fine,' I said, glaring at Max.

Buoyed by my support, Kirk rallied and addressed Max directly. 'If you're not her boyfriend then, who are you? Do you own the place or something?'

'No.' I jumped in, realizing this situation could quickly

get out of hand if I didn't put a stop to it fast. 'Max is a customer. He was probably just looking out for me, but there was no need. You haven't been a pain at all. It's been lovely meeting you.'

Crikey, compared to some of the customers we had through the doors, Kirk was a sweetheart. Definitely the worse for wear, yes, a bit cheeky too, but harmless enough. He'd just been enjoying himself. Where was the harm in that? There'd been no need for Max to be so heavy-handed with him.

'You're all right, you are, Heidi,' said Kirk, marginally appeased. 'You,' he said, stabbing a finger at Max's chest, 'need to learn some manners. And you'd better watch out because she's got a boyfriend. A big geezer by all accounts. He won't be best pleased to hear you've been ordering her about.'

I bit on my lip to stop a smile from spreading across my face. I liked the way my imaginary boyfriend was growing in stature by the minute. I half expected him to waltz through the door and come to my rescue any moment now.

Max's eyebrows lifted, his pupils growing large, as he looked at me as though asking for an explanation.

'And another thing...' Kirk had found his voice and was intent on giving Max the benefit of his advice. 'If she ever breaks up with the big geezer boyfriend, she's going out with me for a drink, so you, matey boy, can do a hike.'

'Right, come on Kirk, the minibus is about to leave,' I said, bundling him out through the front door, anxious to avoid any further confrontation. The cool night air was a welcome distraction from the intense and heady atmosphere inside the pub and I took a moment to gather myself. 'Don't worry about that guy back there,' I told Kirk. 'He can be a bit of an idiot at times.'

'Yeah, a proper knobhead, if you ask me.'

As I waved Kirk, his friends and the minibus into the night, I couldn't help agreeing with Kirk's concise assessment of Max's character; a proper knobhead indeed.

*

With the minibus crew gone, the pub had cleared out to a level that was much more manageable. I had hoped to go to the kitchen in search of a bit of reflective drying up time, but as soon as I'd walked back through the front door, Max was there, lying in wait for me.

'Ellie?'

I felt my skin bristle. I didn't want to deal with this right now. Didn't even know what 'this' was, only knowing that Max had been way out of order. I was still working and the way I felt at the moment I couldn't trust myself not to give Max a piece of mind. 'Yes?' I span round, a core of anger deep down inside, pulling me up tall, my head raised defiantly.

'Oh please, don't look at me like that. I'm sorry. Look he was hassling you. Every time I looked up he had his grubby hands over you. I thought I was helping out.'

'Well, you weren't.' I pulled him to one side, away from the prying eyes of the remaining customers. 'And what makes you think I need your help? This is my job. A job I've been doing on and off for years now. I've dealt with more lairy customers in my time than you'll ever know. If I can't handle the likes of Kirk then I shouldn't be doing this job.'

'He was a drunken fool.'

'Yes, well, he spoke very highly of you too.'

Max grimaced, looking suitably contrite. He raked a hand through his hair, and I wished he hadn't. Wished my body didn't respond to his every movement in a way my head had no part in. 'Sorry, Ellie.' He reached for my arm with his hand, his touch causing our eyes to lock together. I took a step backwards, away from his overwhelming presence. 'I got it wrong,' he admitted. 'I shouldn't have interfered. It was just seeing him, all over you like that, I...'

'Look, forget it,' I said, not wanting to drag this out any more than necessary. 'Apology accepted.' Easier that way or else I might say something I'd end up regretting.

Eric came up beside us, the large set of keys jangling in his hand, to lock the front door. 'Hope you two will be staying for a late one. First chance I've had all night to have a proper drink.'

'Yeah, sure.' Max glanced at his watch, and then briefly towards me, as if asking my permission.

I shrugged and gave a smile. Whatever my personal feelings towards Max, and they seemed to veer from one extreme to the other – he fascinated me, annoyed me, intrigued and dismayed me in equal measure – I certainly didn't want there to be any bad feeling between us or to drag Eric and the pub into our petty disagreements.

'I'll just go and finish up in the kitchen.'

'No you won't, young lady,' said Eric, putting a firm arm around my shoulder. 'It's all done. And you have worked your butt off all evening. Go and sit down. I'll bring you a beer over.'

I didn't need telling twice. The lock-ins weren't a regular

occurrence at the pub, but on nights like tonight, special occasions, when no one wanted the party atmosphere to end, Eric would invite a select few customers and the bar staff to stay behind to enjoy a few extra bevies.

All the bar staff were there, Dan, Andy and Rich, and lots of our lovely locals including Johnny and Polly, Bill, Tony and Dave, and Max now too, sitting on a stool up against the bar. I didn't want to talk or even look at him, best for both our sakes to keep some distance between us.

I slumped down in Noel's rocking chair, my favourite spot in the entire pub, and pulled off my apron and kicked off my shoes, weariness immediately enveloping my body. It was always the same. All the time I was busy working I ran on adrenaline, not noticing the hours rushing by, feeding off the animated atmosphere within the pub, but as soon as I sat down and relaxed for a moment, that's when tiredness hit me. I sighed, stretching my legs out in front of me. Every part of my body ached.

'Here you go, darling. Not sure how we would have managed without you tonight.' Eric handed me a beer and my hands clasped around the ice-cold glass as though it was a lifeline.

'Aw, it was such fun. Weren't the band brilliant? They went down really well with the customers. There was an awful lot of thigh-slapping going on.'

'That probably had something to do with the number of pints we sold tonight.' Eric chuckled. 'There was an awful moment when I thought we might actually run out of beer. Can you imagine what a disaster that would have been? Thankfully it didn't come to that, but it was a close run thing. There's going to be plenty of sore heads in the village tomorrow, that's for sure.'

'You'd have had a riot on your hands if the beer had run out,' said Tony, who'd had more than his fair share over the course of the evening. 'A one-man riot, at least.' He laughed.

Eric settled himself on a stool behind the bar and downed half of his pint of beer. He licked his lips and smiled. Satisfaction was evident on his face as he sat back and relaxed, content in the knowledge he'd put on another great evening for the locals, one that would be talked about for years to come, I didn't doubt.

'I'm going to miss all this,' he said reflectively, his gaze travelling around the pub. We all looked at him, our light-hearted mood suddenly sombre. 'You know,' he said, trying to recover the situation, 'when I do eventually leave here.'

'Nah, it's not really going to happen, is it?' said Dave, shaking his head.

It was common knowledge now that the pub was up for sale, but I think everyone was in denial that such an integral part of our community would move into the hands of someone new, someone we didn't know.

''Fraid so. I've only got two months left on my contract, so I'll be out of here before Christmas. What happens after that is anyone's guess. The pub's been sold by all accounts, but what the new owners have in mind for the place I don't know.'

'They might want to keep you on though?' asked Dave.

'Well, if they do, they're keeping shtum about it.'

'Don't worry Eric,' said Tony. 'We'll boycott the pub if they put someone else in charge.'

'Hear, hear!'

Eric gave a wry smile. 'I appreciate the support, but, you know, every pub has its day and maybe it's the right time for The Dog and Duck to have a change at the helm.'

'No!' came the collective cry.

'Well, at least we know it's not going to be a chain-restaurant which is a relief,' I said, looking at Max. He'd been as interested as anyone in the future of the pub, but tonight he was lost in his own thoughts, nursing his beer. Probably thinking about his earlier behaviour and what a fool he'd made of himself.

'Not a restaurant, but it could still be any number of things. They might change it into a shop or a tearoom or a private house even,' said Johnny, looking directly at Max.

Max looked up and shrugged.

'Come on folks,' said Eric, 'there's no point in all this surmising. What will be will be? And all the time we've got this place then we must celebrate that fact. Who's having another pint?'

*

I'd had a couple of drinks and now I was ready for my bed, before I fell asleep, right there, in Noel's old chair. I stood up and collected my jacket from the hook behind the door. The others were just hitting their stride and were clearly in for a heavy session, but my stamina wasn't up to that. I said my goodbyes and headed for the front door. Max quickly followed me.

'Let me walk you home?'

'No, there's no need,' I said, turning to look at him. 'Stay and enjoy the party. I would, but I'm completely knackered.'

'I was going to head home too. Besides, you shouldn't be walking alone at this time of night. You don't know what kind of weirdos are lurking outside.'

'Oh for goodness sake.' I pulled my jacket over my shoulders and stepped outside. 'You clearly have a very low opinion of me if you think I'm so helpless that I can't handle a lively customer or walk home on my own. Really, Max, I grew up in this village. I've walked home late at night more times than I care to remember and managed to survive so far. I'm really not the helpless creature you think I am.'

'Ellie! Don't be like that. I didn't mean anything by it. And I certainly don't think you're helpless. Quite the opposite in fact.' He paused, frustration evident in his tone. 'It was just one friend looking out for another. Is that such a bad thing?'

I gave Max a sideways glance. He'd shrugged on a big brown moleskin coat, the curl of his hair reaching his upturned collar. He towered over me and I half wished to grab his arm and snuggle up into the warmth of his lovely coat. Instead I shivered beneath my thin pink fleece, attempting not to show Max that I was in the least bit cold.

'No, but really you have no need to worry on my account. I'm perfectly capable of looking after myself.'

'I don't doubt it. Come on, Ellie, give me a break. I wanted to talk to you actually.'

'Oh yes?' I said, unable to hide the sarcasm from my voice.

Well, why should I make this easy for him? He'd seriously annoyed me tonight. What gave him the right to think he could interfere in my life?

Still, whether I wanted him to or not, Max was walking

alongside me. That was up to him. It wasn't hugely out of his way, and besides, I'd be home within a matter of minutes. Whatever Max had to say to me he'd better make it quick.

'Look, sorry about earlier.' He dug his hands deep into his pockets. 'That incident with that other guy. Clearly I'm not cut out for a career in the hospitality business.'

With my arms folded, I was determined not to look at Max, although I was aware of his gaze on my face as we walked along the High Street. When he failed to get my attention, he turned around, making backwards running movements beside me so that I had no choice but to look into his face.

'Come on, Ellie, won't you forgive me?' he pleaded.

It was hard to stay cross with Max for long. He had an unerring knack of inveigling his way beneath my skin, making me feel warm, protected, safe.

'Hmm, I suppose,' I said reluctantly.

He laughed and turned round again, grabbing hold of my hand. 'Crikey, you're freezing. Do you want my coat?'

'No, I'm fine...'

Before I could finish my sentence he'd whipped off his coat and wrapped it around my shoulders, the immediate warmth it provided sending a shiver down my spine.

'You'll get cold now,' I protested.

'Don't worry. I don't really feel the cold.' He grabbed my arm and linked it through his, as though it was the most natural thing in the world. 'So, what's this I hear about a new boyfriend?'

'Sorry?' I said, being deliberately evasive.

'That guy in the pub had great delight in telling me you had a big burly boyfriend. He sounds delightful.' There was no mistaking the humour in his voice. 'When do we get to meet him?'

I shrugged and walked on with more purpose now, still determined not to look Max in the eye. 'I'm not sure that is any of your business. Actually.'

'Come on, Ellie. Don't give me a hard time. I like you. Care about you. I'm interested, that's all.'

God, he had a cheek. Interested to know all the details about my personal life, but reluctant to tell me anything about his. 'Well, to be honest with you, there isn't a lot to tell.'

'But this boyfriend...? Go on. What's his name? Where d'you meet him?'

I stopped, unlinked my arm from his and turned to look at him, open-mouthed at his arrogance. 'Well, if you must know, there isn't a boyfriend. I made him up. Comes in handy when dealing with persistent customers who won't take no for an answer. Works every time, especially when I explain he's a 6 foot 4 rugby player who's the possessive, controlling type.'

'Ah, I see.' Max pursed his lips together as if pondering on that. 'Is that the type you'd go for then? Someone sporty, beefy?'

Max, clearly amused, couldn't help a smile from spreading across his face.

'That's really none of your business either, is it?' I said, riled. 'You stand here wanting to know all about my personal life, but what about you, Max? You're a closed book. I'd go so far as to say secretive even. You never told me about your girlfriend.' The silence that fell between us crackled with tension. 'I only found out about her when I turned up at your house with Amber. It was embarrassing! She clearly knew all about me and yet I didn't even know she existed. You might have thought to tell me.'

I stalked off, not caring if he chose to follow me or not, only relieved that I'd finally got what I wanted to say off my chest. It had been eating me up for ages.

I hoped he would just go home now and leave me alone with my moral superiority intact. Only it dawned on me as I waltzed away that I was still wearing his coat. He might be glad to see the back of me, but I suspected he wouldn't feel the same way about his expensive jacket.

In a moment, Max was at my side again, holding up his hands to me in a gesture of defeat. 'Okay, I'm sorry. I should have told you. That's what I wanted to talk to you about actually. Can I come in? We should discuss this.'

We were standing at the gate to my house and I shrugged off the coat, returning it into Max's arms. The cold night air whipped around me, making my skin bristle with goose-bumps. It wasn't the time to be loitering outside.

'There's absolutely no need to explain. Your personal life is exactly that. As is mine. Perhaps it's best if we keep it that way. Goodnight Max.'

'Please, Ellie.' He touched my arm. 'Let's be friends. Give me fifteen minutes of your time. Let me explain. And then if you still think I'm an arsehole – it's okay, I can see it in your eyes – then I promise you I'll leave you alone and we can pretend we never even had this conversation.'

Twenty

Well, what was I expected to do? I'd already admitted that I found Max hard to resist, and to be honest my curiosity had got the better of me. What was it that he might tell me? Part of me wasn't sure I wanted to put myself through the agony of hearing all about his lovely girlfriend and yet the other part was desperate to know all the details; how long had they been together, where did they meet, what did she do for a living, what was her bra size? He'd been quite content to tell me about Nadine, his long-lost French girlfriend, and while that had been interesting, she was very much in the history category. Sasha was much more fascinating to me, being in the here and now category, but what was stopping Max from being so forthcoming about her? He'd probably come up with some far-fetched excuse as to why he'd omitted to tell me about her in the first place, how it had conveniently slipped his mind and, if I was being truthful, I was looking forward to seeing him squirm.

Indoors, I warmed my hands against the Aga before putting on some milk to heat up for a hot chocolate while Max took up my offer of a glass of red wine. We took our drinks and sat on the squishy sofa next to the Aga. He'd positioned himself with his back against the end of the sofa, his legs gently splayed, his arm laying casually along the top of the cushion, looking directly at me. Eek. The gorgeous underwear model had put in a reappearance. My heart pitter-pattered. I curled my legs up beneath me and backed myself into my end of the sofa. There was nowhere for me to look, other than into the deep dark gaze of Max's eyes. I gulped. Maybe this hadn't been such a good idea after all. Inviting him into my home. My entire body prickled with anticipation. I couldn't make up my mind if it was an enjoyable or terrifying sensation.

'Great night, wasn't it? At the pub?' I said, eager to fill the simmering silence.

'Oh yeah, Eric certainly knows how to put on a good "do". Unfortunately, I didn't get there till late, but I'm glad I caught the band. They were great.'

'Yeah, brilliant,' I gushed, sounding like an overexcited teenager. 'Lovely to see Eric on such good form too – he really is the heart and soul of that place.'

'Yep, and sounds as though things might work out at the pub for him after all.'

'Hmmm, well, I hope so, but we don't really know what will happen yet.'

'No, but we can be cautiously optimistic, I reckon. Always pays to be positive. No point in worrying about what might happen until we know for certain what the situation is.'

That was easy for him to say, it wasn't his livelihood and home at risk. Eric could have his whole world upended in a matter of months, so he wouldn't view it in the same way as Max. There was every chance I would be losing my job too. I stifled a sigh, trying to imagine what that might be like. It would be a real wrench to leave the pub. I'd miss seeing all my lovely customers every day, hearing all their news and keeping up with the village gossip. Aside from missing out on the social side of my job, necessity meant I would need to find another gig pretty quickly to make up the shortfall in my monthly income. But jobs, especially part-time ones, were hard to come by in the area. My best bet might be to expand my fledgling business with dog-training classes or agility groups. Both things I'd considered in the past – a couple of my doggy clients had already asked if I could provide these services – so maybe now was the time to consider it seriously. Or perhaps all of this was a sign from a higher celestial power telling me that I should go back to London after all. Do the job that I'd trained so long and hard for. Wasn't that the sensible solution?

'It isn't always easy to be positive when you don't know what the future holds,' I said, putting my thoughts into words.

'Quite the contrary. It can be exciting.' He flung out his arm with a flourish. 'Sometimes change is good for us. Helps us to grow as individuals.'

I raised my eyebrows doubtfully. 'Hmm, are you a life coach or something in your spare time?'

'No.' Max laughed, his smile lighting up his face, reminding me, if I needed reminding, that I had an extremely good-looking and sexy man sitting only inches away from me. Breathe Ellie, I told myself. 'Just trying to put a positive spin on things, that's all.'

It was hardly surprising that Max had such an outlook. He was an entrepreneur; a property developer and a business man to boot, obviously extremely successful at what he did. Was it so easy to be positive if you were wondering if you would still have your job at the end of the month or if you'd be able to pay the rent? I doubted it somehow.

I stretched my hands above my head unable to stop a massive yawn from taking over my body. It had been a long day and the sofa was way too comfy. My eyes were heavy and those couple of beers and now the hot chocolate had provided the most delightful soporific effect. Max looked at me through narrowed eyes and picked up on my not-so subtle hint.

'Look, I just wanted to clear the air between us. I know things have been a bit awkward ever since that trip to France and I'm guessing that's mainly down to me, what happened in the hotel room.' He raised his eyebrows, a smile resting on his lips.

Awkward? There was me thinking he'd been totally cool about the whole situation and I'd managed to keep my embarrassment and humiliation to myself. Obviously not. And now he'd hinted at that moment, that kiss, that nearly so much more moment. And all that humiliation was rearing its head again.

'Look, I'm sorry too, but had I known you had a girl-friend, there was no way I would have allowed it to happen. Not that anything happened, but... that kiss thing, the smoochy business, I got the wrong idea, that was all.'

'No, don't apologize. It's me who should be apologizing. I suppose it was a heat of the moment thing, we both got carried away and then, well, I thought of Sasha and...' He shrugged, his voice trailing away. 'I handled it badly.'

'Yes, well, I'm glad you remembered, just in time, eh?'

I had to be thankful that I wasn't his poor girlfriend. I wondered if he made a habit of going round getting into intimate clinches with strange women and then suddenly, at the last moment, having an 'oops' moment and remembering he was already in a relationship. What was it Kirk had called him? Yep, he was definitely one of them.

Max had said his piece, regurgitated the whole sordid business and hopefully he felt much better for it. I wasn't certain that I did, but at least he might leave me alone now, safe in the knowledge that he had behaved honourably, right at the last minute. Only now he was looking incredibly at home on my sofa, showing no sign of making his exit, and judging by the expression on his face, finding something incredibly amusing.

'What's so funny?'

'What you said? The kissing thing, the smoochy business, that's been a bit of a problem for me, you see.'

I swallowed hard. He'd obviously been feeling much guiltier over Sasha than I'd thought. 'A problem?'

'Yeah, a really big problem.' His gaze didn't leave my eyes. 'Has it not been a problem for you?'

'No, no, not at all.' For some reason my arms were doing their own thing and waving around in front of my face. 'I mean it happened, obviously, and we can't do anything to change that, but we're both old enough and daft enough to put it down to experience. Just one of those things. How about we don't say another word about it?' I held a finger up to my lips.

'But I can't stop thinking about it. That's the problem. All the time it's there. Taunting me, reminding me.'

'Oh...' What was it he was trying to tell me?

There was a pause, a long lingering pause, full of hidden meaning, I suspected, although what that hidden meaning might be, I had no idea.

'Sasha and I have finished.'

'What!' Whatever I'd been expecting it hadn't been that. 'You have?'

He nodded and I wasn't sure if I should commiserate or congratulate him. Ignoring the fillip in my chest and putting my own feelings to one side, I remembered my manners and how lovely Sasha had been, and realized I should at least try to sound suitably sympathetic.

'I'm sorry about that. Really sorry. Were you together long?'

'About five years. On and off. Although it's been very on and off for the last couple of years. Sasha's a lovely girl. We met through work. She's an interior designer, brilliant actually, and helped me out on a couple of my property developments.' He paused for a moment, examining his fingertips, and I wondered if he might want to sign me up to the lovely Sasha's fan club. 'We have similar interests, mix in the same circles, so I think it was a natural progression for us to take our relationship to the next stage.'

'Yeah,' I nodded encouragingly, not entirely sure how I was supposed to react to this glowing character reference. Hang on... Perhaps I'd misheard him, maybe he hadn't just told me they weren't together any more. I was having difficulty keeping up with all this. Mind you, how any hot-blooded man could resist Sasha's charms, I just didn't know. With her long flowing hair, piercing blue eyes, clear fresh skin and willowy figure she could easily have a second career as a catwalk model.

'But,' Max carried on, leaving me musing over that thought, 'Sasha would be the first to agree with me on this, there has always been something missing. For both of us. We stayed together out of convenience, because it suited us. When I went to London on business I would stay with her at her apartment and she would come and stay with me for long weekends. I don't think either of us believed it would be a long-term arrangement or that we'd end up together for ever. I don't know how your relationship with Johnny was, but Sasha and I, we'd fallen into a pattern of behaviour that was comfortable and safe. It sounds really bad to admit it now but nothing was going to change that until something came along to shake us out of our comfortable rut.'

'Hmm, I guess it was a bit like that for Johnny and me.' Funny though, I still harboured a few pangs of regret at finishing with him. I missed the closeness and familiarity that came from having someone special in my life, someone who looked out for me and put my happiness above their own. I knew that if I hadn't said anything to Johnny we would still be together, but he'd moved on now – a bit too quickly for my liking if I was being honest – finding happiness with Polly.

'It happened, Ellie. Something came along. Something big. And it shook me to the core.'

'It did?' I gulped, wondering where he was going with this. Suddenly the backs of my hands became utterly riveting.

'Yes, why do you think I offered to go to France with you in the first place?'

I started playing with my plaits, taking off the bands and unravelling my hair. Probably not the best idea as I knew it would result in a crimped mess, but I was pleased to let my hair loose from their ties. Besides it gave me some thinking time. I ran my hands through the frizz and shook out the waves, all the time trying to make sense of what Max was telling me.

'I thought you wanted to help out Eric.'

'I did, that was a big part of it, but it was much more than that. I was attracted to you from the moment I met you that day in the lane. You must have realized?' He paused, his gaze unwavering. I shook my head and swallowed hard, my cheeks tingling with a flush of colour. 'The last thing I expected to come upon that day was this beautiful woman with long flowing hair wading about in my river. I thought I'd stumbled upon a water nymph.' He chuckled to himself. 'A water nymph who was having a bad day admittedly, but that only added to the impression you made upon me.'

A water nymph. That was a good thing, right? To be honest, I wasn't entirely sure. Part of me could quite believe all of this was some weird and wonderful dream.

'I didn't know what it was,' Max went on, 'something indefinable, a connection I found hard to ignore. Each occasion I saw you after that, it was there, an insistent probing that left me wanting to find out more about you.'

'Really?' It came out as a squeak, my voice having escaped me. My heart was doing a funny 'slow, slow, quick quick slow' manoeuvre inside my chest. I'd experienced similar sensations to the ones Max was describing. I'd put it down to wistful longing on my part, but I'd had to put those feelings to one side, especially when Max had made it perfectly clear he hadn't wanted to take matters further.

'Yes! That night in the hotel room...' he shook his head. 'You don't how much self-control it took for me to hold back. I wanted you more than anything, you have no idea, but I just couldn't go through with it. I felt really bad. About the whole situation. I didn't want to cheat on Sasha and I didn't want you finding out about her and thinking badly of me.'

'I see.' This very attractive man had just admitted he wanted my body and my body reacted like a teenage girl's at a One Direction concert. Excitement fizzed around my whole being and a warm surge of desire rushed through my veins. Was I hearing him correctly?

Max stood up and walked across the room. His overwhelming masculine presence filled the air with its intensity. He leant his hands on the kitchen table, lifting his head to the ceiling. My eyes were drawn to his tanned forearms, rock solid on the table. 'I didn't want to do anything on the spur of the moment. I wanted to do things properly, if that makes sense?'

Not a lot was making sense. I was beginning to regret those beers and the hot chocolate. I fanned my cheeks with my hand. It was so hot in here. My head was woozy and my body on fire. Looking down at my Bavarian serving wench's costume, I noticed my bosom trying to escape the criss-cross ties that had been holding everything valiantly in place the whole night. It now looked as though the whole elaborate contraption might snap and burst open at the seams at any moment. As soon as Max glanced away, I did a quick bit of careful readjustment squashing my spillage into place. Not that it made the slightest difference.

'Part of me thought that if I got home, saw Sasha again, everything would slot back into place, but it didn't. We struggled on for a few weeks, but we both came to realize it wasn't working. I couldn't get you out of my head, Ellie. I was with Sasha, but I was thinking about you. I realized I couldn't do it any more. I had to go away for a few days on business. Sasha stayed at the house with the dogs and while I was away, from you, from Sasha, from the house and the village, it gave me the distance and the perspective I needed. I knew that I had to go home and tell Sasha that it was over.'

'Oh no! But what about Sasha? That's awful.' I dropped my head into my hands thinking about Sasha, knowing how I would feel in her shoes. 'I feel kind of responsible now,' I told Max.

'There's no need. I know it might seem that way, but really this wasn't your fault. Honestly. Both Sasha and I knew this was going to happen at some time. It was just a question of when.'

This was Max's version of events. He made it sound so simple and straightforward, but relationships never were, especially break-ups. Where was Sasha in all this? Was she sobbing into her pillow right now? I needed to know.

'How did she take it?'

He shrugged, a rueful smile spreading across his lips. 'Funny thing was, I'd geared myself up to tell her, had it straight in my mind what I was going to say, but she beat me to it. When I got home she was waiting for me. All her stuff was packed up and she was ready to go. We spoke about a lot of things, cleared the air and then she mentioned that you'd been round with Amber. What happened. She said how lovely you were.'

'I thought she was lovely too,' I said, feeling a pang of sympathy for Sasha. Thinking how, under different circumstances, we would probably have made good friends.

'Sasha's always been very perceptive. Has always been able to pick up on my moods and my feelings. I have an inkling she may have realized I'd developed feelings for you.'

Developed feelings for me. The words spun in my head. 'Oh...'

'I was pleased though that I could be honest with her. That we could end our relationship still on good terms and with our friendship and respect still intact.'

I smiled inwardly, guessing he hadn't mentioned the kiss we shared, our almost something more moment. Not that anything really happened. *Something of nothing* as my old nan would have said. And Max had shown much more self-control than I would ever possess. He had to be admired for that.

'Well, thanks for telling me,' I said, hugging my arms to my chest.

Max came and sat down on the sofa next to me, much closer now than before and took hold of my hand. It felt strange and natural at the same time. 'Look Ellie, I don't want you getting the wrong idea. I haven't come here to declare my undying love for you.'

Oh! My heart plummeted at the frankness of his words.

'Well, that might be a bit weird,' I said, hiding my disappointment.

'No, nothing like that. I just wanted to explain. After Sasha left I wanted to rush round here and tell you, but it was too soon. I needed to take some time out, wait for the dust to settle. There was unfinished business between us – I wanted you to know what had been going on, that's all.'

'Thank you. I did wonder. One minute everything was going swimmingly, the next... Well, it all makes sense now.'

'Look. Not trying to put any pressure on you at all, but why don't we go out for dinner soon? Tomorrow? That's if you still don't think I'm a complete and utter knobhead.'

Hmmm, he was obviously a bit of a mind-reader too.

'What do you say?' he prompted.

What did I say? I wasn't sure I could find the words. *'Yippee!' 'Oh my god, I'd love to!' 'This is the moment I've been waiting for!' 'What took you so long?'*

If my head was struggling to find something sensible to say, my body had no such difficulties, a warm glow of approval trickling through my veins.

'Lovely,' I said, trying to keep a lid on my excitement.

Think cool, think calm, think collected. A dinner date, that was all. And it wasn't as if I hadn't already been out to dinner with Max. Only this time it would be different. Better. With more of the kissing and smooching stuff. Anticipation bubbled beneath my skin. I sat on my other hand to stop me from flapping it around madly in front of my face. But only for the briefest moment.

However much Max had thought about that night, that kiss, it couldn't have been any more times than I'd re-lived that scene over and over in my head. Imagined what it might have been like had he not brought an untimely halt to proceedings. Now, with him a hair's breadth away, his delicious musky scent teasing my senses, I wasn't about to let him do his disappearing act again. It had been far too long already. Why put off until tomorrow what's within kissing distance today?

I reached across and held my hand to his face, feeling the swathe of stubble across his jawline. That sexy, knowing smile lit up his features. His head came forward to meet mine, our noses gently brushing, his eyes, dark and sensual, promising a thousand hidden delights. I'd seen that look before but only now could I fully appreciate the meaning behind the intensity of that gaze.

'Well, Miss Browne, this is a delightful and unexpected development.' His hand stroked the edge of my face, his touch feather light, his fingers reaching into my hair, gently massaging my skin. His voice was rich with amusement and desire. 'I promise you, I didn't come here for this, but, if you insist, well, I'd hate to disappoint.'

His words sent a warm surge of desire spiralling through my body.

'Well, as you quite rightly said, there's unfinished business between us.'

I kissed him lightly, my lips sweeping his, feeling the warmth of his skin against mine, breathing in his intoxicating scent. My body reacted immediately, all my weariness washing away, every nerve ending now awake with desire. My eyes closed involuntarily as our mouths opened together, Max's tongue sweeping around my lips, teasing and taunting me. His expert kisses were much better, more encompassing than anything I'd ever imagined. We pulled apart, our gazes exploring each other greedily, expectation lighting up our faces as if neither of us could believe this was actually happening.

'You are gorgeous, Ellie Browne, do you know that? Good enough to eat even. Nom, nom, nom, nom, nom.'

He pulled me towards him, his mouth searching out my neck, causing me to squeal with delight as ripples of anticipation ran along my body. We laughed as our bodies tumbled across the sofa, our limbs flailing as we giggled our way into a more comfortable position, trying to avoid falling onto the floor with a bump. Supporting himself on one elbow above me, his other hand stroked my hair away behind my ears, his face up against mine, so beautiful and inviting. Soon we were kissing again, more urgently this time, our breathing fast and abandoned. The months since we'd last been together fell away. Max rolled to one side, pulling me even closer to him, his strong firm hands caressing my curves. His body was hard and sensual against mine and when his hand found the bare skin of my stomach my insides melted. Our legs intertwined and we were lost to the moment until…

Hang on – what was that exactly? I lifted my head for air. That noise? An insistent scrabbling coming from outside. Oh god! Burglars? A wild animal perhaps?

'Coo-ee! It's only me!'

Startled, I rolled off the sofa and landed on the floor with a thump with Max following shortly behind. From my position on all-fours, I strained my neck to look up. Not a wild animal at all.

'Hello Mum.'

Twenty-One

'Hello darling!'

Oh holy crap, it really was my mother. Standing in the hallway as large as life. Dropping her bags to the floor, she lifted her arms to greet me.

'Mum! What are you doing here?' I prised myself up off the floor, leaving Max to his own devices, and threw my arms around her neck, not really believing she was here.

'I thought I'd surprise you!'

'Well, you've certainly done that.' Although I suspected she might be the one on the end of the surprise, finding me half-undressed, the ties to my blouse having finally given up under the strain, and with a strange man in her house. 'Where's Dad?'

'He couldn't come. He's away on some business jaunt for a couple of weeks, so I thought I'd take the opportunity to come home and check up on my favourite daughter.'

'Well, that's amazing. Oh my god it's so lovely to see you.' Seven months since they'd left for their placement abroad and I'd missed them hugely, of course I had, but it was only now seeing Mum with my own eyes, her distinctive and familiar scent of 'Rive Gauche' wafting in the air, transporting me back to my childhood, that the lump in my throat brought home to me just how much I'd missed her. My heart swelled. After what seemed an awful long time of hugging and kissing and squealing and hair patting, Mum extracted herself from my embrace to peer over my shoulder to look at Max.

'I hope I haven't interrupted anything here.' The mischievous grin on her face suggested she knew full well that she had but that she wasn't in the slightest part sorry.

'Mrs Browne. Max Golding. Lovely to meet you?' Max held out his hand managing to look obscenely dishevelled and gorgeous at the same time and I felt a pang of regret for what might have been. What had been so rudely interrupted yet again. Still, it didn't matter – I knew there would be another time for me and Max. Absolutely certain of that fact, even though I was slightly bemused by the whole turn of events.

'And you. And please call me Veronica,' she said, her eyelashes actually fluttering. What the...? But then I could hardly blame her. Max had exactly the same effect upon me.

'Look I'm going to make tracks now and leave you two to catch up,' Max said, 'but I'll see you tomorrow, yeah?'

'Oh, Mum's home now and...'

'Of course, she will,' said Mum gleefully. 'Lovely meeting you Max.'

*

'Good job I came home when I did,' said Mum, after I'd made us a pot of tea and we'd settled at the kitchen table, 'or else I might never have known you had a new boyfriend.'

It was the early hours of the morning and we were both

exhausted. Mum from her long air journey and me from my long day at the pub and the dreamy eventful happenings afterwards, but there was no way either of us would be going to sleep yet, not until we'd caught up on at least some of the news.

'Oh Mum, he isn't my boyfriend.'

Her eyebrows raised in disbelief, as she tilted her head, clearly not believing a word I was saying.

'Really! I know how it must look but tonight was the first night we really got together. Max walked me home from the pub and one thing led to another.'

Mum was smiling, mischievousness lighting up her features. 'And then I waltzed in and spoilt all your fun!'

'Oh that doesn't matter. I was just so thrilled to see you and have you home again. Besides, I'm seeing him again tomorrow night.'

'He seems lovely.'

'He is. And you'll never guess where he lives. Braithwaite Manor. He's a property developer and has two beautiful dogs, oh and a beautiful ex-girlfriend too but we won't mention her. And you'll never guess who he's related to. Noel Golding. He's his grandson.' I could hear the words gushing from my mouth, excitement spilling around my body.

Mum smiled indulgently. 'Well, it's great to see you so happy. That was one of the reasons I came home – to make sure you were doing okay. You've gone through a lot of big changes recently and with us being so far away... well, we worry about you.'

'Oh Mum, I've told you. There's absolutely no need to worry.' I grabbed her hand, checking that she was really here sitting at the table. I still couldn't quite believe it. 'I'm really happy being back home for the time being. The dog-walking is keeping me fit – you wouldn't believe how many new clients I have – and there's plenty of shifts at the pub to keep me busy. Well, for the moment, at least.'

Mum's brow furrowed. I'd kept her up to date on what might be happening at the pub but she was obviously worried what it meant for Eric. Since Miriam had died, Mum had always kept an eye out for him and provided friendship and support when he needed it.

'That's the other thing. I want to see how Eric's doing. Thought he could probably do with a friendly ear. Is there any news on the pub yet?'

'Yeah, there's a new owner, but we don't know who yet or what plans they have for the place. I think Eric's resigned to moving on now.'

'He'll hate that. I don't know what he'll do with himself if he retires. I'll pop down to see him over the weekend. I want to see Josie too and that lovely granddaughter of his. They grow so quickly at this stage.'

'Oh right, so you didn't actually want to see me then,' I quipped. 'It was Stella and Eric you really wanted to visit. Anyway, tell me about Dubai. Are you loving it? The photos always look so amazing!'

'Well, it's as amazing as it looks. The sun always shines. We get to live in a luxury villa complex with everything on site – a gym, tennis courts, swimming pool – and the beach is only down the road. There's a lot of socializing and swanky events. It's everything you imagine an expat lifestyle to be.'

'I feel a but coming on.'

'But… it isn't home.' Mum's gaze flittered around her kitchen, pride and warmth flickering in her eyes as she observed the cream Aga, the old oak dresser that housed all her blue and white crockery collected over many years, the rustic pictures of hens and sheep dotting the walls. 'I miss all this if I'm being honest, our life here, our friends and you especially. I miss our chats. Like this. Around the kitchen table with a glass of wine or a cup of tea. Skyping just isn't the same.'

'Oh Mum! I miss you too. But it's not for long is it? I can't believe how quickly it's gone by already.' Admittedly, the last few months had been a whirlwind what with everything else that had been going on. 'You'll be back before you know it, moaning about the weather and wishing you could have some of that lovely sunshine again.'

'Well, that's the thing.' Mum looked down as she twisted her wedding and engagement ring on her finger, before looking up at me with tired eyes. 'I wasn't going to tell you tonight, but you might as well know. They've offered your dad a further two year contract.'

'Oh… really? Well, that's good isn't it?' I rubbed at my eyes, allowing the news to wash over me. Two years. It had a more permanent and serious ring to it than nine months. 'And how does Dad feel about that?'

'He thinks he should take it. It's crazy money, tax-free, of course. It would take him years to earn that sort of money here. His thinking is that we'd be silly to turn it down. Two years and then we'd be able to come home and your dad could take early retirement. Then we could do all those things we've always wanted to do. Like buying an original camper van and touring the country.'

I grinned, my parents had been talking about their road trip for as long as I could remember. Part of me wished I could go with them. I might still.

'I suppose it makes sense, but what about you, you don't sound so keen?'

'Oh I don't know. I had it in my mind that it was for nine months only, which seemed long enough, but now, another two years? It's such a long time.'

Her gaze scanned my face, observing me thoughtfully, watching for my reaction.

'Mum! I do hope this isn't about me.' She shrugged, looking decidedly sheepish. 'It's not, is it?'

'Well, I wanted to see how you would feel about it. Obviously I wouldn't want to do anything that you weren't happy with.'

'Mum, is this why you've come home?' She gave an innocent shrug. 'How many times do I need to tell you. You don't have to worry about me. If you want to stay in Dubai then go for it. It sounds like an opportunity too good to miss. And another two years will fly by, especially when you're enjoying yourself in the sun.' A part of me felt sad that we'd be apart for such a long time, but I would never want to stand in my parents' way. This was a wonderful chance for them.

'That's exactly what your dad says. And we can come back for holidays. It's not that long a flight. And you must promise to come out and stay with us some time.'

'I will, Mum.' I'd really have to make the effort and get out to see them, next year sometime, perhaps.

Mum rummaged around in her handbag and pulled out a wad of pink tissue, handing it over to me. 'While I remember… a little present for you. Don't get excited, it's only something very small, but I saw it and wanted you to have it.'

I carefully unwrapped the tissue and pulled out the prettiest glass angel intricately decorated with silver filigree, hanging on a silver thread. 'Oh Mum, that is so sweet.'

'Well, I was out doing some shopping and came across this lovely display of decorations and had a bit of a moment realizing that we wouldn't be with you over Christmas.' Oh, that thought stopped me in my tracks. Christmas was still a couple of months away, but with Mum and Dad being away, it would mean spending my first Christmas without them and most likely by myself.

'I saw this and thought how lovely she was. When you're dressing the tree this year you can hang her up and be reminded of us both. Although we won't be able to be here with you in person, we'll definitely be here in spirit.' She held the angel up high in her fingers. 'And hopefully she'll be a guiding light to you over the Christmas period and maybe bring you a bit of luck too.'

'That's such a lovely sentiment,' I said, a warm glow filling my tummy. 'I will definitely be thinking of you both when I put her on the tree.'

A sudden thought occurred to me.

'What will you do about the house? Do you want to rent it out now? I could always find somewhere else to stay if you like. There's plenty of room at the pub.'

'No, not at all. You're welcome to stay here for as long as you like, you know that. We just don't want it standing empty, so if you do decide to go back to London or move in with your new boyfriend,' she raised a mischievous eyebrow at me, 'then just tell us and we can let the property agency know.'

'Don't get your hopes up on the boyfriend front,' I said, laughing.

'Come on,' she said, pushing up her chair and coming over for another hug. 'I can't wait to get into my own bed. And we have a very busy day tomorrow.'

'We do?'

'Oh yes, shopping, lunch, afternoon tea and cake, and probably a glass of wine or two thrown in for good measure.'

'Oh Mum, it's so lovely having you home.'

Twenty-Two

'What do you think to this?'

Mum, true to her word, had dragged me out of bed far earlier than was necessary on a day when I had no dogs to walk or pub shifts to attend, and whisked me off to the shopping centre. Still I didn't really mind, not when our first port of call was the best coffee shop in town where we sat and chatted over delicious French pastries. Afterwards, we hit the shops and Mum insisted on equipping me with new jeans, sweatshirts, knickers and socks, before we'd moved onto the baby section of a big department store where we'd been stuck for the last two hours with Mum oohing and aahing over a never-ending selection of baby-grows and dresses and soft toys.

'It's lovely, but haven't you already bought one just like that?'

'Have I?' Mum laughed, looking down at the collection of carrier bags in her hands. 'A little one can't have too many clothes.'

I shifted my weight from foot to foot, trying to join in Mum's enthusiasm. I wasn't a keen shopper at the best of times. Unlike Mum, who would be guaranteed a place on the national team if retail therapy was ever declared an

Olympic sport. My legs were aching and my head was fuzzy, probably from the events of the previous evening. Images of Max taunted me all day long, him leaning down over me, kissing me, wrapping his strong arms around me – had all of that really happened? In the cold light of day it seemed like a glorious dream. Even his delicious scent haunted me as we walked through the perfumery department, my nose chasing out snatches of his aroma. Probably just as well Mum had brought me out shopping or else I'd have spent my entire day mooning around the house getting myself into a state of heightened anticipation for my date tonight.

Over a lunch of smoked salmon sandwiches and a glass of wine, Mum told me more about their hectic lives in Dubai, the friends they'd made and the events they'd attended, confirming what I already suspected, my parents had a much more active social life than I could ever aspire to. It all seemed a million glamorous miles away from the peace and quiet of Little Leyton. Mid-story, Mum paused and looked at me as though suddenly remembering something important, before quizzing me on my future plans. 'Have you thought what you will do if you lose your job at the pub?'

I shrugged, taking a sip from my cool glass of Sauvignon Blanc. Really, I didn't want to have to face that eventuality. 'Not sure yet. I might try and find some more doggy clients, expand the business, provide more training sessions. Or more likely, I'll probably go back to London and find another job in the city.'

'Is that what you really want to do?'

'It's what I'm trained to do.'

'That's not what I asked, Ellie.'

'I know.' I stretched my legs out beneath our table, looking out at our fellow shoppers as they passed by. I couldn't get anything past Mum. She had that special mother's instinct of knowing if there was a problem and getting to the nub of any issue. In a jiffy. 'Well, it seems the most sensible thing to do,' I said, not meeting her eye.

She reached across the table and took hold of my hand. 'You must do want you to do. Follow your dreams. Do what excites you.'

'Do you really think so? I trained so hard to qualify as an accountant. It was what I always wanted to do, you know that, and you and Dad were brilliant at seeing me through it all, supporting me emotionally and financially. It seems a waste to turn my back on it now.'

'No, you mustn't think about it like that. We supported your education because we wanted you to be in a position where you could make your own choices. And not to have to take the first job that came along because that was the only one you were qualified to do or because you desperately needed the money. No one can take your degree away from you now. That's yours to use as and when you want to. And as a fully qualified accountant, you'll always be able to get a job if you need to. Taking some time out for yourself, being here, it's a good idea. I know you're working just as hard as you were in London, but it's good to get a different perspective. Who knows, you might decide you want to go and do something different, train in a different area. Or else you might want to stay in Little Leyton serving pints and looking after dogs. There's no right or wrong way.'

'And you really wouldn't mind if I did that?'

'Of course not. If it makes you happy then we're happy too. As a parent that's all you want for your children, their happiness and their health.' Her knowing smile gave me a nice fuzzy warm glow inside and relief flooded through me at the knowledge that I would have Mum and Dad's support whatever I decided to do.

'Oh Mum, thanks so much for saying that. For being so understanding. I'm enjoying being back in the village more than I could have imagined, but there's part of me that feels guilty that I'm letting you down somehow.'

'What? Never! Anyway, more importantly,' she curled her fingers around the stem of her glass and tipped back the last of her wine, 'tell me, what are you wearing for your date tonight?'

'I'm not sure. I'll find something in my wardrobe,' I said, waving a hand, trying to sound dead casual, as though I had the whole situation under complete control. When in fact the complete opposite was true. Where Max Golding was concerned, I had little self-control. Just the thought of him sent butterflies fluttering around my stomach and ripples of anticipation to every nerve cell in my body. Deep breaths, I told myself. Get a grip, I reaffirmed. I hated it. That feeling of free-fall. As though nothing could stop me now. My body was working to its own agenda, responding involuntarily to just the memory of Max's touch, his delectable kisses, my head unable to erase the tantalizing images of those moments we shared.

'Hmm, well, I don't think jeans and hoodie are going to cut it,' said Mum, her disapproving face on. 'Let's go and find you something pretty.'

'Mum, I'm all shopped out,' I said, uncertain whether I

could face another marathon shopping session.

'Nonsense. Stamina, that's all you need. Come on,' she said, as though we were going off to do battle. 'Let's go and do this.'

*

Max picked me up from the house at seven-thirty, arriving with a bunch of beautiful flowers which he duly handed to Mum. Honestly, I swear her knees almost buckled, she certainly blushed, flicking her hair behind her ear.

'Oh Max really. You didn't need to do that. They're so beautiful though,' she said, lifting the blooms to her nose to inhale their lovely scent.

'Well, we didn't meet under the best of circumstances, did we?' he said with a wry smile. 'And as I'm whisking your beautiful daughter away for the evening I thought it was the least I could do.'

'That's so very thoughtful of you, Max,' said Mum, positively beaming.

Clearly the charm-o-meter was turned up high. Still, I'd given myself a stern talking-to after my teenage day-dreaming this afternoon. As charming as Max was I wouldn't allow myself to be swept away by the occasion. It was still early days for our relationship. I needed to keep a level head, get to know Max better, the man behind the smooth façade, and not be distracted by his good looks.

'You look absolutely stunning.' Max turned to greet me, planting the lightest of kisses on my cheek, and my insides whirled as our eyes met for the briefest moment, all my good intentions flying straight out the window. In black moleskin trousers and white open-necked shirt, his strong broad frame was visible beneath the crisp fresh fabric, his body looking even better than I remembered. Was that even possible?

I brazened it out, channelling all my innermost self-confidence. Max wasn't to know I was a quivering wreck inside. 'Thank you.' I smiled a bright smile, returning his kiss on his cheek, getting a whiff of his masculine earthy scent. Definitely all man.

If the look on Max's face was anything to go by then it had been a good decision on Mum's part to buy me a new outfit. She'd picked out a floral wrap dress, something I would never have chosen for myself, only trying it on because Mum had actually manhandled me into the changing room, insisting I give it a try. I couldn't hide my surprise when I greeted my reflection in the mirror. The dress fell in soft folds around my body, skimming my curves; it was feminine and flattering in all the right places and surprisingly comfortable too, without being too out-there or looking as though I was trying too hard. Good old Mum.

Now with the three of us stood in the hallway, the dress was definitely working its magic. I felt sexy and flirty, although that probably had more to do with the man standing in front of me rather than the new dress. I was grateful to Mum just for being there. To provide a foil to the sizzling tension emanating between me and Max. I wasn't imagining it. It was real, palpable, tangible, filling the air with its presence. If not for Mum, I think we might have dispensed with the formalities and picked up where we'd left off the previous night; falling onto the sofa, kissing, cuddling, exploring...

No, no, no! Hadn't I told myself I needed to keep a cool head. To ignore the wilful longings of my body and instead concentrate on getting to know the man behind all that gorgeousness. How hard could it be?

Twenty-Three

As it happened, very hard indeed.

Outside, instead of Max's battered old Jeep waiting for us there was a little sporty number, or rather a sleek silver dream machine, parked on the kerbside. Max opened the passenger door with a flourish and saw me inside. Immediately I felt as though I'd been transported into the depths of a romance novel and Max was about to whisk me off to... where exactly?

'Look I have a confession to make,' he said, slipping his seatbelt on. 'I couldn't get us booked in anywhere for dinner. I've tried everywhere within a ten mile radius. What I didn't realize is that it's the county show this weekend and every hotel and restaurant in the area has been booked for weeks.'

'Oh yes, of course it is. Well, it doesn't matter.' To be honest I wasn't hungry, not for food at least. My appetite had clean deserted me and I was running on nervous energy – at the moment I had plenty of it. 'Let's just go for a drink somewhere.'

'No, I promised you dinner so that's what you shall have, madam. Chez moi. If that's okay with you? Although I promise you, hand on heart, this isn't an elaborate ploy to drag you back to my man cave. There's no ulterior motive.'

I laughed, my heart flipping as I looked at his profile. Strong, imposing, impressive. My stomach performed a loop-the-loop manoeuvre and I was beginning to severely doubt my chances of keeping my head tonight. As for my heart, I suspected it was already lost. I turned to look out the window, waving goodbye to Mum.

'Well, only if you're sure?' Excitement trickled through my veins at the thought of visiting Max's house, and a touch of nervousness too. 'I don't want to put you to any trouble.'

'No trouble at all. Besides, I love cooking. It's one of my favourite things to do.'

Well, in the circumstances, there really was only one polite answer to give.

There is something about a man who knows his way expertly around a kitchen that is extremely sexy. Seeing Max in his own home, totally at ease with himself as he poured two glasses of cool white wine, opening cupboards and putting pans onto heat, just confirmed how completely self-assured and competent, how utterly captivating this man was, especially so in the comfort of his own surroundings.

Braithwaite Manor was unlike any other property I'd been inside before. There was a grandeur about the place that could make me believe I'd stepped back in time to another era, an altogether more glamorous and sophisticated age. I made a mental note to keep my mouth closed as I found myself gaping in awe as Max showed me round the ground floor. He spoke proudly of how he'd transformed the derelict crumbling mansion into a warm inviting home, retaining the magnificent splendour of the original house, yet at the same time, breathing new life into the stately old home. Everywhere you looked you could appreciate the workmanship that had gone into the extensive renovations of the rooms; polished wooden floors, intricate detailing in the cornices of the high ceilings and beautifully carved decorations in the exquisite surrounds of the fireplaces. The imposing hallway had a lavish wide staircase with a galleried landing above and a huge central glittering chandelier.

'Oh my goodness, it's like something out of Gone with the Wind. I can just imagine Rhett scooping up Scarlett in his arms and waltzing up those stairs. It's so...' Romantic. I stopped myself right there. Sent that thought packing. Yesterday was one thing, but who knew what might happen today? And if it did, where would that leave us then? Max had said he hadn't stopped thinking about me, but was that just an itch that needed scratching? Was I strong enough if this turned out to be just a heady reckless fling to be able to walk away with my heart intact? Would the thrill of one night with Max be worth the inevitable aftermath?

'... so, so magnificent!' I said, managing to salvage the moment.

Max gave me a sideways glance as though he hadn't the first idea what I was talking about, which was just as well really.

He took me into the vast drawing room at the rear of the property, which had tall Georgian windows offering panoramic views of the valley. Despite the sheer scale of the property, it still felt like a proper home with plenty of warm touches such as colourful cushions, vibrant rugs and bold paintings, which gave a welcoming and comforting vibe. Was that Sasha's influence? I wondered. I suppressed a sigh. She kept entering my head, taunting me with her memory. I could just imagine her wafting around here, totally at home in these beautiful surroundings.

There was a huge farmhouse table in the kitchen, but it looked as though we wouldn't be sitting there for our dinner. In a small turreted bay, with cushioned seats fitted in the curve of the window overlooking the garden, Max had chosen to dress a small round table with a heavy white linen cloth, fairy lights suspended overhead and an array of sparkling tea lights at its centre.

'Wow! This all looks amazing. Honestly, I'm over-whelmed,' I said, my head not knowing which way to turn first. 'It's all so beautiful.'

'Good. I'm glad you think so. That was very much the intention.'

'This is what you do for a living then, presumably,' I said, gesturing at the workmanship around us. 'Make beautiful houses.'

'I guess you could say that. New developments mainly, but some individual properties too. I still get excited about finding an old run-down property and being able to transform it into something special. This though,' he held up his palms to the ceiling, 'was very much a personal project. I had a great team of guys working with me, but I was very much involved in the design of the project and in every aspect of the build on a day-to-day basis. I still like to get my hands dirty when I can.'

'Amazing! Where did you learn to do all this? Was your dad in the building trade?'

He gave a hollow laugh. 'My dad? No, he didn't know one end of a screwdriver from another. He was an academic, highly respected in his field, so we travelled a lot when I was growing up, as Dad had various university placements around the world.

'Were you very close to him?'

He paused a moment, as though considering the question. 'Not really. I admired him, everyone did. From an early age I was told what a brilliant man he was, what an amazing intellect he had, but I wasn't like him at all. I was a sporty kid who wanted to be outside all the time, running riot. I don't think Dad really knew how to relate to me.'

'Well, I'm sure he'd be very proud of you now if he could see all this.'

Max shrugged. 'I don't know. Maybe.' He paused, a wry smile on his lips. 'Probably not.' There was a wistful tone to his voice. 'Gramps, Noel, was the one who nurtured my love for making things. In the summer holidays I would come and stay with my grandparents and I'd spend so much time with Gramps in his shed, helping him on different little projects or just watching him work with his hands. Making cupboards, building a bird table, fixing the gate to his allotment. He always gave me something to do and I used to love those long summer days. His toolbox was like a treasure chest to me. I would take the tools out one by one and examine them. Just the feel of them in my hands brought me so much pleasure.' Max pulled out a couple of colourful plates from the oak dresser. 'Anyway, it looks as though dinner's ready to be served.'

My nose twitched as the aromas of garlic and olive oil wafted in the air. Max beckoned me to sit at the table and I took my place on the cushioned window seat overlooking the garden, suffused in warm lighting. This little nook within

Max's huge home was delightful, intimate and cosy. You could almost forget that you were in a huge manor house.

Max served up a delicious starter of pan-fried scallops and came and sat down beside me. Afterwards we ate a sea bass main with crispy sauté potatoes and buttered asparagus. It was sublime, comparable to anything I'd ever eaten in a restaurant. Was there really no end to this man's talents?

There'd been a shift in the air from the previous evening when we'd been spontaneous and carefree. Tonight I'd been enjoying getting to know Max better, hearing about his childhood in a more formal, restrained manner. I sensed we were both being careful around one another, gently pulling away the layers, discovering more about each other.

'Do you want to take a look outside?' asked Max, after we'd finished our meal, noticing me peering out through the window.

'I'd love to.'

Bella and Holly, who had been comatose in front of the Aga all evening, jumped up as soon as we made moves to go outside. Max slipped his coat around my shoulders and took hold of my hand, leading me into the garden. Even in the half-light I could see what a wonderful space it was, with perfectly tended lawns sweeping into the distance as far as the eye could see. Classical statues overlooked the lawns, and ornamental box plants lined the path that meandered around the edges. Max told me that beyond the old wall on the right-hand side was a vegetable garden and a wildflower garden. Somewhere, behind the scenes, must be a team of full-time gardeners to see to the maintenance of the extensive grounds.

We watched the dogs lolloping into the distance as we wandered slowly around the garden, talking, laughing, all the time our hands clasped tightly together.

'Thanks for coming tonight, Ellie. I've really enjoyed having you here.'

'No, it's me who should be thanking you. I've had a great time. The food was amazing and seeing your beautiful house, well, honestly, it's completely knocked me out.'

'Come on, there's more to see yet.' He whistled and the dogs came bounding back, pushing past us to beat us back into the house, skidding as their paws hit the kitchen floor. I laughed, giving them both a hug before Max led me through the kitchen and into the magnificent hallway.

'You did want to see upstairs?' He stopped, one foot on the first step and turned to look at me. The way he asked, his voice sexy, warm and persuasive, made me wonder if there was a hidden meaning to his question. I was definitely more than happy to find out.

'Yes, of course. I'd love to see the rest of house.'

'Good.'

Before I had time to protest, Max bent down and in one fell swoop scooped me off my feet and into his arms.

'Whoa! What...'

He laughed and swung me round in his arms. 'Well, you were the one who mentioned a romantic fantasy involving Rhett Butler. Isn't this what you had in mind?'

'Yes, but I didn't mean... And no, it's not my romantic fantasy. Oh, Max just put me down, you've made your point,' I said giggling, flapping my legs helplessly in the air, not wanting him to put me down for a moment. 'You'll do your back in.'

'Nonsense, it's fine,' he said, swaying on the spot, pretending his knees were buckling beneath him. He then proceeded to carry me upstairs as though I really was just a slip of a girl, when in fact I wasn't – too many beers and slices of cake had put paid to that – but Max made the trek upstairs seem remarkably easy. From my vantage position of his arms, I had a terrific view of the ornate ceiling and the numerous paintings lining the walls, although I couldn't really appreciate the beauty of them, focussed as I was on Max's all-encompassing presence above me, my arms clinging tightly around his neck. He was far too distracting for me to want to concentrate on anything else.

At the top of the stairs he turned left onto the galleried landing, striding past a number of doors until he reached a door at the very end of the walkway, gently pushing it open with his knee.

'And this is the master bedroom,' he said, standing on the threshold to a beautiful big room, decorated in muted creams and beiges. Good job I wasn't standing or else my knees would have buckled beneath me at the giddy realization that I was actually in Max's magnificent bedroom. Taking centre stage was a huge four-poster bed adorned with a gold silk eiderdown, bright white pillows and lots of plump cushions. In the pretty bay window, framed with abundant luxurious drapes, was a charming chaise longue overlooking the garden.

'Lovely,' I sighed, feeling at something of a disadvantage, still held aloft in Max's arms. 'You can put me down now, you know.'

Ignoring my muted protests, he walked over to the bed and laid me in the centre. As I sank into its glorious depths,

Max's head hovered over me, close enough for me to inhale his delicious scent and just within kissing distance of his mouth. My eyes closed and my hands clutched the feather duvet beneath me as a wave of desire washed over me. My body tingled with anticipation as I waited to feel his breath on my face, his wide full lips upon mine. And waited... And waited. Nothing. I opened half an eye, expecting to see Max preparing to kiss me, but instead he was over on the other side of the room. He flung open the patio windows, allowing a cold rush of air to flood in to the room, revealing a pretty balcony.

'The view from up here is even better. Come and take a look.'

Quashing my disappointment, I rolled over and clambered out of the bed and joined Max at his side. 'It's beautiful,' I agreed.

So too were the other numerous bedrooms he showed me – I stopped counting at ten – all decorated to individual themes, with highly specified bathrooms or wet-rooms. Admittedly my heart wasn't quite in it after leaving the master bedroom behind. For a moment, I'd imagined we were going to continue where we'd left off the other night, but Max seemed more interested in carrying on with the guided tour. Maybe seeing me in his bedroom where Sasha had previously been had given him second thoughts about the wisdom of this whole idea?

'All these bedrooms?' I really couldn't make sense of it. 'There's only you living here,' I said incredulously. 'Why do you need so much space?'

'I do have friends come to stay from time to time,' he said, clearly amused by my question. 'Besides, this was always intended to be a family home. I'd like lots of kids one day.'

Crikey. I'd pity the poor woman who needed to produce all those children. Suddenly, I was struck by the disparity in our lifestyles. Max belonged in a different world entirely. Honestly, it made me wonder what was I doing here?

It hadn't been that long ago that Sasha had been padding about this beautiful home, sharing her daily life with Max, sharing his bed too, no doubt, and her influence was probably all around me still in the lovely furnishings. What was I? A temporary distraction? Someone who had come into Max's life to serve as a catalyst for him to make some overdue changes, changes he admitted he would have made anyway at some point.

'I think I should go.' The words escaped my lips, startling me as much as they caught Max off-guard.

'Really, already? Oh God, I'm being a bore, aren't I? Sorry. Look, I know I can get carried away talking about the house. It's a bit of a passion of mine if you hadn't already guessed, and sometimes I just don't know when to stop.'

He raised a hand to my face and ran his fingers across my cheek.

'No, it's not that.' His touch sent shock waves coursing around my body. 'Thanks for inviting me, Max. I've loved looking round your house, hearing how you've made the renovations, it's just...' I paused, standing at the top of the beautiful staircase. It was just what? That I suddenly felt uncertain. Vulnerable at being alone here with Max, not knowing what he expected from me. I couldn't compete with Sasha and I certainly didn't want to be just a fling for him. I felt as though Max was about to rip out my heart and throw it into the night sky, and I wanted to run out of the house and not come back or see Max ever again. Thinking about it sent my head into a fuzzy spin, especially with Max's deeply intense gaze fixed hard upon me. Yesterday, I hadn't the time to think, everything had happened so quickly, but now, it was as if we were standing on the edge of a precipice.

'I don't want you to go, Ellie.' He grabbed my arms and pulled me closer to his body, our eyes locked together. My head tried to think rationally, but my body responded in the way it only knew how to this man, relinquishing into his embrace. 'What's wrong?'

'Nothing.' And everything. 'It just feels...' How could I possibly explain when I could barely make sense of it myself.

He kissed me lightly on the lips before pulling back to look at me. 'How does *that* feel, Ellie? Tell me.' I felt his breath upon my face, his voice husky as he stroked my cheek.

'Oh...' He could have no idea the effect he had upon me deep down inside. 'Lovely,' I said, with a sigh, all rational thought leaving my head. 'Just lovely.'

Max smiled warmly. 'Look, Ellie, I meant every word I said last night. I'm crazy about you. Haven't been able to stop thinking about you. But if you'd rather not be here, if you want me to take you home, then just say.' His gaze challenged me. He cupped my chin with his thumb and forefinger, his eyes observing me imploringly. 'It's your decision, Ellie.'

Twenty-Four

'Kiss me again, Max,' I murmured.

His handsome face smiled down on me. 'Oh, I am more than happy to oblige.'

That seductive smile curled on his lips as he took my face in his hands, his dark eyes open, but hooded with desire. His mouth found mine and my lips parted, the sensation of his taste on my tongue igniting all my senses. He kissed me softly, as though for the first time, and I felt my body sway under his attentive embrace. My hands reached out for his head, pulling him closer, wanting more of him, more of his delicious kisses, feeling lost to everything around me but the intensity of this gorgeous man currently sending my entire being into spirals of delight. His body was firm and hard against mine, my hands running over his broad shoulders, eager to discover every inch of him. Our kisses came faster now, more urgently, our breathing ragged, as we occasionally surfaced for air, looking imploringly into each other's eyes.

'You're beautiful, Ellie, do you know that?'

I laughed away the compliment, but my skin prickled in acknowledgment of his words and with it the realization that under Max's adoring gaze, seeing for myself the light in his eyes and the effect I was having on him, I felt beautiful too.

He laid a trail of kisses from my mouth, down my neck and across my collarbone, making my toes curl in delight. His hand brushed against the curve of my breast and I gasped, taken by surprise by the intensity of his touch. His masculine scent was intoxicating, my head lost to everything but the moment. I grabbed onto the balustrade to steady myself, thinking my legs might buckle beneath me.

'Have I shown you my bedroom?' said Max with a glint in his eye. He scooped me up again in his arms, my body feeling as light as a feather in his hold. Unable to stop a big smile of contentment from spreading over my face, I clasped my arms around Max's neck not wanting to let go. Ever.

'Oh, I could definitely get used to this,' I teased.

'Really? Well, I can see I'm going to have to increase my sessions at the gym then to keep my strength up.'

'Oi,' I said, digging my heel into his thigh.

He laughed too as he strode along the landing towards his bedroom, carrying me comfortably in his arms. He pushed open the door and walked across to the bed, dropping me down gently into the depths of the fluffy white linen. This time he didn't turn away, he leant over me, his brown eyes looking deeply into mine, his weight on my arms pinning me to the bed. He whispered my name in my ear, making my whole body tingle with anticipation, before proceeding to kiss me, tentatively at first, small sweet kisses on my mouth and on my neck, making me squirm with delight until I thought I wouldn't be able to tolerate the exquisite sensations any more. Then his kisses became more insistent, his tongue exploring my mouth, his evident hard desire for me fuelling my own passion.

His hands ran over my body and when his hand cupped my breast, my nipples hardened immediately to his touch. My hands reached out for him, eager to feel the strong lines of him and the firmness of the muscles in his chest and arms. Oh, and his thighs. Strong, muscular thighs. Everything about this man was irresistible and I felt spellbound by the magical effect he wove on my body and soul.

Max rolled over onto his back pulling me on top of him. I sat astride him, and his hands, strong hands with a gentle touch, which had already brought me such pleasure, fondled my breasts through the fabric of my dress, driving me to heavenly distraction, before he found the tie at my waist.

'May I?' he asked, a wry smile on his lips.

Such a gentleman. I nodded, unable to contain my excitement, desperate now for him to rip it off me.

Max pulled the two ends apart and my lovely new dress fell open. Max watched as I shrugged the dress off my shoulders, letting it slip down to my waist. Keeping eye contact, I pulled down my bra straps and unclipped the catch at the back, throwing my bra to the side, all the time revelling in the adoration of Max's unwavering gaze. I didn't feel self-conscious at all, just totally at ease. All powerful in my feminine potency. His hands reached up, his fingers tracing my breasts with the lightest of touches, my body arching involuntarily.

'Mmm, come here you gorgeous creature.'

Max grabbed my arms and pulled me down on top of him, rolling me onto my side to face him. His expressive eyes devoured me greedily as he used one hand to smooth my hair behind my ear while the other cupped my breast, taking my breath away. I undid the buttons on his shirt, my hands discovering the hardness of his torso beneath, my fingers running along the highly toned ripples of his stomach muscles. He pulled me to his body, our legs intertwining, and I relished the sensation of his naked flesh up against mine. His thumb and forefinger found my nipple and I gasped. He gently squeezed, pulled and twisted at my breasts in a way that had me writhing in pleasure. I reached down to his waistband, undoing the button to his trousers, my hand grasping his full-on hardness, bringing a smile of warm satisfaction to my lips and eliciting a groan from Max. With an urgency now, he pulled off his trousers and boxers and threw them aside, sweeping my dress to the floor at the same time. He pulled me into his embrace, our bodies in unison, our mouths coming together in an explosion of kisses. His hand travelled from my breast down to my stomach and then to the waistband of my knickers, each smooth movement causing my insides to melt further until his fingers were tracing a trail beneath the elastic, taunting and teasing me with their promise.

He pulled away from me, his hands grasping my head, his gaze observing me fervently. 'God, Ellie. You do something to me. Do you know that? Something deep down in here.' His voice was heavy with emotion as he tapped on his chest with the flat of his hand. I smiled, pulling his head to mine and kissing his lips, full wide lips that seemed to have a magnetic pull. I simply couldn't get enough of his delicious sensual kisses.

His hand ran down my leg, hitching his thumb onto my knickers and pulling them down over my thighs so that I could wriggle free of them. We were both fully naked now, our legs wrapped around each other, our bodies seeming to meld together perfectly. His hand travelled along the inside of my thigh, up and down, his thumb stroking my flesh in a slow rhythmic movement that sent me into ever-increasing spirals of delight.

I called his name, pulling him closer, reaching down to feel him, my hand grasping onto his hardness, wanting more of him, all of him, my heart thumping with a passion I'd never experienced in my life before.

'Max,' I said, breathlessly.

'What do you want, Ellie?' he said, his voice taunting me.

'Please, Max,' I gasped, feeling as though my heart might not take any more.

Max reached above me, pulling out a small packet from the pillow behind my head. 'Are you absolutely sure this is what you want, Ellie?'

'Yes.'

'Did you mention something about going home?'

'No! Max, please,' I begged him. 'I want you. So, so much.' His gaze held mine, desire simmering between us. 'Please. Now.'

He slid his hands under my hips, lifting my body to his, gently inching his way into me, slowly, surely, my body yielding to his weight on top of mine, our bodies melding together, each movement bringing a gasp of pleasure to my lips. He drove deeper into my body, at first slowly, but then with more intent, more purpose, with infinite skill, again and again, so that I couldn't concentrate on anything else but the exquisite sensations tormenting my entire body. My mind was lost to everything but Max and the highly charged significance of the moment.

Max's focus was fixed entirely on me, taking his pleasure from the thrills he delivered to me, his hands caressing and fondling the contours of my body, while he thrust hard inside me, each deep movement pushing my body further and further towards a teetering edge, ebbing and flowing relentlessly until I couldn't contain the delicious sensations any longer, my whole being relinquishing to a final shuddering wave that overwhelmed me completely, my beautiful sweet release bringing Max to a total-encompassing peak too. He collapsed down on top of me, falling into my embrace. We both exhaled together in harmony, our bodies warm and glowing in satisfaction.

Max rolled onto his side to look at me, our gazes still locked together, our limbs still entwined, neither of us wanting to break the intensity of the moment. He reached up with his hand to caress my face and swept his fingers through my hair, tidying it behind my ears, before kissing me on my lips. 'I may have lied. About having an ulterior motive in bringing you here.' His voice was husky and edged with humour.

'Is that so?' I said, running my finger around the outline of jaw, drinking in all the gorgeousness of his lovely face. 'That's absolutely terrible. I'm shocked. Totally shocked.'

'Will you stay?'

I stretched out my body in his lovely huge bed, not wanting to ever leave it, but knowing that I'd have to soon, breaking the magic spell we'd created between us. 'I'd love to, but Mum's at home so I should really get back.'

'Aw shame. I wanted to have you all to myself. Some other time, eh?'

'Yeah, definitely,' I said, thinking it couldn't come soon enough, the very idea sending a warm pool of delight to the depths of my stomach.

Twenty-Five

'It's good to see you looking so happy.'

Mum grabbed my hand from across the other side of the pub table and gave it a little squeeze. Her taxi would be arriving soon to take her to the airport and Eric, Josie, Ethan, Betty, Johnny and Polly, and Paul and Caroline, and some other friends had gathered for a farewell drink.

Admittedly ever since that glorious evening spent in Max's bed I hadn't been able to stop grinning. At random moments when I was least expecting it a big dreamy smile would take over my face and people would look at me oddly asking if everything was okay.

Hmmm, everything was just perfect.

It was hard not to stop thinking about Max though, reliving in glorious detail every moment of that night, each delicious kiss, every caress of his hand over my body, every snippet of conversation we shared. I knew it all, frame by frame. He'd invited me to lunch the following day but I'd already made plans with Mum and then he'd been tied up with work for a few days and was away on business now so we hadn't seen each other since, but I was sure it was only a matter of time until we did.

'Oh, I am happy, Mum. I've told you. Everything's going

well at the moment and having you home these last few days has been such a lovely treat. I'm going to miss you so much when you're gone though.'

'Oh, me too. Let's not talk about it. We've still got...' she glanced at her watch '... twenty minutes left.'

Funny thing was I'd often thought about Mum and Dad in the intervening months when they'd been away, of course I had, but it was only spending time with Mum these last few days that I'd appreciated just how much I'd missed them. There would be a huge gap in her place when she left, but I had to keep reminding myself that we'd still be keeping in contact by email and Skype, and it was only for... two years. *Two years?* Who knew where I'd be or what I'd be doing in two years' time, if I'd still be in Little Leyton or if I would have returned to London, if Max would still be a feature in my life, or if he would just be a distant wonderful memory. The thought made my stomach lurch.

Now, as I watched Mum making her way around the pub saying her goodbyes in her inimitable style, with hugs and kisses, and much laughter, I had to turn my head away to stop the tears from rolling.

'Come on,' I said to Josie who was sitting next to me, 'let me have a cuddle with this little one.' I took Stella from her mum's arms and buried my head in the gorgeous scent of her baby-grow, before holding her up in the air, her little face gurgling happily at me. My heart lifted, amazed at how much she'd changed in such a short space of time.

'Oh, I can't leave without having one last special cuddle with my favourite little girl, can I?' said Mum, suddenly back at my side. She sat down on the other side of me and indulged in a bit of baby snatching. 'You know how proud your mum would be, Josie, to see this little one, don't you? You're doing a fabulous job, you really are.'

We shared a look between us – me, Mum and Josie – and I think we were all in danger of dissolving into tears there and then. Instead we picked up our glasses and raised a toast to each other.

'You'll keep an eye on Ellie for me, won't you Eric?' Mum asked.

'Of course I will, you know that.'

'And I'll keep an eye on Eric,' I said, laughing.

'Yes, well, make sure you do. I want to be kept updated on what's happening here at the pub. You know you can come and stay with us, Eric, if ever you want to.'

Eric raised his eyes at me in amusement. Over the last few days, Mum had invited everyone, and their grandmother, to visit her in Dubai.

'I might just take you up on that, Veronica. Anyway,' he said, peering out of the window, 'you'd better get a move on. Looks like your taxi's here.'

We all moved out from the table, picked up Mum's bags and congregated outside the pub, standing in an awkward huddle, taking it in turns to say our goodbyes. I waited until the end when Mum wrapped her arms around me and gave me a huge hug, squeezing me until it hurt.

'Goodbye, love.'

'Bye Mum. Send my love to Dad, won't you?' I said, unable to hide the emotion from my voice.

'I will.'

I turned away, noticing the tears in her eyes and allowed Eric to bundle her into the back of the taxi. As it pulled away and drew out of sight, Eric put his arm round my shoulder and I wrapped my arms around his waist.

'Come on you, let's get you inside and we'll have another drink.'

What would I do without my friends? I was so grateful to them all for being there, for me and Mum, for making our farewell almost bearable just by their presence. These people were like a second family to me and the pub a second home. That was one of the good things about being in Little Leyton, I had a support network around me. If I'd been in London it would have been much harder to deal with, going back to an empty lonely flat. I had much to be grateful for, especially now I had an extra exciting dimension in my life in the form of Max.

I had another couple of soft drinks, before people slowly began to drift away. It was early afternoon and thankfully I had no pub shifts or dog walks planned for the rest of day. Just as well probably in my heightened emotional state. When Polly left to go and visit her parents, Johnny stayed to keep me company and later he joined me on the walk home.

'Can I ask you something?' he said, as we strolled leisurely through the village.

'Sure.'

'Your mum mentioned that you were out with Max Golding the other night. Are you two an item now?'

Surely I couldn't be blushing in front of Johnny? I knew him too well and yet suddenly I felt laid bare under the scrutiny of his direct question.

Of course I'd told Mum what a lovely evening I'd had with Max, reiterating that we were good friends only and ignoring her subsequent doubtful expression, and I'd told Josie probably more details than she'd wanted to hear, but then I knew she wouldn't whisper a word to anyone. What could I tell Johnny though?

Part of me wanted to spill the beans and tell him everything. Probably not the best idea considering our past history. I wanted to tell the whole world about my wonderful evening with Max, in all its glorious detail, but discretion got the better of me. It was still early days. Effectively a one-night stand at the moment. Neither I nor Max knew what the future held for us and perhaps until we did it was best to keep our budding relationship under wraps.

'Not an item,' I decided upon, as I pulled mugs out of cupboards and spooned coffee into them. 'We've spent some time together, yes, but we're just friends,' I said, dishing the same old line out again. Judging by the expression on Johnny's face it seemed I wasn't convincing him any more than I had Mum.

'Look Ellie, just be careful. How much do you actually know about Max? He's had a long-term girlfriend until very recently, did you know that?'

I turned to look at Johnny, scanning his expression. There was a time when we shared everything with each other, all our innermost secrets, our hopes and our fears, but I could hardly confess my true feelings for Max. It didn't seem right.

'Sasha? Yes, of course I know about her. They separated recently. We're both single now, Johnny. We're not hurting anyone.'

'I'm not concerned about anyone else, Ellie. I'm just worried about you getting hurt. That's all.'

I felt my skin bristle, my good mood doing a vanishing act. What was it to do with Johnny, anyway?

'Well, thanks for the concern, but I'm more than capable of looking after myself.' I handed him his mug of coffee. 'You didn't waste any time in going off with Polly. You weren't so worried about me getting hurt then, were you?'

He shrugged, his shoulders slumped as he nursed his coffee. 'I wouldn't have got together with Polly in the first place if you hadn't blown me out.'

'Oh, right, I see. Is that what all this is about? You've moved on, found someone new, but you don't want me to do the same. Are you jealous, is that it? Oh, Johnny, you disappoint me. I thought you were bigger than that.'

He sighed, shaking his head. 'Look I'm sorry. I'm not explaining myself properly. I'm happy with Polly and the way things are going, she's a great girl, but I still have feelings for you, Ellie. I can't switch those off just because we're not together any more. You were my teenage sweetheart!' He looked up at me from under long dark eyelashes and my heart tugged at the poignancy of his words. 'I'm not daft. I know there's no future for us romantically any more, but I still care about you and what happens to you? Is that such a bad thing?'

'No.' I sighed, matching his smile. Johnny and I went back a long way. The last thing I wanted was to fall out with him. 'What, and you don't think Max Golding is a good move for me?' I said, wryly.

'All I'm saying is, be careful. He's a businessman, motivated by money and I'm not certain he's too fussy who he tramples over to get what he wants.'

I appreciated Johnny's concerns, but if he'd witnessed the Max I'd seen the other night, the kind and sensitive man, then I felt sure he would have to reassess his opinion of him.

Max was good-looking, charming and rich, to boot. No wonder he'd ruffled a few feathers in the village.

'Look, I'll promise to be careful, if that makes you feel better?'

Johnny nodded resignedly, an awkward silence hanging between us. 'So, what do you know about him buying the pub then?'

'What?' I looked up, my fingers momentarily caught in the handle of the mug, scorching my knuckles. 'Ouch, shit! What are you talking about?'

'Ahh.' Johnny nodded sagely. 'Not a lot then, I'm guessing.'

I put the mug back down again, fanning my hand in front of my face. I looked at Johnny, perplexed, eager for an explanation, my heart suddenly racing in my chest.

'I've had my suspicions for a while now,' he went on, 'ever since I saw him snooping around the place with his surveyor and his accountant.'

'Oh honestly, Johnny, that doesn't mean anything.'

'I asked him, this morning. I ran into him in the High Street. Apparently the contracts have been signed today. Max Golding is the new owner of The Dog and Duck, I'm surprised he didn't mention it to you.'

Surprise didn't even come close. Shock, more like. Followed by a good dose of anger. My stomach fell to the floor and a sharp pain stabbed at my chest. Could it really be true? Or was Johnny making up stories about Max in an attempt to jeopardize our relationship. I looked across at Johnny. No, never. If there was one thing I knew about Johnny it was that he would never lie to me.

'Well, I don't know why you're surprised,' I said, trying

desperately hard not to show just how gobsmacked I was. 'I told you, we're only friends. And I haven't seen him in days. Besides, he doesn't have to tell me everything that's going on in his life. Why would he tell me about his business dealings?'

Why wouldn't he? We'd had plenty of discussions about the future of the pub and not once had Max intimated he wanted to buy it for himself. I couldn't believe it. I thought there was something between us, a special connection. He knew how concerned I'd been about Eric and yet he hadn't said a word. First he'd kept the fact he had a girlfriend to himself and now he'd failed to tell me he was buying the pub, something he knew I would be desperate to hear about. And if what Johnny was telling me was true, then it meant Max would be my new boss – where would that leave our relationship, if there was any chance we still had one?

'Well, I just assumed that he would. Knowing how close you two have been recently.'

I wasn't about to admit it to Johnny, but I would have made the same assumption too.

'He does seem to like his pubs.'

'Does he?' I said, still reeling from the news.

'Yep. He bought The Bell in Upper Leyton and The White Horse at Fletton. Completely gutted and renovated them into luxurious homes and sold them for a tidy profit, so I understand.'

Bile rose in the back of my throat. 'Well, he wouldn't do that with The Dog and Duck. Not to Eric. They're good friends.'

'Oh right. Well, you obviously know him much better than I do. You should ask him.'

At that moment I felt as though I didn't know Max at all. He'd asked me an awful lot of questions about the pub. About Eric too. I'd thought he'd just been showing an interest, but perhaps he'd been using me to get some background information. The thought made me shudder with disgust.

'Oh don't worry, I intend to do exactly that.'

Twenty-Six

As soon as Johnny left, I felt totally adrift, not knowing what to do. Part of me wanted to go straight round to Max's and demand to know what was going on but, as I'd told Johnny, Max didn't owe me any explanations. I would have hoped he'd wanted to tell me, but clearly not. That hurt. The other night I'd felt so close to Max, as close as it's possible to feel to someone. I'd trusted in him, feeling as though I could have told him anything. I'd opened up to him completely and yet he hadn't done the same. Now I felt used and foolish.

What plans did he have for the pub? Was he really going to rip the heart out of it and sell it on to the highest bidder? And what about Eric? He hadn't seemed worried when I'd spoken to him earlier, but he'd probably been putting on an act for the sake of Mum and me, not wanting to upset either of us, knowing we'd both be feeling emotional anyway.

I paced up and down the kitchen only then spotting the envelope on the fireplace, snatching it up as though it were a lifeline. I ripped open the paper and pulled out a card. It showed a grumpy-looking pug with her puppy, sitting side by side. My heart melted.

To my darling daughter, thank you for such an amazing time! Remember, although we're apart in distance, you're always very close to our hearts. We are very proud to have you as our daughter and whatever you decide to do in life is fine with Dad and me. Just have fun! Lots of love, Mum xxx

Tears pricked at my eyes as a huge swell of emotion rose in my chest. In the short time since I'd waved Mum off in her taxi, all the joy seemed to have been sucked from my life. Oh Mum! What wouldn't I give to have her back here for just another half an hour. Time to share a cup of tea or a bottle of wine. To chat and ask her advice over this latest bit of gossip that would be sweeping through the village like wildfire. My heart sank at an awful realization. Would the pub even still be here when Mum next came home?

Just as I was wondering what to do next the phone rang, making me jump out of my reverie. Maybe it was Max with an explanation? Or Eric or Josie wanting to tell me the news. Or Mum telling me she'd missed her plane and was coming home to give me a much-needed cuddle.

'Hello, is that Ellie Browne?'

'Yes.' I didn't recognize the woman's voice at all.

'Ah, hello Ellie, it's Rhoda Dexter here.' There was a pause where I was obviously expected to realize who this person was. A dozen different dog faces flittered into my mind as I tried to match an owner with the pictures; the cockapoo, the lab, the pointer, the collie cross, the Bitsa – no, none of those.

'From Firman Brothers?' she finally added.

My mind quickly played catch-up. A couple of months

ago I'd applied for a job with the biggest global consultancy firm of them all, Firman Brothers. It was just a punt really. Something of a whim. It was round about the time of Amber's accident, when I'd just met Sasha and I'd had a severe case of the hump with Max and was wondering if my future did belong in Little Leyton after all. The job was at management level and I really didn't have the wealth of experience they were looking for. I'd assumed my application had gone straight in the bin. It was no big shakes.

'Oh yes, of course, hello.'

'I know it's short notice, but I wondered if you'd be available for an interview tomorrow afternoon? Say 2.30 p.m.'

My little world in Little Leyton span round me in a blur. London and the heady heights of corporate finance were a million miles away from the life I lived now. Wasn't my future firmly planted in the village or was Fate wading in with her size-nine wellies and telling me to get the hell out of here?

'Yes. Yes, I would.'

'Super. Look forward to meeting you then.'

*

After a restless night where I got absolutely no sleep whatsoever while my mind played over and over Johnny's revelation about Max, my poor brain trying, and failing, to make sense of it, I crawled out of bed early the next morning knowing I had an extremely busy day ahead of me. Before I caught the train to London, I had four dogs to walk and I decided it would be easier and quicker to walk them together, so with Amber, Digby, Hugo and Monty as company I headed out.

The temperature had dropped significantly in the last couple of weeks, but this morning, down in the back lanes, the sun was making a valiant attempt at breaking through the trees, dappling the ground in a golden glow. Underfoot, a carpet of leaves, rich in hues of amber, brown and yellow crunched satisfyingly. With the dogs mooching at my feet, I couldn't think of any better way, or any better place, to start the day. Well, apart from having a clearer head and knowing what the hell Max Golding was up to. It was eating me up inside. Still there'd been no word from him, and however much I tried to put it all out of my head, I couldn't. Tonight I'd be doing a shift at the pub and no doubt Eric would fill me in on what was going on, but I was still smarting that Max hadn't deigned to mention anything to me. Wasn't I at least owed an explanation?

I walked into Max's field, which was part of my daily dog-walking routine now, and let the dogs off their leads, watching as they galloped across the grass chasing each other, their tails wagging furiously. My heart melted at the sight of them. I loved each and every one of my dogs, more so now since I'd come to know their different personalities and their funny idiosyncrasies. Amber was a proper lady and hated to get her feet wet, refusing to budge if faced with a muddy patch down the lane, which often ended with me having to carry her through any puddles on our walk. Saying that, she had improved immensely with our training sessions and her recall was so much better than when I first started working with her. Digby was driven by one thing alone and that was his stomach and he would often sidle away and latch onto any suspecting passer-by if they had a whiff of anything remotely edible on them. Hugo and Monty were like a comedy double-act, leaping around, chasing each other in circles and disappearing into bushes, emerging covered in brambles. I sighed. If only people could be more like dogs. Trustworthy, loving and loyal.

In the distance I saw Max's house, the memories of the night we spent together flooding into my mind. I thought something special had happened that night, that we'd made a connection, but obviously I was wrong. I'd read far more into the situation than was actually there. Max could easily have contacted me if he'd wanted to, but he hadn't. Didn't that say it all?

Despite feeling the warmth of the sun of my face, a shiver ran down my spine, stirring my resolve. Hell, why was I spending so much time wondering what was going on in Max Golding's mind? I shouldn't have to guess. The one thing I really cared about was the pub and if Max didn't have the decency to come and tell me what his plans were for The Dog and Duck, then I wasn't about to waste any more time second-guessing his intentions. Life was too short. I needed to know today. Right this minute. Quite simply, I would go and ask him straight.

'Amber, Digby, Hugo, Monty!' I called the dogs' names and, as one, their ears pricked and they came bounding towards me. I clipped their leads on and waltzed across the field and down the hill towards the Braithwaite Estate, a firm intention stirring in my chest. I don't know why I hadn't done it sooner. I wasn't prepared to wait around any longer, hoping Max might grace me with his company. Any reminders of that night spent in his bed were to be put firmly out of my mind; the feel of him, the touch of him, the scent of him, all of that was irrelevant now. All I wanted was to know the truth about the pub.

Emerging out of the cutaway from the field I stopped in my tracks, seeing Max in his driveway talking to another man. Treacherously my body reacted violently to the sight of him; his tall broad frame and the cut of his jaw stirring something instinctive deep down inside me. I took a deep breath and steadied my nerves. I couldn't be distracted by anything but the job in hand.

'Come on,' I said to the dogs, tugging on their leads. We must have looked quite a sight crunching down the driveway, especially when Max's dogs, Bella and Holly, ran to greet us, giving us a noisily enthusiastic welcome. Max and the other man turned to watch our arrival.

'Ellie! How are you?'

If Max was surprised to see me he didn't show it. He was all charm and sophistication and the epitome of country-style living, standing there in his padded gilet. Our night of passion evaporated in the morning air seeing him looking so pleased with himself and all I could think about was the pub that had always played such an important part in my life, and in the lives of my parents and all my friends too. I owed it as much to them to get an explanation. At that moment I think I may have hated Max.

'Is it true?' I asked, ignoring his question.

'Sorry?' He tilted his head in a way that suggested he had no idea what I was talking about. Infuriating, when clearly he did.

'Is it true about the pub? Have you bought The Dog and Duck?'

'Ah well, I was just talking to Peter here about that. He's my...'

'Yes or no, Max. That's all I need to know.'

If he thought he might intimidate me with that penetrating gaze of his then he was very much mistaken.

'Right.' He nodded slowly. 'That would be a yes then.'

It was only Max's friend and the six dogs dancing the maypole around my feet that stopped me from launching myself at Max and banging my fists on his chest.

'And you didn't think to tell me?'

'Look, I was going to tell you, of course. You're on my list, I promise. I've been busy, that's all.' He made a move towards me, but I recoiled from his approach. 'Come inside, I'll only be a few minutes, we can chat it through.'

'Yes, I was about to go, anyway,' said Peter, looking more uncomfortable with every moment.

'No. Don't leave on my account. Max and I have nothing to talk about.'

I was on his list? Bloody cheek. Right down the bottom of it by the sounds of it. What annoyed me most was that he would have known about the deal the other night when we were together. We could have 'chatted it through' then. Only Max had obviously decided that wouldn't have been a good idea when he'd clearly had other more carnal pursuits on his mind.

I turned on the spot with what I intended as a flourish, but instead just tripped over one of the six dogs, who were all growing more excitable by the moment and jumping up madly at my legs.

'You all right there,' asked Peter, holding out a hand to steady me, while Max tried to hide that annoying, irritating smile spreading across his face.

'Absolutely fine,' I said, only just managing to keep a lid on my fizzing temper. 'Just one thing,' I asked, unable to help myself, 'are you going to do one of your special renovation projects on the place?'

'Well, even you would have to agree that the pub is well overdue a facelift.'

'I see. Well, thank you, you've told me everything I need to know.'

'Come on, Ellie, don't be like that. We need to talk.'

No, we didn't. Honestly, the way I felt now, if I never saw Max Golding again, it would be a day too soon.

Twenty-Seven

Grrr. I spent the whole walk home grumbling to the dogs about what a complete and utter waste of space Max Golding was. Judging by the way they lifted their heads to listen to me and the continued wagging of their tails, they were in total agreement, well that's how I interpreted it anyway. To think I'd been taken in by his sophisticated, charming ways. What an idiot! I should have realized, when he'd failed to tell me he had a girlfriend, that he wasn't to be trusted. Wasn't that warning enough? What made me think he would be honest about anything else? Wishful thinking, obviously.

After dropping off the dogs with their respective owners, I dashed home and jumped in the shower, washed off the bad odour left from my meeting with Max this morning, tamed my wild frizz with the straighteners and pulled out my favourite skirt suit from the back of the wardrobe.

As soon as I slipped on my patent court shoes and applied some mascara and lippy, I was back in professional services mode, but I must admit it felt strange, as if I was dressing up in my mum's clothes and pretending to be someone else. Still, the dog-walking girl in jeans and sweatshirt would be left behind in Little Leyton for the day. Along with any thoughts of Max Golding. Thank goodness.

Twenty minutes later and I was on the train to London, relieved to be leaving the village for the first time in weeks, something I would never have expected to feel only a few days ago. Gazing out of the window at the landscape rushing past, I wondered if my love affair with the simple life had come to an abrupt end. Not that it had proven to be such a simple life after all. Returning home was only ever meant to be a temporary thing and while it had been fun while it lasted, perhaps now was a good time as any to return to my city life. Especially with Mum and Dad away for another couple of years, big changes happening at the pub and the spectre of a life-changing one-night stand hanging over me. Did I really belong in the village any more?

I sighed, only then giving some thought to the enormity of what lay ahead of me today. Talk about punching above your weight. I'd blindly agreed to an interview, at a time when I hadn't been thinking straight and still reeling from the news that Max was buying the pub, without any real hope of being offered the job. Still, it would be good practice if indeed my future did lie back in London.

Walking from the Tube stop to the offices of Firmans, my heels click-clacking on the pavements, a shiver of anticipation ran over my skin as I soaked up the buzz in the air. The London traffic swarmed past me, cyclists weaving in and out of the cars and buses as they navigated the busy roads, a soundtrack of horns filling the air. As I walked along the pavement, swept along by the swell, people side-stepped me as they rushed on their way to their next pressing appointment. The shops, with their window displays tantalizing with the promise of the perfect Christmas, were already busy with shoppers. There was still some weeks to go to Christmas but looking at the crowds you could almost imagine it to be Christmas Eve. Mmm, it felt good to be alive. There was an energy, a purpose and a sense of excitement in the atmosphere that came from being part of a busy vibrant city.

It wasn't as if I'd ever hated living and working in London. I'd loved my job at one time and loved my flat too. If I hadn't been made redundant then I would still be working there. It was only when change was forced upon me that I realized that my life had been pretty much all work and no play. Perhaps that was all I'd needed. A bit of perspective. The chance to get a bit of balance back in my life. Hadn't I achieved that now? Maybe it was time for me to get back into the swing of things in London after all.

'If you'd like to go up to the seventeenth floor. Miss Dexter will be waiting for you.'

Firmans head office was in the heart of the city in a huge modern skyscraper with swishy lifts, vast open-floored offices and full-length windows offering panoramic views of the London skyline. Even on a grey and overcast day like today it was still a breathtaking sight. It would be no hardship to work in such amazing premises.

Rhoda Dexter, a petite blonde, with killer heels and a figure to die for greeted me warmly and showed me to a huge boardroom where I was introduced to the three people who would be conducting my interview. A flutter of trepidation washed over me. I took a deep breath, smiled broadly and shook hands with everyone, wondering whether perhaps I should have done a bit more preparation than I had, which had been absolutely none. Never mind, too late to worry about that now. I sat down in the chair opposite them, crossed my legs at my ankles and rested my hands in my lap, a picture of assured professionalism.

If I could handle four wilful dogs at one time, then I reckoned three senior managers had to be an absolute breeze.

Maybe because of that and the fact that I had no hope of getting this job, I just seemed to waltz my way through their questions. Even to my own ears I sounded collected and confident. I realized as I told them about my experience and the array of clients I'd worked with, that I had much to feel proud about.

It all passed in a blur and when it was over I was almost disappointed. My interviewers stood, thanked me for coming and told me they'd be in touch soon, although I still believed I didn't have a hope in hell of being offered their job.

Not that it mattered. If not this job then there'd be another one. Nothing today was going to puncture my mood of optimism. Not Firman Brothers. Not the thought of an uncertain future. And definitely not Max Golding. Because, in spite of recent events, I was feeling hopeful. London had welcomed me back into its arms and I wanted to savour the moment.

Instead of heading straight home, I went to the nearest cafe and bought a goat's cheese and beetroot panini and a skinny latte, settling myself into a seat by the window where I could sit and watch the world go by. What a treat. To see the mums with their tots in buggies out for some Christmas shopping and a visit to Santa perhaps? The young lovers walking hand in hand. The elderly couples helping each other along. A motley selection of dogs having a good old mooch around. The office workers taking their lunch breaks. I was one of them not so long ago and could imagine being one again in the not too distant future. For the first time in weeks it seemed a likely option. The New Year was not long off and suddenly a whole new life beckoned on the horizon. A new job, a new set of friends and a new social life and suddenly my future would be looking rosy again. Not that I would do anything hasty. I needed to take some time to make sure the next decision I made was the right one. When I got home I would register with some employment agencies and scan the job sites to see exactly what was out there.

My phone vibrated in my pocket and I pulled it out to see who was calling me. Max Golding. Dismiss. I certainly didn't feel like talking to him – ever again. I would just have to put that whole episode down to experience. Admittedly the evening spent in his bed was an experience that would stay in my mind for a long time to come, one I'd first hoped would be repeated, but not any more. If there was one thing I knew I needed from a relationship it was honesty and transparency. I couldn't be doing with Max's secretive, underhand ways.

I closed my eyes and relished the sensation of the sun caressing my face through the window of the cafe. My body relaxed and, unbidden, thoughts of Max flooded my head. Even in the middle of London, fifty miles away from the village, I couldn't get away from him. Reminders of his delicious enticing scent, the memory of his expert touch on my skin, his breath on my face... I snapped my eyes open again, shutting out the thoughts.

Okay, it might take me a little while to get Max Golding out of my system.

As I took the train home, I came to the conclusion that

it might be easier to do that in London rather than in Little Leyton. Still, my decision about whether to stay or go had nothing to do with Max. He was just a distraction. An annoying, frustrating, temporary distraction. Mind you, if he continued to call and text me at the rate he had been today then I might never be able to escape his clutches. I'd had half a dozen texts asking me to call him and a couple of missed calls. Funny how he expected me to jump to attention when he called the shots, after keeping me waiting for days. There were no words to describe the arrogance of the man.

As the train pulled into Little Leyton, I picked up my bag and headed for the door. Walking over the bridge to the car park, my phone buzzed again, shredding my nerves for the umpteenth time that day. In desperation, and in a bid to get rid of him once and for all, I yanked the phone from my pocket and stabbed at the answer button.

'Yes. What is it you want exactly?'

'Oh, hello Ellie,' said a voice clearly not belonging to Max. 'Sorry if I've rung at a bad time, but I just wanted to say thank you for coming in to see us today.' I gulped, a heat burning on my cheeks at the realization that Rhoda Dexter was on the end of the line.

'Ooh, sorry, I thought you were someone else,' I said, laughing lightly, wondering if I'd left something behind in their offices. Why else would she be ringing me? Quickly I checked my bag for my purse, my keys, my umbrella. No. All present and correct.

'No problem,' said Rhoda, her voice warm. 'I was just ringing to congratulate you on a successful interview. We'd like to offer you a job with Firmans.'

'You would?' It was all I could manage to say. The air

whooshed out of my chest. Honestly I couldn't have been more surprised if I'd been offered a place on the national football team.

'Yes. The formal offer will be going out in the post to you today. If you could have a look through the terms and return the signed acceptance to me before Christmas that would be great. Any queries, then just let me know.'

'Thank you,' I said, wondering why I didn't feel more excited by this unexpected news. After all, wasn't this the opportunity I'd been dreaming about all day long? 'That's just brilliant news,' I said, conjuring up a tiny bit of excitement from somewhere.

Twenty-Eight

After my shift at the pub I was ready to collapse. It had been a long and eventful day that had included my run-in with Max, a jaunt to London, an interview which I'd attended just for the hell of it and then a job offer I had no expectation of receiving – what on earth was I going to do about that? Did I really want the job? It sounded like a good idea all the time I had no hope of getting it, but now? Would I be a fool to even consider turning such an amazing opportunity? And why was it such a difficult choice anyway? What was there to keep me in Little Leyton now? Too many questions. My head hurt just thinking about it.

Turning up at the pub for what I thought would be an easy shift I found Andy had called in sick, Dan had taken a day's holiday and Eric was huddled with his friends around a table in the front bar for one of their mammoth card sessions, so I was left to man the bar pretty much on my own. There was no chance of me having a quiet word with Eric either. He was far too busy having a good time. If he was worried about his future at the pub then he wasn't showing it, laughing and joking along with his friends. Finally, after five long hours, with my legs feeling they were about to buckle beneath me, the last of the customers left for home and Eric came along, rattling his keys before locking up the main door. I breathed a huge sigh of relief.

'Well done, love,' he said, giving me a squeeze around my shoulder. 'You've worked bloomin' hard tonight. Not sure how we'd manage here without you.'

I smiled, grateful for Eric's appreciation. I wondered if I should mention that I might not be around much longer. That I might be heading back to London. Not that I was under misapprehension that I was indispensable. If it wasn't me pulling pints then there were plenty of others waiting to fill my place. Who knew, though, there might not even be a job here for me much longer.

'Do you have to rush off?' he asked.

'No, not at all,' I said cheerily, even though I was desperate to fall in to my bed. I was much more desperate to know what the gossip was. Luckily I didn't have any plans until tomorrow afternoon so I could look forward to a lie-in.

'Fancy a nightcap?'

Eric made two milky coffees and poured a nip of brandy into each of them. We took the coffees and went and sat on the wooden pew in the front bar. I tucked a cushion beneath my bottom and one behind my back and kicked off my shoes, grateful to get the weight off my feet. I took a small tentative sip of my coffee, the alcohol blazing a trail down my chest.

'You've heard the news,' he said, with a wry smile on his face. Eric seemed remarkably blasé about this latest turn of events.

'About Max buying the pub? Yes, Johnny told me. I still can't quite believe it. I'm so cross with Max. That he didn't mention anything, even when we had dinner together.' I paused, hearing the words tumbling from me. 'What do you think about it?'

'Well, we knew someone was going to buy it. To my mind, I'd rather someone I know buy the place than a complete stranger or a big chain.'

'Yes, but you know what Max has done with the other pubs he's bought in the past? He's done them up and sold them as houses.'

Eric nodded and lifted his coffee cup to his mouth. 'Not this time though. I've talked it all through with Max and he wants to keep the place as a pub. Good news, eh?'

'Really?' I heard the note of surprise in my own voice.

'Yep.'

I'd imagined this conversation with Eric, played out the different scenarios over in my head, how we'd both be suitably outraged at Max's temerity at coming in from outside the village and having the audacity to think he could take over the pub, *our* pub. Our outrage at what he might do with the historic building. Not once had I imagined that there would be a positive outcome to the scenario. Had I completely over-reacted and misread the whole situation? It wouldn't be the first time. Mind you, if it was such good news, as Eric was suggesting, why wasn't he jumping up and down with excitement?

I curled my hands around my cup and took another sip of coffee. The brandy was going down well. At this rate, I might need another one.

'So, you're absolutely certain, Max doesn't intend changing the use of the pub?' I still couldn't believe I was getting the full story here.

'As certain as I can be.'

'Wow, I can't quite believe it. And where does that leave you, Eric? Does Max want you to stay on as landlord or has he got other plans?'

'No, he came round earlier today. We had a long chat. He wants to keep things running just the same as they always have. Business as usual.'

'Well, that's terrific news,' I said, feeling a pang of guilt that I'd ever maligned Max and his intentions in the first place. Still though, Eric appeared thoughtful, contemplative. Not how I would have expected him to be – there was something he wasn't telling me.

'Fancy another coffee?' he asked, standing to clear the cups.

'Yes please,' I said, getting up to join him. 'And you're happy with that arrangement, Eric?' I probed.

He turned round to face me, his arms behind him, resting back on the kitchen worktop. 'Look, Ellie, with all the uncertainty over the last couple of months and whether or not I still had a future here, it's given me time to think.' He gave a wry smile. 'The thing is I've decided that it's time for me to leave the pub. Seeing your mum again and hearing what a great time she and Harry are having out in Dubai brought it home to me. There's a whole other world out there that I should be exploring. I'm still young enough and fit enough to travel, enjoy life, maybe meet someone new. I feel ready to do that now. I want to take advantage of those possibilities while I still can.'

I watched as he opened the brandy, pouring a bigger glug this time into our coffees. He handed me my cup and we wandered back and settled ourselves on the pew again, me still reeling from what I thought Eric was trying to tell me.

'And this has got nothing to do with Max?'

He shook his head. 'No, I'd made up my mind before I even knew Max was buying the place.'

'Crikey.' My shoulders slumped and I heard a sigh escape my lips. First Mum and Dad had moved away to begin a new life, then Johnny and Polly had come together and were in the delicious throes of new love, Max was blazing a trail in his own single-minded way, and now Eric was wanting to break away and make a new life for himself. I couldn't help feeling as though I was being left behind. 'I never thought I'd see the day.'

'Me neither. But things can't stay the same forever, Ellie. I realize that now. Circumstances change. People change. It's time for me to move on.'

Oh God! Eric said it so matter-of-factly, as though it was of little consequence. To me, it felt as though my whole world had shifted beneath my feet.

'Right.' I clasped onto my coffee cup as though it was a lifeline. All the time I'd been panicking that an outsider was going to come in and change the face of the pub forever when in the end Eric had decided to call it a day. That meant my future at the pub would now lie in the hands of Max Golding, the last person in the world I'd want deciding my fate. 'You know you'll be playing straight into Max's hands by walking away. He won't have any obligation to keep it running as a pub if you're not going to be around.'

'Ellie!' He scolded me with a disapproving look. 'I'm sure he won't. He told me he wants to keep the pub going and I've no reason not to believe him.'

'Hmmm, well, I'm not sure I share your faith in Max Golding.' Maybe Max was much cleverer than we all thought. Perhaps he'd been banking on Eric leaving and that's why he told him they'd keep things running the same as they always had. The way things seemed at the moment, I wouldn't put it past him.

'Don't make me feel guilty about this, Ellie. Just give Max a chance. I know you must be worried about what it means for you, but I'm sure you'll still have a job here with Max as the owner.'

My gaze flitted around the pub, taking in the wood-panelled walls, the comfy chairs and tables, the countryside scenes on the wall mingling with caricatures. All so familiar, all so reassuring.

'Oh Eric, it's not about me at all. I don't care about my job. It's more about the pub and what it will mean for the local community.'

'Well, I'm sorry, Ellie. I'd hate to see the pub close just as much as you would, probably more so, but I can't put my life on hold just in case that might happen one day. Max has assured me that he'll keep the pub running as it is for now, but what happens months or years down the line, who knows? None of us do. I've given the best years of my life to this place. And now it's time for me to do what I want to do while I still can.'

I looked across into Eric's kindly eyes and felt a fluttering of shame. I reached over and grabbed his hand. 'No, I didn't mean it like that. Of course I didn't. You've been amazing. And you've done so much for this place. I would never begrudge you doing what you want to do now. No way. You deserve to get out there and have a good time and find some happiness. I guess I'm just being selfish. If it was up to me I'd like everything to stay the same as it's always been.'

Eric squeezed my hand, a rueful smile on his lips. 'Change doesn't have to be a bad thing, you know.'

'No, I know. I'm sure everything will work out fine,' I said, not really believing my own words. 'Everyone's going to miss you so much though. Me especially.'

'And I'm going to miss you too, but I'll still be around. You won't get rid of me that easily. Thought I might find a little cottage in the village as a base for when I come home from my travelling. I'll go and visit your mum and dad first.'

'Really?'

'Yep.' His face lit up in a wide mile. 'Your mum did an amazing sales job on Dubai.'

'Oh right, so I have her to blame for all of this,' I teased.

'Not entirely.' He paused, his gaze drifting out the window, clearly already off on his travels. 'And then I fancy going inter-railing around Europe for a couple of months. Don't worry though, I'll be back regularly to check up on Josie and Stella, and you of course, and to see how this place is doing. I'm looking forward to sitting this side of the bar with my old mates and catching up on the news.'

'Hmm, you make it sound wonderful,' I said, with a sigh. I glanced at my watch and groaned. 'Crikey, look at the time, I should get a move on.'

Eric stood up and opened his arms up to me for a hug. 'We're still good, aren't we, Ells?'

'Too true,' I said, burying myself into Eric's broad chest. Whatever my feelings about the pub, my relationship with Eric was much more important.

'And don't worry about the pub. It's been standing a few hundred years, long before we were even thought of, and I'm sure it will still be standing long after we're gone too.'

Perhaps Eric had a point. All things come to their natural end and Eric had decided it was time for him to end his association with the pub. Maybe it was time for me to move on too. Hopefully, the pub would always play an important role in the village, and we would always have our memories of the special times spent there.

I kissed Eric goodbye and closed the door of the pub behind me, glad to be out in the cool night air. I looked up at the faded sign of the dog and duck swinging in the cool evening breeze and shivered, pulling my jacket over my shoulders. As I started on my walk home, I pulled out my phone from my pocket and turned it on to check my messages. Almost immediately it rang and for a fleeting moment I thought it might be Rhoda calling to say they'd made a mistake and they hadn't meant to offer me the job at all. But then I realized it was hardly likely, considering it was half past midnight. Max's name flashed on my screen instead and I felt a stab of regret. Had I been too hasty in my treatment of him? I didn't know, but I wasn't ready to talk to him yet. I was far too exhausted and, just at that moment, emotional as well. I switched my phone off. I'd think about Max Golding tomorrow.

Twenty-Nine

It was becoming a habit, a most annoying one. A loud banging on the door rousing me from my bed at some unearthly hour. I rolled over and waved an arm around, trying to find the clock. I picked it up and glared at it accusingly. *Eugh*. 8.30 a.m. on a day when I could quite legitimately stay in bed until midday. What sort of crazy person was hammering at my door at this time. Muttering under my breath, I pulled on some clothes and padded downstairs, hoping it wasn't a dog with an emergency walk requirement. Just as soon as I got rid of whoever it was, I'd make myself a mug of tea and climb back into bed.

I pulled open my front door to find Max Golding.

'Morning!'

He stood on the doorstep looking obscenely handsome for first thing in the morning – oh God – was that even allowed? I steeled myself, trying to keep a cool head and attempting to work out what exactly Max was playing at, but whenever I saw him like this I couldn't help but give in a little.

He clutched a bottle of champagne in one hand and a wicker basket full of goodies in the other. I couldn't stop myself from peering over to look inside at the contents spilling over: yoghurts, fresh orange juice, croissants, cinnamon and orange muffins, jams, strawberries and melon. His gaze ran up and down my trackies, a fetching shade of washed-out blue today, and took in my mussed-up hair and sleep-deprived, make-up-free face.

'Don't tell me you forgot about our breakfast meeting?'

'What breakfast meeting?'

'The one I would have told you about if only you'd picked up the phone to me yesterday?'

I crossed my arms huffily in front of my chest, twisting my mouth to stop the smile twitching at my lips. I was so angry at him, furious that he'd kept me in the dark about his plans to buy the pub and yet now, with him standing here in front of me, in all his romantic gorgeousness, everything was becoming so muddled in my head.

'Yes, well, I was very busy yesterday.'

'I gathered that. Look, if you don't want to come out, can I at least come in? I just want to talk to you and bring you up to date on all the news.'

Reluctantly, I pulled back the door to let Max through, wandering ahead of him to the kitchen and parking my bum on a kitchen stool. I rubbed at my eyes, trying to force myself awake. 'I know it all already. You've bought the pub. Eric is leaving. The pub might stay as it is or else it might be transformed into a lovely home for some outsider coming into the village looking to find their country idyll. Not that I'm worried about that because no one else round here seems to be concerned, so why should I?' I let out a deep breath. 'What else is there to know?'

'Are you working today?' asked Max, totally ignoring my mini rant.

'Later. This afternoon.'

'Great. We can have some of this then,' he said, proceeding to ease the cork from the champagne. 'Some Bucks Fizz! Well, it is almost Christmas.' I laughed. Now we were nearing November, the weeks would fly by quickly enough. I hadn't really given it much thought until now, but maybe it was time for me to get my Christmas spirit out from the cupboard.

I watched as he made himself at home in my kitchen, amazed at his arrogance. I'd only let him in because I'd wanted to know one way or the other what his intentions were and here he was opening cupboards and pulling out glasses and bowls as if he owned the place. Clearly he was a man used to doing exactly what he wanted, where he wanted and when he wanted. He poured two glasses of champagne, topping up the fizz with fresh orange juice before handing one to me, our eyes locking for a moment, catching me off-guard, my body suddenly remembering what such a look had promised and delivered once before.

'Thanks,' I said, stifling a yawn, wishing I'd been better prepared, half wishing I'd ignored the door and gone back to sleep. Then again, I would have missed Max in all his early-morning glory. In jeans and black polo shirt, he looked effortlessly stylish. Gorgeous, in fact. I swallowed hard, wondering how long it took him to perfect his 'breakfast meeting' look. I suspected he hadn't even given it a second thought. Probably just fell out of bed looking like that. His mussed up hair oozed sexiness and my fingers twitched to run through it.

What was I thinking? I gave myself a stern talking-to,

remembering I had good reason to be irritated and annoyed at Max, and the way he'd treated me. Yes, I was very annoyed at him. Serious and grumpy face back on.

From his basket he pulled out a checked tablecloth and laid it over the breakfast bar, along with all the goodies he'd brought along. I watched in awe as he laid out all the different items, although I pretended to be wholly unimpressed. I popped a strawberry into my mouth relishing its sweetness and washed it down with some champagne. It was hard to stay cross with someone when they were bribing you with such delightful treats.

'I know I've upset you and I wanted to apologize, to make it up to you. I promise you there was no intention to mislead you or lie to you. Really.'

He looked contrite enough, but if there was one thing I'd learned about Max in the short time that I'd known him it was that he was totally convincing and totally charming. The same charm he'd no doubt used in his extensive business dealings to date. It was part of what he did, part of who he was. The charm wasn't for my benefit alone and I needed to remember that if I wasn't to be swayed by it.

'You knew how concerned I was about the pub and you didn't say a thing. The other night when we had dinner together you could have mentioned something.'

'Well, the other night over dinner I had more pressing things on my mind.'

His dark eyes flashed with desire as his gaze ran over my face.

'See! That's exactly what I mean. You're evasive. I don't like it when you're not being straight with me. First you failed to mention you had a very attractive girlfriend waiting for you at home, then you forget to tell me you'd actually bought the local pub, the one where I work, the one you knew I had a vested interest in. I just don't understand. What other secrets are you keeping from me, Max? Do you have a wife hidden away, three children at boarding school and a secret gambling addiction you haven't told me about?'

'Ah well, that thing I wanted to talk to you about...' His dark eyebrows lifted, his brown eyes growing wide with amusement. I glowered at him, failing to see the funny side and he held up his hands in a gesture of defence. 'I'm only kidding. No, I don't have any of those things, I promise.' He reached across and took hold of my hand. Part of me wanted to snatch it away again, but I was enjoying the physical contact too much. 'There'll be no more secrets. It's unfortunate that you learned about Sasha and the pub the way you did, before I'd had a real chance to explain the situation and I apologize for that. I guess I'm a bit of a control freak. I like to get everything sorted and organized before showing my hand. I've done enough business deals to know that nothing is confirmed until the paperwork is signed. Things fall through at the last minute all the time. I was waiting for the contracts for The Dog and Duck to be signed before saying anything. That's all it was.'

He was looking at me intently while I distracted myself with a Danish pastry, littering crumbs over the worktop. It sounded convincing enough and Max was always so plausible. The trouble was my personal feelings for Max had got in the way of any logical thought process and I found it hard to think straight in his company. I found it hard to concentrate on anything but the look of him, the scent of him, the fact that his hand was still entwined with mine.

'Okay. I guess,' I said giving him the benefit of the doubt. I gave a small smile, our eyes meeting across the breakfast bar, my insides burning with heat. Quickly, I dropped my gaze. 'So you're now the proud owner of a pub?' I said, extracting my hand.

'Yes. And I couldn't be more pleased.'

He'd said there would be no more secrets, so I just had to ask him straight.

'And will it be staying as a pub or are you planning on renovating it into a home and selling it on?'

'What!' Max grabbed hold of my hand again. 'That's crazy. Where on earth did you got that idea from?'

'Well, it wouldn't be the first time, would it? Johnny told me you'd already bought a couple of pubs and sold them on as private homes.'

'Ahh right, Johnny. The same Johnny who was in love with you. The Johnny who looks out for you and worries about you, the man who thinks I will end up hurting you because he believes I might be falling in love with you too.'

He paused, looking at me intently, a thousand fireworks alighting in my head.

Falling in love? No! Stop it right there. Just breathe. And think. Stop being so stupid. *He didn't say he was falling in love with me. He said Johnny thought Max might be falling in love with me. Something quite different.* I steadied my breathing as Max gave a rueful smile, resting his hands on the stool between his legs.

'It's true what he says, but they were purely business deals. And they were pubs that ceased trading months before and had been standing derelict for some time. I'm not the monster you seem to think I am. I don't go around taking over thriving businesses and throwing the landlords out on the street.'

I shifted on my stool, feeling uncomfortable. When he said it like that I wondered if I hadn't been a bit hasty in my judgement of him.

'And you should know me well enough by now to know that The Dog and Duck has a special place in my heart. I bought the pub precisely because I wanted to secure its future. Granddad would be turning in his grave if he thought I'd be turning the pub into housing. I could never do that. I want to keep the pub at the centre of our community just as much as you do.'

'Really?' The relief in my chest escaped in a sigh.

'Yes. Absolutely.'

'Well, I'm sorry,' I said, taking a sip of my bucks fizz, as though it was a minor understanding on my part. As though I was totally in control. As though my heart wasn't thumping loudly in my chest. He couldn't possibly know the maelstrom of feelings I'd been wrestling with inside.

'Apology accepted.'

'And I'm sorry too about confronting you yesterday when you were with your colleague. I shouldn't have done that. That poor man, what he must have thought of me?'

'Oh don't worry about it,' said Max, with a dismissive wave of his hand. 'I explained to Peter.' A look of amusement was back on Max's face, the smile on his lips teasing me.

'What did you explain to Peter exactly?'

'You know, that you were the mad dog lady of the village, prone to random bursts of outrage and he wasn't to worry about you. I would check up on you later.'

'You didn't?' I stood, placing my hands on my hips.

'I may have done. Totally believed it actually. And true to my word I'm here checking up on my favourite dog lady.'

Max came over and pulled me towards him, placing one hand on my waist, the other tilting my chin up to meet his lips. He leaned forward kissing me gently.

'No don't!' I pushed him away, taking a step backwards from his approach.

'Ellie?' Concern flashed over his features. 'What's the matter? I was joking! I didn't really tell him you were a crazy dog lady.'

'Yes, well, please don't kiss me.'

'Why not?'

'Because I haven't brushed my teeth. And I haven't showered either.' My nostrils twitched involuntarily. 'If you must know, I think I'm smelling a bit iffy.'

'Oh, is that all?' He leaned in, nuzzling his nose into the crook of my neck, sending shivers around my body. He sniffed exaggeratedly, making, quite frankly, disgusting slurping noises, his tongue caressing my skin, which had me backing away from him and squirming in delight at the same time. 'Mmm, you smell absolutely delicious to me, good enough to eat, in fact.'

Thirty

Managing to escape Max's clutches, I ran upstairs giggling.

'Just wait there! I won't be long, I promise,' I called from the top of the stairs.

'Should I come up with you?'

'No! Just wait.' Although I have to say, Max's offer sounded very tempting.

I jumped in the shower, quickly washing myself down, feeling inexplicably happy that Max was here, that he'd explained about the pub, that Christmas was coming, that my future was looking rosy and bright again. Today wasn't the day to be thinking about my new job offer. Best to wait until the paperwork came through, let the idea ferment in my mind for a day or two so that I could come to a considered decision as to what to do next.

The main thing was that The Dog and Duck, a place that held such a special place in my heart, would be staying as a pub, with or without Eric at the helm. I was just overjoyed that Max and I were friends again.

I stepped out of the shower, anticipation fizzing round my veins at the thought of Max waiting for me downstairs. Quickly, I dried myself off, found some clean clothes, brushed my teeth, put a lick of mascara and bronzer on, brushed my hair, and raced back down the stairs again, all in about five minutes flat.

'Right,' I said, with a smile. 'Now I'm ready for our breakfast meeting.'

An even bigger smile lit up Max's lovely features. 'Come here, you,' he said, taking a deep breath of my scent as he pulled me into his embrace. 'Hmm, that's even better,' he said, drinking in my scent. He laid a trail of kisses from my collarbone up to my neck, along my jawline and then behind my ear, his breath warm and heavy on my skin. My body arched to his touch and my hand sought out the firm outline of his body.

'No, stop.'

'What now?' I heard the frustration in Max's voice as he held my upper arms, looking at me imploringly.

'I was just wondering. Now that you own the pub does that effectively mean that you're my new boss?'

Max screwed up his face as though contemplating this very difficult question. 'Erm, yes. I suppose it does.' He nodded, his lips curling in amusement. 'Great, isn't it?'

'Well, in that case, I'm not sure we should be doing this.' I folded my arms, enjoying the intimacy of teasing him. 'There must be some company regulation that states no kissing allowed between working colleagues.'

He narrowed his eyes and shook his head. 'Absolutely not. The only company regulation that must be adhered to is the one which states that you,' he tapped me on the nose, 'must do exactly what your boss tells you to do. And right now, I'm ordering you to let me kiss you.' He picked up the first random piece of paper that came to hand from the kitchen worktop. 'It says so right here on our breakfast meeting agenda. Item No. 4. Kissing and any other smooching business.'

I picked up the piece of paper, scrunched it into a ball and threw it across the room. 'I can see this new relationship isn't going to work at all. I don't take orders from anyone. Well, only Eric, but then he doesn't really give orders, he just asks nicely. I couldn't possibly take orders from you.'

'Oh, is that so?' Max was so close, I could feel his breath upon my face, his nose gently grazing my cheek. 'We might have to rethink this arrangement then.' His voice was low and husky making my insides melt. 'How about you give the orders and I do exactly as you say?'

'That sounds a much better idea,' I said, as we now stood chest to chest, our lips a hair's breadth away. 'You'd better kiss me then.'

'Really?' He swept a finger over the curve of my jaw while the other hand played with my hair. 'Are you absolutely sure? I'd hate to overstep the mark here.'

'Absolutely sure. Kiss me, Max. Kiss me now.'

His eyes were heavy with desire as his lips found mine and he kissed me fervently in a way that had me forgetting about everything but the moment, as if we were the only two people who mattered in the world. Never before had anyone been able to touch me emotionally and physically in the way Max did, stripping me of all my self-consciousness, reaching me deep down inside, discovering a part of me that I hadn't even known existed.

His hands dropped to my waist and in one fell swoop he lifted my T-shirt up over my breasts and over my head, before effortlessly undoing the buttons to my jeans and pulling them down over my hips and knees. At that moment

I think I may have done anything Max told me to. If I thought I'd managed to get dressed quickly, Max undid all my good work so much faster. I stepped out of my trousers into Max's embrace, his warm and appraising gaze making me feel powerful and beautiful.

He held my arms out to my side as his gaze swept the length of my body before he quickly shrugged off his polo shirt and stepped out of his jeans. I gasped at the sight of him, bronzed and lean and muscular, standing there in only his boxers, his desire for me all too evident. He pulled me to him again, his hardness pressing against me. Then he kissed me passionately, his tongue in my mouth taking me to heightened pleasures as our hands eagerly roamed each other's bodies. We fell down onto the sofa together, my legs wrapping around his, our fever for one another making us breathless. The other evening we had taken pleasure in the slowness of the dance, our movements tentative and gentle. Exploratory. Not now. Our base desire, an intense need firing our souls, drove us on with a reckless abandon.

Max's hand swept up my inner thigh, my desire increasing with every second, until he found the warm moist softness between my legs. My hand reached out for him, pulling him towards me. My whole body throbbed in exquisite anticipation of what was to come next. Our eyes met in recognition of the moment and my legs parted as Max guided his way inside me, my body yielding to his, accommodating his thickness. His dark, seductive eyes held mine the entire time, as he watched my reaction, thrusting hard inside me, over and over, each movement taking me to a new peak of pleasure, climbing higher and higher, until I could hold on no longer. I cried out his name, my sweet delicious release coming in an utterly overwhelming shudder. As I let go, so did Max, a deep guttural groan escaping his lips as he fell into my arms. My whole body surrendered beneath him, my limbs weightless, a warm fuggy cloud of satisfaction enveloping me. Exhausted and elated, I kissed the hair on his head, soaking up his delicious masculine scent.

'Oh. My. God. That. Was. Amazing.'

'And so are you, Ellie, my beautiful, sexy, funny, crazy dog lady.'

I elbowed him in the side, giggling, as I huddled into his embrace. Max reached over the side of the sofa and retrieved the charcoal fleece blanket off the floor and placed it over my bare legs. We snuggled up, our arms clasped around each other, Max stroking my hair, feeding me Danish pastries and topping up my champagne with orange juice, the fizz on my tongue making me light-headed. It felt hugely decadent to be drinking champagne mid-morning. Mind you, sitting naked on the sofa with a gorgeous hunk was pretty decadent too, although I wasn't about to complain about that.

Much later, after we'd reluctantly got up and dressed, Max mentioned that he ought to be getting back home.

'I haven't walked the dogs yet. Fancy coming with me?'

Well, wasn't that my favourite thing in the world to do?

With Max at my side, dog-walking took on a whole new dimension. The world looked a different place this morning. Brighter, clearer. We climbed over the stile at the bottom of Max's field and walked over the small bridge across the stream, stopping for a moment to watch the water flowing beneath us. We then crossed another field, the dogs leading the way, until we reached the canal. Hand-in-hand we meandered along the towpath, chatting and laughing, stopping occasionally to watch the boats navigate the locks and to chat to the canal folk going about their business.

'So do you have any plans for the pub yet?' I asked.

'Ah well, I needed to talk you about that. First off, I want to give the place a facelift. That's going to mean closing the pub down for a couple of weeks, which is a shame, but I think it will be worth it in the end. I don't intend to make any major changes to the fabric of the building, but I want to put new kitchens and bathrooms in, strip and re-polish the floors and repoint some of the brickwork. The furniture needs updating too. I thought I'd get Johnny to help out with that.'

It all sounded brilliant and it was such a relief to know that Max didn't intend to gut the place or change the underlying character of the building.

'What a great idea. I'm sure Johnny will be grateful for the work.'

'Well, I hope so. I know I'm not his favourite person at the moment.' He gave me a wry sidewards glance. 'Anyway, hopefully the work won't take too long. What I have in mind is that, first and foremost, the pub will retain its essence and charm. I'd like to think if Granddad were able to walk through the doors of The Dog and Duck, he would find the place just as he remembered it. He'd be able to wander up to the bar, order a pint of Best and go and sit in his favourite chair as he always did.'

'Aw, that's so lovely.' Hearing Max talk so fondly about his granddad and the pub made me wonder how I could ever have doubted him. Our vision for the future of the pub was exactly the same.

'I do have a bit of a problem now though.'

'Really?' Anxiety stirred in my chest. I knew there had to be something.

We'd just reached the lock-keeper's cottage and Max beckoned for me to sit down on the wooden bench overlooking the canal. The dogs mooched around at the water's edge, their snouts seduced by the scents, and their ears pricked to the different sounds permeating the air. Max placed an arm around my shoulder.

'Yes, well now Eric has indicated that he wants to leave the pub, I'm without a manager.'

'Do you think he might be persuaded to stay?'

'I've tried, Ellie. Offered to increase his salary and to make any changes to the staff levels he feels are needed, but he's not interested. I think his mind's made up. He's at a time in his life when he wants new challenges, a different focus. I can understand that.'

'Me too, I suppose. Although I find it hard to imagine the pub without Eric behind the bar.'

'He's said he's willing to stay on for a while until I've appointed a new manager. But I think Eric has plans to travel so I know he won't be hanging around too long.'

I sighed inwardly. 'Where will you look?' I asked. 'Will you advertise?'

'Actually I've got someone in mind, but I wanted to run it past you first. Someone who I think might be ideal.'

'That's great. Who?'

I had a sneaky suspicion I knew who it was. Peter. That guy I'd met briefly at Max's house. The one who thought I was a mad dog lady. He'd seemed nice enough, but I wasn't sure I fancied him much as my new boss. Another sign perhaps that it was time for me to move on from Little Leyton.

Max shifted on the bench, turning his body to face me and picking up my hand. 'You Ellie.'

'ME?' I blurted, far too loudly, causing the dogs to come running to my side and a man steering a passing narrowboat to look at me oddly. The way Max was holding my hand, looking at me intently, the man might well have imagined he was witnessing a marriage proposal.

'Yes, you Ellie,' said Max, a smile on his face. 'I don't know anyone better qualified to run the place than you.'

'You're mad, Max.' Which made us both smile. 'I don't know the first thing about keeping a cellar or buying beer.'

'All stuff that Eric can teach you. You've got a great business head on you, Ellie, it would take you no time whatsoever to pick up that side of things. More than that though, the pub is in your blood. You love the place. Anyone can tell that just from talking to you. You know how it works. You can control a jam-packed bar of noisy revellers better than anyone I know. With your years of experience of working there, you know what works and what doesn't work. What goes down well the customers. The beers, the events, the meetings. It would be great to carry on doing all those things and more. Getting involved in the charity run to France was an eye-opener for me. Showed me how much you can do when you all pull together as a community.'

'Wow!' I was knocked sideways by Max's enthusiasm and his belief that I could actually run the pub. I'd sometimes stood in for Eric when he'd been away, but I'd always had Dan or Andy around to help if needed.

'When I bought the pub I never had any intention of running it myself. I wouldn't want to. I bought it for personal reasons, a gesture to my granddad's memory. I love the pub but I only want to be on the right side of the bar, enjoying a pint or two. You saw what I was like the night of the beer festival. If it was down to me we wouldn't have any customers left. I'd go round upsetting them all. Not you though. You're a natural with the punters. A real people's person. You really are the best person for the job, Ellie.'

I took my hand from his and stretched it out along the back of the bench. My gaze was fixed on the gentle undulating movement of the water in front of me. I inhaled a deep breath of cool morning air, different thoughts struggling for attention in my head.

'I'm flattered, Max, that you would ask me. Thank you. You're right, I do love the pub and I love working there. It never actually feels like work to me. The thing is...' I didn't want to look him in the eye. 'I'm not even sure I'm going to be staying around Little Leyton now.'

I loved the time I'd spent with Max this morning, it felt magical and exciting and full of promise, but I couldn't base my plans on what was only a fledgling relationship. It was still too early to say where it was going or if we had a long-term future together. I needed to start rebuilding my life and I suspected I would need to do that in London with a new job and all the opportunities if afforded.

'Oh.' There was a perceptible pause that cut through the air. 'Really? I thought you were staying now.'

I turned to look at him. Into those deep dark eyes that had the power to seduce and inveigle me. 'I've been offered a job in London. It's a great opportunity. At Firman Brothers.'

Max let out a long slow whistle, clearly impressed. Without missing a beat, he said, 'Wow, that's great. Congratulations.' He gave a rueful shrug, his mouth twisting in thought. 'Now, who's guilty of keeping things to themselves?'

'Oh Max, I just haven't had a chance to tell you.' I felt my cheeks redden. 'I only went for the interview yesterday. It all happened rather quickly. I'm just waiting for the formal offer to come through.'

'And you're going to take it?'

I clasped my fingers and stretched my arms out in front of me. 'Well, yes, I think so. Or maybe I won't, but... Oh, I really don't know yet. I need to think about it.'

'I guess you'd be a fool not to.'

'Mmmm.' Those were my thoughts exactly. 'I can't really make any firm decisions until I've got the contract in front of me. I'm sorry, Max.'

'Don't worry, there's absolutely nothing to be sorry about. You must do what's best for you. I'll be able to find someone else to run the pub.' I nodded. I didn't doubt it, so why did the thought make me inexplicably sad? 'I just wanted to give you first refusal.'

'Thanks. I'm really grateful for that. Honestly, I am.'

Max stood up, calling the dogs to his side. 'Come on, we ought to be getting back.'

We turned for home, lost in our own thoughts for a moment before Max said, 'Thought I'd organize a bit of a get-together at the pub to celebrate my new ownership. Just the regular crowd. To spread the news in case there's anyone who won't have heard. We'll have a proper re-opening party when the refurb work's been done, but it'll be good to get everyone together now.'

'Yes. Sounds fab,' I said brightly, wondering why my mood didn't quite match my words.

Thirty-One

The trouble was I couldn't turn down a fabulous job at one of the most prestigious consulting firms in the world for the sake of a man. Never. I was mad to even consider it. Only I had been considering it. For days now. Every time I was out with one of the dogs my mind would go back to that conversation with Max on the bench. What it meant for us and our relationship if I did, as I'd told him, take the job and move back to London. Only a few days ago I'd been bad-mouthing Max and thinking the very worst of him, but that had all changed when he'd come to the house and told me his plans. That I'd featured in those plans, as his potential manager of the pub, was something I could never have anticipated. But really, what was there to think about? Manager of the local pub on a so-so salary or a senior management role in a top-notch city firm with a huge salary plus bonuses. Honestly, it was a no-brainer.

My personal feelings for Max were getting in the way of making a rational decision. The memory of his breath on my skin, the caress of his touch on my body, his distinctive and enticing scent were all conspiring to make my head fuzzy and giddy. But could I really trust my emotions? It was still early days for me and Max. What was to say that the flame burning so strongly between us at the moment wouldn't fizzle out just as quickly as it ignited?

Now I only had until Christmas to decide what to do about the job offer from Firmans. The envelope with my offer of employment had sat on the mantelpiece at home ever since it had arrived, although I'd taken it down to re-read the letter several times. The terms they were offering were amazing, better than anything I could have imagined, £10K more than I was earning in my previous job and twice yearly bonuses with a clearly projected career path. All the perks that come from working with a big firm; gym, executive restaurants and private health care. Beautiful central London offices too.

My mind ran ahead thinking of all the possibilities. The people I would meet, the clients I would get to work with, the glitzy social events, the overseas travel. I would find a new flat. I could even think about getting a mortgage now – putting down some proper roots.

What was it Mum had said about Dad's job offer in Dubai? They would be silly to turn it down. Wasn't it the same for me? Even if I only did the job for a few years. Enough time to make a sizeable nest egg and to gain the experience to add to my CV that would be invaluable for my career. There would be plenty of time in my thirties and forties to act out my countryside dream.

Carefully, I pulled out the envelope from the shelf again, tapping it against my hand. My mind was made up. There was only one sensible decision I could make. I would be accepting the job with Firmans, with a start date of 5th January, less than two months away now. I placed the envelope back on the shelf, pushing aside the stab of trepidation I felt in my chest. Instead I needed to focus on the bubbling excitement shooting around my body. Eek! Look out London, here I come!

*

Now I was late. I'd spent so much time this morning mooning about, pacing up and down the kitchen, trying to come to a decision, that I'd completely lost track of the time. Gemma Jones had rung me earlier, in a bit of state actually, asking to see me, saying that she had something important to tell me. Would I mind having Digby to stay again, I didn't doubt. Still I didn't mind at all. I knew she was struggling at the moment. Hardly surprising with everything she had on her plate. And I wanted to make the most of the few remaining weeks I'd have left with my four-legged friends. I was determined to squeeze in as many walks as possible.

Dread filled my stomach at the thought of having to notify Gemma and my doggy other clients that I'd be closing down my business. I shook my head, not wanting to face that just yet. It could all wait for another day.

I rushed out the door feeling suddenly lighter at having made my decision. The uncertainty about what to do had been driving me mad, making me restless and agitated. Now, my mind was set, I could look ahead with optimism and start to make some plans. Obviously there was a huge part of me that would be sad to be leaving Little Leyton. I was going to miss the village hugely, my lovely friends, all my lovely doggy friends too, the pub especially, but I could always come home for the occasional weekend when I wanted to. It would be the best of both worlds. Yes, definitely. What it would mean for Max and me I just didn't know, but I'd never planned my life around a man before and I wasn't about to start now, especially when there was nothing to suggest our friendship was going to develop into anything more serious. Perhaps it was good that I'd be taking a step backwards before I got too involved with Max.

I walked up the path to Gemma's beautiful home and rapped on the brass knocker.

'Oh Ellie, come in.' Gemma's beautiful blue eyes were reddened and her face, bare of make-up, looked strained. Digby came running up to greet me, his tail thumping wildly against my leg. The baby yelled from his rocker on the floor and two adorable little girls offered me tea and cake from their colourful plastic tea set.

'Girls, will you go into the playroom please. Just for a few minutes. I need to speak to Ellie.' She whipped the baby out of the rocker and held him under her arm, although it did nothing to stop his relentless wailing. I pretended to ignore the incessant crying and instead I gave Digby a big cuddle as he was looking up at me with a forlorn look in his chocolate brown eyes.

'Sit down,' said Gemma.

It was only then I noticed the dozens of cardboard boxes littered over the floor.

'Excuse the mess,' she said with half a smile. She ran a hand through her blonde hair, exhaustion clear to see on her pretty features. She sank down on the sofa. 'I'm so sorry, Ellie,' she said, clutching her head in her hands.

'Whatever's the matter?' I asked, as Digby sidled up beside me, and planted his head on my lap.

'As you can see, we're on the move. It's all happened a bit

quickly but...' She let out a huge sigh. 'The house is being repossessed.'

'No!' My hand flew to my mouth. 'How come?'

'Well, I knew Nigel was having problems in his business, but I didn't know the extent of it. He's been keeping the worst of it from me and I've only just found out this week that we're in all sorts of debt. You wouldn't believe it. So much so, I don't know how we're ever going to get out of it. Our lovely house will have to go, along with the cars and there's no way we'll be able to afford the school fees any more. It's heartbreaking.'

'Oh, Gemma. How awful. I'm so so sorry.'

She shrugged resignedly. 'We'll get through it somehow. I hope. For richer, for poorer. For better, for worse, and all of that. People go through much worse, don't they?'

I suppose they did. My mind immediately went back to our trip to France, to the refugees in Calais, and though this was nowhere near as bad as that, for Gemma and her family it must be a completely awful and frightening situation to find themselves in. It certainly put my little niggles and worries into perspective.

'Anyway, I wanted to let you know the situation. We're moving out in a couple of weeks, just in time for Christmas. Great timing, eh? The thing is, and this is so embarrassing, Ellie, but I just can't afford to pay your bill. I feel so awful about it. I'm furious with Nigel. If he'd told me how bad our finances were, I would never have kept using you to walk Digby. Honestly, I had no idea things were this dire. Once we're back on our feet, I promise you, we'll pay you then.'

'Please don't worry about it. Just forget about the money. Really.' Seeing Gemma's obvious distress and knowing what a difficult time she'd be facing in the coming months, it was the least I could do in the circumstances.

'Thanks for being so understanding, Ellie. I'm not sure how I would have coped these last few weeks without you.' She looked across at Digby who'd slumped into a heap at my foot, enjoying my constant petting of his back. 'Poor boy. We're going to have to let him go. The kids will be devastated, but the rented house we're moving into won't accept pets. Besides, Digby deserves a better home, somewhere they'll be able to give him the time and attention he needs. I've been in touch with the local dogs home and they're confident that they'll be able to rehome him quickly. Hopefully they can find him a new family in time for Christmas.'

'Oh no!' My stomach twisted. I could hardly bear it.

'Don't Ellie,' said Gemma, holding up a hand to stop me from saying anything more. Tears gathered in her eyes and I think she noticed the tears welling in mine too. She stood up and began gathering toys up from the floor.

'Look, I can see you're busy here,' I said, looking around at the books, crockery and linen spilling out of boxes. 'Why don't I take Digby for a walk, get him out from under your feet.' This could be the very last opportunity I'd have to take Digby out, I realized with a pang of sadness.

'But I can't afford to pay you, Ellie.'

'I know that. There's no need. Honestly. Just one friend helping out another. That's all.'

She came across and gave me a hug. 'Thanks Ellie. You're a star.'

I slipped Digby's lead on and we headed outside towards the back lanes, both of us eager to set out on our favourite walk for one last time.

Poor Gemma and her family. Poor old Digby too.

*

Walking into the pub on a Friday night always lifted my spirits, but tonight there was an extra buzz about the place. An end of term feeling. A Christmas is coming feeling. Happiness soared in my chest to see the pub heaving with so many familiar faces. Dan, Andy and Rich were working flat out behind the bar and Eric was patrolling the front bars chatting to all his friends and customers, his spirits high, a big smile spread across his face. Just like old times.

Across the room sitting round the large circular table, I saw Josie and Ethan, Polly and Johnny, Bill and Tony, Paul and Caroline, and Max too. Our eyes literally met across a crowded room and it was though I'd been struck by a force of lightning, my whole body igniting with desire. He acknowledged me with a nod of his head and immediately stood up, weaving his way through the throng of people to greet me.

'Hello Ellie,' he said, wrapping his arms around me and kissing me on the lips, oblivious to the stares from everyone around us. I could have stayed like that, safe in his embrace, for the entire evening, but Max pulled away to look at me, stroking me gently on the cheek. 'Let me get you a drink.'

What a fabulous feeling to be amongst my friends to celebrate the new ownership of the pub. With a glass of wine in hand, I raised a toast to Max.

'To the new gorgeous owner of The Dog and Duck.' I paused to kiss him lightly on the lips. 'Wishing you every success and many happy years ahead in this beautiful pub.'

'Thanks Ellie.' Max smiled, raising his glass back at me.

'You do know that you're taking the pub on at the best possible time. Christmas is always such a vibrant and exciting time here. Especially once we have the tree in position and all the decorations up on the beams and over the fireplace. With the fire blazing it looks so magical. We'll have some special Christmas beers on too. And it gets so busy, every single night of the month. On Christmas Eve we have the annual outdoor Christmas carol concert in the High Street and everyone piles in here before and afterwards for mulled wine and mince pies. Honestly Max, you'll love it. I'm getting so excited just thinking about it, I can't wait.'

'Well, it's certainly a new adventure,' said Max, clearly amused by my enthusiasm. 'And talking of new adventures, what about you, will you be accepting the job offer from Firmans?'

I opened my mouth to reply, but the words stuck in my throat. Something stopped me from just coming out and telling him straight – yes I would be taking the job. For some reason it felt that saying it aloud might give it a validity that I hadn't come to terms with myself yet.

'Probably,' I said, copping out. 'You've reminded me though, I need to go through the paperwork, sign it and return to them. They want me to start in the New Year.'

'Well, it sounds like an excellent opportunity. Too good to miss.'

I couldn't disagree with him, but I supposed there was a small part of me that hoped he might try and persuade me to stay. Still, tonight wasn't the time to be thinking about my new job. I shut the thought out of my mind. Tonight was all about my friends, the pub and Max.

We wandered back over to the big table, stopping on our way to chat to different people. I introduced Max to the few he didn't already know, but word had quickly spread around the village that Max had bought the pub and the news seemed to have been welcomed positively from all quarters. There was even a positive energy emanating from the old oak beams and the stone flag floors, as if the building was welcoming this new development in its history with open arms.

'You all right, lovely?'

Eric's warm and familiar voice resonated in my ear and I span round to see him, throwing my arms around his neck.

'Just fine, Eric. I'm so sorry if I gave you a hard time the other night.'

'Nah. You didn't. I know you only want what's best for the pub.'

'Yes, and for you too, Eric. That's just as important. You've been so good to me. Like a second dad. I'm going to miss having you around this place so much. You're allowed to go off on your travels, but only on the promise that you'll come back regularly to see us all.'

'Just try and keep me away.' He laughed, rubbing me gently on the back. 'This place is in good hands now, you know that, don't you?'

'Yes, I'm sure it is,' I said, as we both turned to watch Max as he mingled happily with the clientele, getting to know his customers.

'Does it feel strange,' I asked him, 'to be passing the pub over into someone else's custody?'

Eric gave a wry smile. 'Do you know, Ellie, it doesn't feel strange at all. It just feels right, as though it's the natural thing for me to do now.'

Funnily enough, I knew exactly what Eric meant. Despite my initial misgivings about Max taking over the pub, suddenly everything seemed to be falling into place. The pub was in safe hands and would continue serving the residents of Little Leyton, hopefully for years to come, Eric was happy in his decision to take time out to travel the world, Johnny and Polly's relationship seemed to be growing stronger with each passing day, Josie and Ethan were full of love and pride for their new daughter, Mum and Dad were living the high life in Dubai and I had a fabulous new job and life to look forward to in London.

Everything was going swimmingly for now, but maybe the decision between my new job in London and a future in the village with Max wasn't so straightforward as I first thought after all.

Thirty-Two

"It's the most wonderful time of the year!" Humming beneath my breath, I placed the advent candle on the shelf in front of the optics and stood back to admire its beauty. *Perfect.* I struck a match, holding the flame to the wick, watching it flicker into life, its amber glow reflected in the mirror behind.

It was the first day of December and there'd been such a happy and exciting air of anticipation wafting around the old oak beams in the last couple of weeks. Everyone was so pleased that the pub's future had been secured and now the Christmas preparations really could start in earnest.

'You sound happy,' said Dan chuckling, who wandered into the bar behind me, ready for the evening shift.

'Oh, I just love this time of year, don't you? The whole build-up to Christmas is just so magical. I love seeing all the houses decorated in twinkling festive lights and the Christmas trees glimmering in the windows. We should probably get our tree tomorrow morning, don't you think? I see some people in the village have got theirs up already. We can put it in the bay window where it usually goes – and then I can get it decorated before we open at lunchtime.'

'Sure, I can give you a hand if you like.'

Earlier in the day Polly had dropped off a beautiful wreath brimming with holly and ivy, spruce, mistletoe, pine and various coloured stems of willow and dogwood. I'd hung it carefully on the nail on the front door, the addition of dried orange slices and cinnamon sticks tied with ribbons emitting the most delicious aroma, providing the perfect welcome to The Dog and Duck over the festive season.

I threw another log on the fire and stoked the flames with the iron poker.

"It's the most wonderful time of the year!"

'Do you know any other words to that song?' asked Dan, ruefully.

'Oh sorry.' The tune had been going over and over in my head all day long as I'd begun to place a few decorations around the pub. Pine cones in the hearth. Swags of holly and ivy around the picture frames. Mistletoe above the door frames.

Maybe it was time for me to dig out the Christmas CDs, so I could sing along to something else, although I might have to wait until Dan was out of the way as I suspected he wasn't feeling the goodwill of the season in quite the same way as I was just yet.

'So what are you doing for Christmas this year, then?' he asked.

'I've not made any firm plans yet. It will be strange with Mum and Dad being away. It'll be the first time ever that I won't be spending it with them.'

Usually on Christmas Day we would wake early, opening our stocking presents to the sounds of Christmas carols on the radio. Dad would pour glasses of Buck's Fizz and raise a toast to us all. Afterwards we'd have a light breakfast of scrambled eggs with smoked salmon, before heading out to St Cuthbert's for the morning service. Then we'd make the short walk to the pub where we'd join our friends and neighbours for a few festive drinks, and much laughter. Back at home, we would be greeted by the most delicious smell of the turkey roasting in the Aga, and then we'd all get busy putting on the vegetables, heating up the cranberry and bread sauces, and putting the Christmas pudding on to steam. Some years it would be just the three of us; other times Nanny Browne and Aunty Sue and Uncle Vic would come to stay, or sometimes Eric, Josie and Ethan would join us for the day. How ever many people we had around our Christmas table it was always the most wonderful occasion, a sumptuous meal that was drawn out over several hours, where we pulled crackers, sang songs, told tales and went on, getting steadily merrier, long into the night. After we finished our puddings, we moved on to crackers and cheese and Dad would break open the port, ending up playing card games into the early hours of the morning.

A pang of regret tore at my heart. This year it would be oh so different.

'Well, if you're at a loose end, you're very welcome to come and join me and Silke down on the boat for Christmas dinner. I've volunteered to work over lunchtime, but we'd love to have you come back with us, if you'd like to.'

'Aw thanks Dan, that's really lovely of you to offer, but Josie and Ethan have invited me round to theirs to spend it with Eric and baby Stella, so I'll probably end up going to them.' I'd been holding off making firms plans just in case...

Well, if I was being honest, just in case I received a better offer. Part of me was disappointed that Max hadn't made any mention of his Christmas plans yet.

My gaze drifted around the pub which was looking even more warm and welcoming than usual with the few festive touches I'd added today. Tomorrow it would look even more Christmassy once the tree was in place. Strange to think that the pub still looked and felt the same as it had ever done, but Eric was no longer officially the landlord of The Dog and Duck. His contract had come to an end and despite Max's best efforts, he'd been unable to persuade him to sign up to a new one. It was definitely the end of an era. Eric had agreed to help out and oversee the running of the pub until he went off on his travels in the New Year. Whether we liked it or not there would definitely be a new manager behind the bar within a few weeks. If whoever came in as the new landlord could do half as good a job as Eric had done these last few years then we'd know the pub would be in very safe hands indeed.

'You do know they're forecasting a white Christmas this year?' Dan was arranging a display of the new Christmas craft beers at the end of the bar.

'Really?' I turned to look at him. 'No, I hadn't heard that. That would be amazing. Although I'm sure they forecast a white Christmas every year and it never actually happens. Usually it's grey and damp. Have you tried any of those beers yet?' I asked him.

'No, although I think perhaps we should,' he said, looking up at me with a smile on his face. He picked up the bottles, one by one, and read from their labels. 'There's a "Yuletide Special Ale" brewed with winter fruits and spices, "Santa's Special" which is a rich malty ale that has chocolate undertones, the perfect accompaniment to mince pies, apparently, and a "Winter Delight" that's flavoured with cinnamon and ginger.'

'Mmm, I suppose we ought to sample one for ourselves, just in the name of research and for the good of the locals.'

'What do you fancy?'

'Well, Betty Masters dropped off a box of her mince pies today so I think it will have to be a "Santa's Special", don't you?'

Dan poured our beers, while I put the money into the till and came back with a couple of Betty's mince pies. It was early evening and we didn't have any customers in yet so we pulled up a couple of stools behind the bar, and indulged. Well, it was almost Christmas, after all.

'Do you mind if I put on a Christmas CD?' I asked Dan.

'If you must,' he said, with a wry shake of his head.

'Hmmm, these are delicious.' I took a bite into the crisp sugar-coated pie, the pastry melting in my mouth and the hit of fruits mingling with spices on my tongue was just lovely. Washed down with a mouthful of the chocolatey beer, I had to agree it was the perfect combination.

Not long after, a cold shaft of air whooshed though the snug as the front door opened and I looked up to greet our first customer of the evening, or as I soon found out, not a customer but my new boss, Max Golding. My heart gave a little fillip, as it always did, at the sight of him. As he dropped his head to avoid the low beams I was reminded of the first time I'd spoken to him in here. Then I'd been totally overawed, my body responding strongly and immediately to his presence. Nothing had changed in the months since.

If anything my feelings for him had only grown stronger, if my beating heart and flushed cheeks were anything to go by now.

He looked over his shoulder and past us into the bars, checking to see if we had any customers in. When he saw there weren't any he turned and locked the front door behind him.

'Look, I'm glad I've caught you both here. There's something I need to tell you. It's all a bit short notice, I know, but I'm closing the pub with immediate effect.'

'What?' I spluttered, looking at Dan for support. 'You can't do that!'

'Sorry Ellie, but my contractors will be here first thing in the morning to make a start on the renovations.'

'Not now, surely Max? It's Christmas for heaven's sake. We're always so busy at this time of year. All our customers will be so disappointed if they can't come in for their festive pint – it's madness to do it now. Why not wait until after the New Year, when it will be so much quieter?'

'I know it's not ideal, but my guys have got a gap in their schedule. If we don't do it now, it's going to mean a wait of another couple of months. And I really don't want to have to do that.'

I glared at Max, anger bristling along the length of my body, hardly able to believe that he could pull such a stunt. Why hadn't he discussed this with me? I knew this was his business now, but weren't we supposed to be friends – more than friends – and hadn't he promised me there would be no more secrets. If only he'd run his plans past me or Dan we could have told him this was absolutely the worst time to close the pub. I dropped my head in my hands.

'But I was going to get the Christmas tree tomorrow. And then there's the carol concert in the High Street on Christmas Eve. And what about Christmas Day? The pub has never been closed on Christmas Day. It's a Little Leyton tradition to have pre-Christmas dinner drinks. Tell him, Dan!'

'It does seem a shame,' said Dan, noncommittally.

'A shame! It's a bloody disaster. Please, Max, don't close down the pub. Not now. I'm begging you.'

'Sorry Ellie.' He dropped his gaze. 'I've lined the guys up now. They're all ready to go. You need to trust me on this. Once the work's done, you'll see that all the upheaval will have been worth it.'

'But Max...' I sighed. It was futile trying to appeal to his better nature. At the moment I wasn't sure he even had one. He was definitely the Grinch who was walking off with my Christmas.

'Look if it's the money you're worried about, then obviously I'll honour all the staff's wages while the pub is closed.'

'You just don't get it, do you Max?' I blew out the candle behind me. 'It's not about the money. It's about what's best for the pub. For the community. We're letting them down by not being open over Christmas.'

I thought I'd come to know Max, understood him, but yet again he'd managed to totally sideswipe me with his behaviour. He'd clearly given no thought to how I might feel in all of this, not to mention Dan, the rest of the staff and our customers too.

'That's the way it has to be, Ellie. I know it's disappointing, but it won't be for long. I promise you. I'm the new management now, and with that comes inevitable change.' I couldn't help noticing the steely intent in his voice. 'A case of "out with the old and in with the new".'

Frank Sinatra was crooning in my ear, urging me to 'Have yourself a merry little Christmas' There wasn't much chance of that now, not with Max closing the pub for the Christmas period.

'Well, there doesn't seem much point in us hanging around here now then.'

'No, you get off.' Max almost seemed relieved. 'I'll lock up and put a notice up on the front door. I'll give you a call later, Ellie, we can talk more then, if you like.'

Tears swelled in my eyes and my whole body shook with frustration and rage. Dan and I shared a look and his fingers reached out for mine behind the bar, giving them a supportive squeeze. With Mum and Dad away, I'd been banking on the pub and its lovely customers filling the hole my parents' absence would make over Christmas. I'd been so looking forward to being at the heart of the community's celebrations and now Max had dashed all my Christmas plans in one fell swoop. It was heartbreaking.

I thought we'd finally got over our differences. I thought Max shared the same vision for the pub as me. I thought... How wrong could you be?

Frank was still warbling in my ear, telling me all my troubles would soon be out of sight. I glared accusingly at the CD player, stabbing at the button to turn it off. For once, even Frank Sinatra couldn't make everything better.

Thirty-Three

The next morning I woke with a heavy heart and a throbbing headache on account of all the crying I'd done the previous night. After Max had dropped his bombshell, I'd walked straight home and as soon as I'd got through my front door, I'd slumped down onto the floor and cried. Tears of anger, disappointment and regret. Once I started I couldn't stop. I just couldn't believe Max had taken the decision to close the pub, it made no sense whatsoever.

Why would he choose to have the renovations done now at the busiest and most profitable time of year? After everything I'd told him about the importance of the festive season to the pub. Unless that didn't matter to him any more. With Eric now out of the picture and with his name on the deeds to the pub, Max could do exactly what he wanted with the place. First and foremost, he was a businessman, an entrepreneur. You didn't get to acquire his level of wealth by being emotional or sentimental over business decisions. Perhaps, as Johnny had suggested, Max had other plans for the pub after all and was intending on turning it into a luxury home before selling it on for a tidy profit.

My heart tore. Maybe Max had the perfect excuse now

to do exactly that. He'd given me the opportunity to take up the role of manager and when I hadn't given my heartfelt consent, he'd seen that as a chance to offload the business, to do what he knew best, turn the pub into a lovely family home. A lot less aggravation. Tons more profit.

In between bouts of sobbing last night, I'd made myself a mug of cinnamon hot chocolate, stirring marshmallows into the delicious sweetness when there was a knock on the door. From the heavy intent of the brass knocker and the feelings it stirred within me, I knew immediately it was Max. It could be no one else. He knocked once, twice and then again. I stayed stock-still, hardly daring to breathe, not wanting to make the slightest movement. Max knew I was there, and he knew that I knew he was there, but I had no intention whatsoever of speaking to him. When my phone rang, I switched it off and went upstairs to take a bubble-filled bath.

This morning, with the scent of the cranberry body wash I'd used tugging at my senses, I pulled back the curtains to look at the winter scene outside. A layer of frost covered the ground and the chill of the December morning penetrated the window, sending a shiver down my spine. In the garden below a robin bobbed about happily, before taking up position on the flowering winterberry, surveying the scene around him. Through the houses, I could see the spire of St Cuthbert's reaching up into the sky. I still intended going along to the Christingle service, Midnight Mass and the Christmas morning service, as I'd done every other year, but looking out over Little Leyton this morning, Christmas seemed to have lost a little of its shine.

Damn Max Golding! Why was I standing here moping when I should be full of joy and excitement for the coming few weeks? I wouldn't give Max the satisfaction of spoiling my enjoyment of the holiday season, even if the pub was closed. Little Leyton was so much more than the pub, it was a warm and supportive community, who rallied round each other to help out through tough times. Max might be happy to rattle around in his big stately pile without a friend to his name, spending his nights counting his money no doubt, but to the rest of us Little Leytoners, friendship, loyalty and respect counted for so much more than making money.

Quickly I pulled on my jeans, my thermal vest and my pink fluffy fleece. I had Amber to walk later this morning, but there was something I needed to do first. Dashing out of the front door, I ran straight into Pete the postman who handed a wad of letters to me.

'Looks like you've got plenty of Christmas cards in there, Ellie,' he said with a smile.

Oh, that reminded me! I needed to post Firmans letter. I ran back inside and grabbed the envelope, placing it inside my jacket pocket.

'Already? How lovely. Thanks Pete. I'll look forward to opening those later. How are you? Looking forward to Christmas?'

'Can't wait. It's the best time of the year, I reckon. Especially with the little ones. They're so excited.'

Pete had twin boys of about three years old, so I could just imagine how special Christmas would be in their household this year.

'See you soon,' I called, running down the High Street.

It was silly, I knew, but I wanted to see the pub, to check

for myself that it was still standing, that Max hadn't been in the middle of the night and torn it down with a bulldozer. When I reached the front door I tried the handle, hoping against hope, that it might actually open, but of course it didn't. I pressed my nose against the glass of the door to see inside, just able to make out the pumps, the bar stools, my advent candle on the shelf which wouldn't have the chance to burn now. I felt a huge pang of sadness that I couldn't just walk inside and start preparing for the day's trade. That I wouldn't get the chance to decorate the Christmas tree for the window.

I stood back to read the notice that Max must have stuck to the door.

SORRY. THE PUB WILL BE CLOSED FOR RENOVATIONS FOR THE FORESEEABLE FUTURE. APOLOGIES FOR ANY INCONVENIENCE.

That was short and to the point and gave no indication as to when the pub would re-open, or even if it would re-open. My hand reached up to touch the beautiful wreath – at least people would still get to see its loveliness when they came to read the notice on the door. I was just about to turn away and head for home when a van pulled up at the kerb. Two men climbed out, opening up the back doors to pull out their toolboxes.

'Morning, love,' they called.

'What's going on here then?' I asked, hopeful that I might get more insight from them.

'Er...' One of the men pointed to the notice as if I was asking a stupid question. 'The pub's having a facelift.'

'And when will it be re-opening again, do you know?'

The guy shrugged and smiled. 'No idea. You'd have to ask the gaffer about that.'

Dejectedly, I walked away, my hand turning over the envelope in my pocket. There was no point in surmising. Max obviously had his plans for the pub and from the sounds of it, nothing or no one would stand in his way. The sooner I got used to the idea that The Dog and Duck wouldn't be featuring in my Christmas for this year, then the better.

On my way home I popped into the newsagents to buy a newspaper and just as I was leaving I bumped into Betty Masters.

'Hello lovely, how are you today?'

'Okay, I suppose, although you'll have heard the news that the pub has closed down.'

'Yes. It's a shame, but I'm sure it'll look lovely when it's all done. I've heard that the new owner is good at that sort of thing.' A big smile swept across her face. 'Anyway, I must tell you, Pip is coming home at the weekend.'

'Really? Well, that's just marvellous news,' I said, giving her a big hug, thrilled to share in her joy. 'And do you know how long he's staying for?'

'Until the New Year apparently. It'll be so lovely to have the whole family together for Christmas. It's been such a long time.'

'I'm so happy for you Betty. Oh, and thank you for the mince pies by the way. They were absolutely delicious.'

'I'll drop some more off to your house,' she said conspiratorially. Clearly Betty had much more important things to be thinking about than the closure of the pub. It had been a huge body blow to me, but I was beginning to realize that life and Christmas would go on in Little Leyton regardless of what was happening at The Dog and Duck.

*

There was a real cold nip to the air as I took Amber across to the field, what I would always think of as Max's field now, for our training session. I dug my hands deep into the pockets of my padded jacket, grateful for its fur-trimmed collar as I snuggled into its comforting warmth. The ground was crisp and hard beneath my feet and the branches of the trees were tipped in frost, creating a winter wonderland effect. As I gazed across the fields with sheep dotting the landscape, I took a deep breath, admiring the beauty of the countryside, a scene that wouldn't have looked out of place on a Christmas card.

Talking of which, my Christmas cards were all written and ready to go. I'd been so organized this year, hardly able to wait for the festive season to start. Now, I wondered what the hurry had been about. With only my dog-walking duties to keep me busy in the run-up to Christmas, I would have plenty of free time on my hands. Still, that just meant more time to savour and enjoy the delights of the season. This afternoon I would get out in the village to hand-deliver the cards for my friends and neighbours.

Amber ran off gaily, her previous accident now well and truly forgotten. She hadn't suffered any ill-effects from her run-in with the bush, apart from a small scar on her side which she had to show for her adventure. She still insisted on having a good old sniff around that part of the field, but carefully avoided going into the deepest depths of the shrubbery there. Seeing her from a distance, her nose to the ground, her tail held straight behind her, filled me with a warm swirl of pride. The little dog had come on in leaps and bounds since I'd first started working with her.

Today though was the first time since I'd been using the field that I was keeping my fingers tightly crossed that I wouldn't bump into Max Golding. He'd phoned me already this morning, but really, what did we have to say to each other? Nothing was going to change the fact that the pub was now closed. What Max and I needed was some distance from each other. Our personal lives had become too embroiled with the future of the pub. My head was telling me one thing; that I needed to go back to London to take up my career again and leave the fate of The Dog and Duck in the hands of its new owner, while my heart was telling me something else entirely; that I needed to stay in the village, to oversee what would happen to the pub – maybe just until a new landlord was in place. Didn't I owe it to my parents, to Eric and to all our lovely customers to see the pub through this period of change? I laughed out loud. Who was I kidding? The only reason I wanted to stay was to satisfy my own curiosity and desires. And then there was Max, of course. Always Max. Messing up my head with his all-pervading presence. I tucked a hand inside my jacket to check my envelope for Firman's was still there, with a mental note to myself to post it later.

'Come on, Amber,' I called, as a cold shudder ran the length of my body.

Walking always cleared my head, so I picked up the pace. I definitely needed to clear my head – of the pub and all thoughts of Max Golding.

Later, on my way home, after dropping Amber off with Cathy, I walked to the other end of the village and called in at Beck's Farm Shop. Today I should have been collecting the Christmas tree for the pub and, with Dan's help, decorating it too, but Max had put paid to those plans. Instead I decided, not wanting to be completely deprived of the pleasure, I'd decorate my own Christmas tree at home. It wouldn't be quite the same without Mum and Dad around to help out, but at least I knew once the tree was up, twinkling away brightly in the window, that it would feel as if the Christmas season had well and truly arrived.

'Hi Ellie, how are you?'

Ryan Lockwood was making easy work of lugging Christmas trees over his shoulder and putting them through the netting machine, bagging them up ready to sell to his customers. I hadn't seen him in years. Hadn't even realized he was back in the village. Back when I'd known him, years ago now, he had a reputation as a bit of a wild boy. A known truant, the school grew tired of his continued absences and he was eventually expelled. Afterwards there were all sorts of rumours about him – drink and drugs, run-ins with the police – but whether there was any truth in those stories I didn't know. Standing in front of me now was a strong and fit young man, with a wide handsome face, almost unrecognizable from that wild and wayward teenager.

'Hi Ryan, it's great to see you.'

'Yep, you too. After a Christmas tree?'

'Please. Nothing too big. Maybe about five foot or so

and something that won't drop all its needles.'

'Over there.' Ryan pointed to a row of trees leaning against the fence. 'Pick out the one you fancy and I'll bag it up for you.'

'Thanks. I didn't think you'd be so busy already.'

'Oh yeah, Christmas seems to have come early to Little Leyton.' He rolled up the sleeves of his sweatshirt and wiped his brow with his forearm. 'I've already sold over twenty trees today.'

'Wow!' I laughed. 'Well, it's really good seeing you back in the village, Ryan. Are you sticking around for a while?'

'Yep,' he nodded. 'There are worst places to live. And you?'

'I'm here until at least the New Year but after that who knows...'

Ryan had a point. There were much worse places to live than Little Leyton and for me the village would always have a special hold over my heart, waiting to welcome me back in the fold – at any time in the future.

Thirty-Four

I stood back to admire the tree which was standing tall with a myriad of colourful lights twinkling in its branches. It was perfect. Well, almost. I leant down to pick out a small silver frosted bauble that was lost within the lush green foliage and placed it towards the top of the tree where it had a better chance to shine. I sighed in full and utter appreciation of its beauty.

In previous years, along with Mum, we'd chosen a colour scheme for the tree; one year we'd gone for all silver, the next all gold, then red and green, we'd even had a purple year, which we'd thought was a terribly good idea in the middle of November, although by the end of the festive season, the allure of the bright purple had worn a little thin, and we'd declared that from then on it would be traditional colours all the way.

I'd had a brief moment this morning when I'd toyed with the idea of trying the purple again, maybe with some silver to break up the purpleness, but then the red and green was always so lovely and festive, and the baubles and toy soldiers and jolly Santas were glistening at me, shouting, 'pick me, pick me.' In the end when I simply couldn't choose between the different colours, I thought, *to hell with it, why shouldn't all those bright and shiny baubles mingle happily together on the tree*. Once I started I couldn't stop, overtaken as I was by an enthusiasm to hang as many as possible of the decorations we'd collected over the years onto the tree. Eschewing our usual tasteful white candle lights too, I found some old multi-coloured flashing lights in the loft and draped those over the tree, even adding some silver and turquoise tinsel around the bottom.

I smiled, feeling inordinately proud of my handiwork. The whole effect was gorgeous; bright and brash, the colours clashing wildly, a joyful explosion of festivity nestling in the window of No. 2 Ivy Lane Cottages.

In fact, at that moment, I thought it was probably the best and most beautiful tree I'd ever seen. I pulled out my phone to take a photo of it to send to Mum. She would most definitely not approve, I thought smiling, but then Mum wasn't here...

Suddenly I remembered the gift she'd given to me on her last trip over. I went over to the dresser and opened the top drawer, pulling out the wad of pink tissue. Inside, I uncovered the little glass angel, my fingers tracing a trail around her halo and on the delicate carving of her wings. What was it Mum had said? That she hoped the angel might bring me a little luck over the Christmas period. That would be nice. Carefully, I hung the decoration on one of the top branches of the tree, where it could be seen, the light through the glazed windowpane reflecting through its wings. Perfect. My work here was done.

Without my parents around to help me in the tree-dressing ceremony, Michael Buble had heroically stepped up to the plate and was giving his full and heartfelt support as he hummed his approval in the background.

'It's beginning to look a lot like Christmas...'

Just as I pressed send on the photo to Mum I noticed a text from Max, his name on my phone always eliciting a quiver of anticipation inside me.

Hi Ellie! Sorry... I know I've upset you by closing the pub, but it had to be done! Don't let this spoil things between us. Please? I'm going to be pretty busy in the run-up to Xmas, but hopefully we can catch up over the break? Missing you. Speak soon, yeah? Love Max xxx

Grrr. Upset me? That didn't even come close. I sank down on the sofa, unable to drag my eyes away from my masterpiece of a tree. Oh God, but I missed Max too. I didn't want to admit it to myself but that man took up so much space inside my head. This wasn't only about the pub, it was about us, our relationship. Clearly I hadn't meant anything to him. Every minute of the day, he was there, infiltrating my mind and senses with the memory of his scent, his touch, his whole being. He'd upset me and infuriated me and really I had half a mind never to see or speak to him again. That would teach him. And yet... oh how he'd mesmerized me too.

I read his text over and over again, all the time lingering over those most important words. *Missing you* and *love*. I sighed and switched my phone off. It was never a good idea to read too much in to these things.

*

Johnny, Polly, Josie, Ethan, Dan, Silke, Andy and I had gathered in Polly's cosy cottage for a pre-Christmas soirée. We'd all brought a supper dish along, and there was plenty of booze available too; Prosecco and beers and a cranberry-infused fizz which had been going down very easily all night long. In the middle of the coffee table was a plate of mince pies baked by Josie and we were now tucking into those as we went round the group for the Secret Santa. The others had opened their presents already – Johnny had opened his Santa Claus boxer shorts and roll of toilet paper in the same design to much hilarity – it was only left to me now to undo the prettily wrapped box in front of me. Everyone was looking at me expectantly, urging me to get a move on, but nothing was going to stop me from savouring the moment. I turned the parcel over in my hands to try and get some clue as to what might be inside. I shook it to my ear to see if it made any noise – it didn't – and I held it to my nose to see if it had any scent – it hadn't.

'Come on, Ells, just get on with it, would you? We're all dying of suspense here,' said Johnny, who was now looking slightly the worse for wear, having slumped halfway off the sofa.

Quickly I untied the ribbon, my fingers tearing at the reindeer paper and pulled off the lid to the pretty floral box to find a pair of pink ribbed walking socks inside with paw prints on the soles.

'Oh my goodness they are gorgeous,' I said, deciding there and then that I had to put them on. I pulled them over my feet and wiggled my toes in the air. 'Thank you to whoever chose these. They're brilliant and will be perfect for my dog-walking.'

'Don't suppose you'll be doing much dog-walking though when you take up your new high-flying job in the city,' said Josie.

'No.' A life in London would be so different to the one I'd made here in Little Leyton. No dogs, no close friends, no beautiful countryside, no Max Golding – I suppose there had to be some perks. 'But I will wear these socks regardless,' I said, pushing the black cloud away. 'They will look very sexy with my pencil skirt and heels.'

Digby, who had come along this evening as my plus-one, sniffed at them curiously and wagged his tail in approval. I glanced at my watch, wondering how Gemma and her family were getting on. Today was their moving day and they would be in their new, rented home by now. A new start for them too, and a more secure future, I hoped.

'Ha ha, any news on the pub?' Ethan asked.

Dan, Andy and I shared a look and shrugged.

'No, nothing,' I said.

'Although we are still being paid,' said Andy, 'which takes the sting out of it a bit.'

'Yeah, but for how long? Has Max not said anything to you, Ellie, about when the pub will re-open again?'

I had to admit that he hadn't and I was in the dark as much as anyone else.

'Seems strange though, don't you think,' said Johnny, 'that he's chosen to do his so-called renovations now when it's the busiest time of the year for the pub. And he's not giving any idea of when it'll be open for business again. Unless he's got other plans for the place now?'

I hated the way Johnny had a habit of putting a voice to all my innermost fears and worries.

'Nah, I don't think so,' said Dan. 'There's no need to worry. The Dog and Duck will open again once the place has had a facelift and he's got a new manager lined up. Admittedly the village seems a bit sad with the pub out of action but in the grand scheme of things, for the sake of a couple of months, it's not really such a big deal, is it?'

There was a reluctant murmur of agreement from the others.

'I suppose,' I sighed, wondering if I hadn't over-reacted to Max's plans for the renovations. After all, he'd told me that he'd intended to close the pub for refurbishment, I just hadn't expected it to be so soon, and over the Christmas period too. By the time the pub was open again, I could be back in London.

'I'm just disappointed that the pub won't be open for the carol concert,' I said, 'that's always such a good night, or Christmas Day drinks, and then there's New Year's Eve too...'

I knew I was in danger of sounding whiney on the subject, but it still saddened me to think of all those lovely occasions we'd be missing out on.

'There's nothing stopping us from doing the whole mulled wine and mince pie thing ourselves on Christmas Eve if we wanted to. We could set up stalls outside the pub and at different points along the High Street. The locals would love it. What do you reckon?'

'Yep, great idea,' said Andy, clearly enthused by Dan's suggestion. 'Let's do it. What do you say, Ells?'

'Yeah, I'd love that.' In the absence of the pub being open, it would be the next best thing. The carol concert just wouldn't be the same without a warming mug of mulled wine and a mince pie to enjoy afterwards and now the locals would get their Christmas Eve refreshments after all. It would be lovely, I knew, just not the way I would want it to be.

As Digby and I made the short walk home I rummaged around in the inside pockets of my jacket looking for my gloves and pulled out the letter to Firmans. I'd completely forgotten to post it. Walking past The Dog and Duck I looked up to the top window to see a light glowing dimly in the front bedroom. Either the builders were working very late or else someone had already moved into the pub. Who knew? I was way past second-guessing Max Golding's intentions. When I got to the post office, I ran my fingers along the edges of the envelope, tapping it against my hand for one last time. I really couldn't put this moment off any longer. I felt a small smile of satisfaction appear on my lips at the realization that I was making absolutely the right decision before popping the letter in the box.

Thirty-Five

I woke early on Christmas Eve morning and padded over to the bedroom window to draw back the curtains. I shivered at the cold winter's scene greeting me outside and wrapped my arms around my chest. A sharp frost covered the ground and muted white clouds hung low in a grey sky. I craned my head upwards, just as I'd done when I was a little girl, searching for Father Christmas, wondering if he was on his way yet. The thrill of the anticipation I felt back then stirred in my stomach even now. I could never imagine a time when I would tire of the excitement of Christmas, even if things would be very different this year without Mum and Dad around and with the pub being closed too.

Downstairs, I switched on the lights on the tree, gave Digby his early morning hug and flicked on the kettle. I was just putting a teabag into a mug when the phone rang.

'Hi,' I said distractedly, grabbing the phone to my ear as I pulled open the fridge door with my other hand.

'Ellie, it's Max.'

'Max!' Treacherously, my heart soared. I hadn't spoken to him in weeks, ever since that night he'd broken my heart when he'd closed the pub down, and yet now I was ridiculously pleased to hear from him.

'I need to see you. Can you come down to the pub?'

'What, now? It's seven o'clock on Christmas Eve morning, Max. I haven't heard from you in weeks. What's so important? Can it not wait until after Christmas?'

'No, it really can't, Ellie. I need to speak to you now.'

'I don't know, Max, I...'

'It's an emergency.' There was a steely determination to Max's voice that unnerved me.

Dread swept through my body. 'What sort of an emergency?'

'Um,' he wavered, obviously wondering whether to tell me or not, before saying, 'a flood kind of emergency.'

'Oh God! Right, I'll be straight down.'

Why Max was calling me out to help, I had no idea. Surely a plumber would be much more useful in these circumstances. To be honest, I wasn't sure I even knew where the stopcock was. Still, no matter, maybe he just needed me there for some moral support. I raced upstairs and threw on some clothes, not even bothering to shower. With Digby at my side, eager at the prospect of an early morning walk, I pulled on my wellington boots and we rushed outside. The cold made me gasp and I rubbed my hands together before finding gloves inside the pockets of my coat. We half-ran, half-skipped, our way down the High Street – not easy in wellies – and within minutes we were standing outside The Dog and Duck, my heart beating wildly, whether at the exertion from my early morning run or from the knowledge that I would be seeing Max again any moment now, I wasn't sure. I tried the door but it wouldn't open. Anxiety stirred within me standing in front of the place that had always meant so much to me. What if water came gushing out as soon as the door was opened? What if everything had been completely wrecked inside. I'd seen the devastation caused by flooding on the TV and that was the last thing the pub needed. Urgently, I rapped on the door with my curled fist. Hearing footsteps from inside the building, my pulse quickened as they became noticeably louder the closer they got. The door swung open and there was Max, dressed in jeans and a black T-shirt splattered with white paint. He raked a hand through mussed-up hair and sawdust fell in a snow cloud around him. Weariness etched his features, but his face lit up in the biggest warmest smile when he saw me.

'Ellie!'

He opened up his arms to beckon me into his embrace and even if I'd wanted to resist, I wouldn't have been able to. His body held a magnetic pull and soon his arms were wrapped around me, my head falling onto the firmness of his hard chest, my body reacting in the only way it knew how. I looked up at his warm and beautiful eyes seeing my own longing reflected there. I pulled away, looking up into his gaze, his dark eyes filled with affection.

'Max, what's happened? Where's the flood?'

'Oh.' He ran his hand through my hair, looking into my eyes beseechingly. His gaze dropped the length of my body to look at my pink wellies, the sight clearly amusing to him. 'I may have got you here on false pretences.'

'What? There is no flood?' He shook his head, and I looked at him aghast, wondering what I was doing here after all. 'But you rang. You said…'

'Have you seen?' he asked, pointing above my head.

'Oh my goodness!' In my haste to get here, I'd completely missed the new pub sign. Despite the greyness of the sky, the image of the dog and duck rich in colours of black and green and red and brown, gave a blaze of colour to the High Street. The beauty of it took my breath away. Digby, beside me, looked up too wondering what all the fuss was about.

'That's amazing,' I said, 'oh, and the front door too!' My fingers ran over the newly painted woodwork. Still in black, as I'd always known it, but now shiny and glossy, the old peeling crumbling paintwork nowhere to be seen.

'Do you want to take a look inside?'

'What? But, I don't understand.' A mix of anger, relief and confusion swarmed around my body.

My head too was having trouble making sense of all this. Max had lied about the flood and now he was inviting me inside to see what exactly? What was he playing at? Damn that man. Always messing with my head and tugging at my heart strings.

'Come on, let me show you.'

Max led me by the hand into the pub, the building that I knew so well. Reluctantly, I took tentative steps, anxious at what I might find waiting inside. Would the pub be unrecognizable to me now? I looked all around, up to the highest reaches of the ceiling and down to the furthest corners of the floor, around the bar and into the seating areas. All so familiar and yet it was as if I was seeing it all for the first time. Everything was just as it had ever been, but the whole place had been brought into a sharper focus now. The woodwork had been stripped back and re-varnished, the walls freshly painted, bringing out the vibrancy of the deep red hue, the floors polished and the upholstery revitalized with new purple tartan covers on some of the seats and red velvet on the others. It was better than I could ever have imagined.

Tears gathered in my eyes and I turned to look at Max, as his gaze scanned my face for my reaction. 'Oh Max, this is amazing. I can't believe what you've done.' His hands were covered in dust and grime, and it looked as though he hadn't changed his clothes in days. 'This is your handiwork, isn't it?'

'Well, me and the guys too. We've been working through the nights to get this done. I wanted you to see it first. There's lots more to see upstairs.'

I followed Max up, my whole body quivering at the realization at what he and his team had done here. The stair-rail with its intricate spindles had been given a whole new lease of life stripped back to its natural beauty. The old avocado bathroom suite had been ripped out and replaced with a new white one, including a power shower and there was no more wobbly loo seat either. All the bedrooms had been re-decorated in light, neutral colours giving the illusion that there was so much more space now.

'I've not chucked anything out,' said Max, as we stood in the doorway to the bedroom where I used to stay with Josie. The daisy sprigged curtains were now folded neatly over a ladder in the corner. I felt a pang of nostalgia for those lost days. Things here would never be the same again, that was for sure.

'What's the matter,' asked Max, turning me round to

face him, his gaze searching my features. 'Do you not like it or something?'

'No, I do.' I took a step backwards. He was too close, way too close.

'But...?'

I ran my hands through my hair, suppressing a sigh.

'Oh Max!' I span round on the spot, drinking it all in. 'It's all so lovely what you've done here, but I just don't know why you couldn't have discussed it with me, or Dan, or Eric first. Asked our opinions. I know you're the owner now but, between us, we've got years of experience working here and know much more about The Dog and Duck than you ever will. You showed absolutely no respect to our opinions or feelings. Or to the feelings of our customers. They're the people who make this pub work and if we didn't have them we wouldn't even have a business.'

Maybe it wasn't my place to say, but I was still smarting at the way he'd closed the pub so suddenly with scant regard to anyone else.

'Sorry, Ellie.' He tilted his head to the ceiling, obviously disappointed at my reaction. What had he expected, for me to simply forget about everything that had happened in the past? 'I know you didn't agree with that decision, but I did what I thought was best. Honestly. Don't you think it's been worth it? Come on, take a look at the kitchen.'

It was hard not to get swept away by Max's enthusiasm. Everything I'd seen so far had convinced me that he couldn't have done any better job. The kitchen had been transformed with new units and worktops, a gleaming white double sink, a new range cooker and new appliances too. Eric was gone now, but I knew he'd be so impressed when he saw what Max had done with the pub. I tried to picture someone new here, buzzing about the kitchen, serving behind the bar, bringing their new ideas for the pub with them, but the thought just made me inexplicably sad. Had Max made any new plans on that front, I wondered.

'Let me make you a coffee,' said Max now. 'We have so much to catch up on.'

I wandered through to the bar and sat down at the table in the bay window, my head turning each and every way still soaking up all the loveliness of the renovations. Max brought me a coffee, sat down next to me and took hold of my hand.

'Look Ellie, I'm really sorry. For the way I went about these renovations. The last thing I wanted to do was to upset you. You must know what this place means to me, what with it being Granddad's favourite old haunt. I suppose in my enthusiasm at finally getting my hands on the place, I got a bit carried away.'

'But Max it's every time. First you forgot to tell me about Sasha, then you failed to mention that you'd bought the pub and then you went steaming ahead with renovations without even discussing it with anyone first. I know what happens here now has nothing to do with me any more, but I just wished you'd talked to me, let me in.'

'Guilty,' said Max with a wry smile, holding his hands up to the air. 'The thing is I'm not used to doing that. I'm used to just getting on and doing things. I realize now I should have spoken to you first. I want to change, Ellie, and I will, I promise you, if you'll just give me the chance. This place is important to me, but what's more important to me is you.

You and me. What these last couple of weeks has taught me is how much you've come to mean me.'

'Oh...' my skin prickled with heat at the enormity of his words. 'Do you mean that?'

Max laughed and touched my face with his hand.

'Of course I mean it. I absolutely adore you, Ellie, and want you in my life. I'm so bloody proud of you getting that job. You're amazing and I wanted to tell you that. To wish you the very best of luck. Not that you'll need it, because I know you'll absolutely ace it. London's not a million miles away – I know we could make it work, if you wanted it to.'

I turned my head to look at Max, my insides melting at the imploring look in his eyes, hardly able to believe what I was hearing.

'Oh Max, it's what I want too. You're the first thing I think about in the morning and the last thing I think of at night.'

'Well, that's very good to hear, Ellie Browne, because even if you were going to the other side of the world, we'd find a way to make it work. You and me, we could have something special together.'

My skin tingled. They were words I could only ever have dreamt of hearing.

'Oh, Max, I'm not going to London after all. I've thought about it long and hard and I've decided that I need to stay in Little Leyton.'

'What?' His face clouded. 'No way! You can't give up that fantastic opportunity. You need to go to London and take up that job. The pub will still be here, I'll still be here. We'll find a way to make it work out between us, really.'

'You don't understand, Max. My mind's made up. I've

already written to Firmans telling them I won't be taking up their offer.' Admittedly it had taken me a little time, but in the end the decision had been a very easy one to make. There was no way I was going to let my life be dictated to by a man, but when Gemma told me Digby would have to go the kennels, I knew in an instance that I couldn't let that happen. Mum told me I needed to follow my heart and that was precisely what I intended to do. 'If that job offer is still open,' I told Max now, 'I'd love to take you up on it.'

'Are you kidding me? Max looked genuinely taken aback. 'The job's yours. I've been holding back from finding a new manager in the hope that you would change your mind, but I didn't want to put any undue pressure on you. I wanted you to take the job here because it was something you really wanted to do.'

'Oh I do. I've been thinking about all the amazing things we could do here and I'm so excited to be a part of it.' I could feel the excitement now fizzing in my stomach.

'You don't know how happy that makes me. And don't worry about me interfering. You'll have free rein to do exactly what you want to do here. Although there is one thing – I really think we should do another trip to Calais as soon as we can in the New Year.'

I smiled – wasn't that how all this had started?

'Definitely. There could be no other co-driver for me, Max.' I paused, transfixed by the sight of our hands clasped together on the table. 'Although before we finalize anything, I would need to negotiate some terms.'

Max lifted his eyebrows, a look of puzzlement on his face.

'Such as…?'

'Well, there's something you must know.' I paused, my gaze lingering on his. 'It's something very important to me. Something you need to be okay with if we're going to move forward together. The thing is Max, there's another man in my life.'

Max narrowed his eyes, his mouth curling at the corners. 'Is that so?' He dropped his gaze to his side, where Digby was laying contentedly at his feet.

'Yes. If I'm going to be managing the pub then I need to know Digby would be welcome here too.'

'You know what,' said Max laughing. 'I've always thought that there was something missing at The Dog and Duck and now I know exactly what it is. A resident dog.'

Max took my face in his hands and kissed me long and hard, the reminder of his touch setting off an explosion of exquisite sensations within me that reached the far ends of my fingers and toes. His scent, fresh paint mingled with wood shavings and hard toil, taunted my nostrils, inflaming my hunger. His kisses even more intoxicating than I remembered.

'Look,' Max pulled away, glancing at his watch, fired up by a sudden urgency. 'If we're going to get this pub open in time for the lunchtime rush, then we need to get a move on.'

'Really?' I asked, in desperate danger of dissolving into tears again.

'Really,' said Max, with a broad smile.

Thirty-Six

By lunchtime, the mulled wine was simmering on the stove, we'd taken delivery of a huge batch of warmed mince pies and the Christmas tree was shining brightly in the window of the pub. Dan, Andy and Eric were manning the bars and it seemed as though all my friends and neighbours in Little Leyton had turned up to celebrate the re-opening of The Dog and Duck.

Max, who'd changed out of his old work clothes and was now wearing a pair of black cords and a red plaid shirt, looked more handsome than one man should be decently allowed to look. He stood up on a stool to address the crowd.

'Ladies and Gentlemen, can I just have your attention for a moment please.' A good-hearted cheer reverberated around the bar. 'I'm not going to bore you with a long speech, I promise.'

'Thank goodness for that,' interrupted Johnny.

'No.' Max laughed. 'But I would like to welcome you all to our informal re-opening of the pub. Thanks to everyone for coming and showing your support. I want to reassure you that there'll be no further changes or closures here at The Dog and Duck – although I hope you'll agree that the improvements we've made have been worth the small inconvenience of having to keep the pub closed for a short while.'

Max looked over at me, a glint in his eye and I gave a sheepish smile in return.

'Business will continue in much the same way as it's always done under the great leadership of Eric, our departing landlord.' A huge round of applause went up and Eric took a bow in front of all his friends and customers. 'I'm also hugely excited to introduce you to our new manager, or should I say landlady, someone who is known to most of you here already, I'm sure, the lovely and very capable Miss Ellie Browne.'

'Whoop, whoop, whoop,' Johnny was the most vocal in his support, but everyone cheered and clapped and Eric manhandled me to Max's side where I gave a slightly self-conscious wave and bow.

'All it remains for me to say is to wish you all a very happy Christmas and ask you to join me in a toast to The Dog and Duck.'

'The Dog and Duck!'

Honestly it felt as though all my Christmases had come at once. I was besieged by congratulations and hugs from the locals and if there'd been any doubt in my mind that I was making the wrong decision, then that afternoon in the pub, amongst all my friends, with Digby at my side, any inkling of doubt was wiped clean away.

'Oh Max,' I said, when we snatched a moment to ourselves later. 'Thank you so much for everything. I'm so sorry for ever doubting you. This is the best Christmas present I could ever have wished for.'

'Ah, talking of Christmas presents, I have something for you. Come with me.' Max took my hand and led me over to the bar, reaching behind to retrieve a small box wrapped in red tissue which he handed to me. I looked down at the pretty box feeling overwhelmed by this morning's events and guilty at having misjudged and maligned Max. He'd gone to so much trouble, not only working all hours to get the work on the pub completed, but also taking time out to go and find me a Christmas present.

'Oh, I feel awful now. I haven't got you anything.'

'It doesn't matter. By agreeing to take up the job of manager here and more importantly, giving our relationship a chance, you've already given me everything I could ever have wished for this Christmas.'

'Oh Max. Will you come round tomorrow night after I get home from Josie's? For champagne and cheeses and...'

'Just try and stop me,' he said, kissing me on the nose. 'Come on, over here,' he said, leading me into the doorway to the back corridor where a sprig of mistletoe conveniently was placed. He looked up before kissing me again, on the lips this time. 'Go on then. Aren't you going to open it?'

'Should I though? It's not strictly Christmas yet.'

'Well, if you don't want it,' he said, teasingly.

'No,' I laughed, grabbing it back off him again. 'I want to open it please.' I ripped off the tissue, my fingers fumbling in my haste, revealing a small black velvet box. I prised off the lid and gasped. On the end of the most stunning and delicate gold chain nestled a beautiful dog and duck pendant. I turned it over in my hands, over-awed by its gorgeousness.

'Oh my goodness, that is the most beautiful thing I've ever seen.'

'I had it made specially. Should I put it on you?'

Happiness fluttered through my entire body. I could never have expected to find myself in this position and felt so lucky that Max was back in my life and we could pick up where we'd left off with our relationship, carving a sparkling future out for ourselves. Max lifted my hair, his fingertips on my neck sending shivers down my spine, before fastening the necklace in place.

'Let's have a look,' he said, turning me around to face him. 'Perfect,' he declared, 'just like you.'

*

Later as the carols sung by the Salvation Army wafted in to the pub from the High Street, I looked all around me, at the fire blazing in the hearth, the tree glimmering in the window and my lovely advent candle flickering behind the bar, finally being given its rightful chance to burn, and wondered if there'd been a time when I'd ever been happier. Everyone was here tonight. Betty Masters had been in with all her family, including Pip, who had made it home in the end. Victoria Evans from the newspaper had turned up with a group of friends and had been joined later by her mum, the Reverend Evans, who only stayed for one drink, before dashing off on church business. Our neighbours Paul and Caroline were there, sitting on a table with, Eric, Josie and Nathan, with baby Stella, asleep in her buggy. I'd already had a couple of sneaky cuddles. Even Ryan Lockwood turned up with a pretty young girl in tow, who I presumed to be his girlfriend. Most surprisingly though, Sasha, Max's ex popped in for an orange juice and to wish us both all the best in our new venture. Which was very lovely of her, I thought. Disappointingly, she hadn't grown any less beautiful since the last time I'd seen her. If anything, she looked more radiant and glowing than ever, although Max was quick to reassure me he only had eyes for me these days.

'Ellie,' he called now, as we were just finishing cleaning up after the last of our customers had left, either to make their short journeys home or to set off on their way to St Cuthbert's for the midnight mass service, where we'd shortly be going too. 'Come here and have a look at this.'

He stood in the doorway of the pub and pulled me into his embrace as he pointed up into the night sky. A blast of cold air greeted me and I gasped.

'Oh. My. Word. Did you arrange this specially?' I asked, as I watched transfixed, thick snow falling all around us.

'Well, you know... For you, Ellie darling, nothing is too much trouble.' He chuckled, squeezing me tight, and planted a kiss on my cheek. 'Come on, we should get a move on, we don't want to be late for church.'

Locking up the doors to the pub, I took a glance up at the new Dog and Duck sign and felt a huge swell of pride. Landlady of The Dog and Duck. *Fancy that*. And with the most gorgeous and loving man at my side – make that two gorgeous men – it felt as if all my Christmas wishes had come true. For tonight only, I was leaving Digby in his new basket snuggled up by the fire at the pub, but I suspected he wouldn't have any trouble whatsoever in settling into his new home. I tucked my arm into Max's and we set off, walking huddled together through the snow, which was already blanketing the ground in a thick and heavy layer. I looked up into the night sky, relishing the sensation of snowflakes falling on my face, and wondered if Father Christmas might be up there somewhere after all. For now, I really could believe it to be true because the one thing I'd learnt from today was that miracles, they really can happen.

Acknowledgements

I love pubs – well, I did spend a great deal of my formative years outside drinking establishments with a bottle of pop and a packet of crisps in hand, waiting for the grown ups to reappear – so that's probably why they've etched a special place in my heart. I love dogs and I love Christmas too, so you can imagine the fun I had writing this book.

A big thank you to the Aria team, in particular Caroline Ridding and Sarah Ritherdon, for giving me the opportunity to share these characters with you, and for their brilliant editorial expertise and advice in helping to turn my story into what it has become today. To Jade Craddock too, for waving her magic wand over my manuscript.

I must definitely give a shout-out to my lovely four-legged friends at the Thursday morning agility class who gave me the inspiration for the dogs in this book and whose names I may have borrowed for the purpose.

To my husband, Nick, and my kids, Tom and Ellie – thank you for all your encouragement and support, I really couldn't have done it without you all.

And to everyone who has picked this book off the shelves to read – thank you! It means a lot and I really hope you enjoy it!

Finally, in the inimitable words of Noddy Holder, Merry Christmas Everybody!

Jill xxx